The Beersheba Triangle

The Beersheba Triangle

Md. Yamani

Quartet Books
London   Melbourne   New York

First published by Quartet Books Limited 1986
A member of the Namara Group
27/29 Goodge Street, London W1P 1FD

Copyright © 1986 Md. Yamani

British Library Cataloguing in Publication Data
Yamani, Md.
   The Beersheba triangle.
   I. Title
   823'.914[F]   PR6075.A4/

ISBN 0 7043 2490 3

Phototypeset by AKM Associates (UK) Ltd
Ajmal House, Hayes Road, Southall, London
Printed and bound in Great Britain by
Nene Litho and Woolnough Bookbinding, both of Wellingborough, Northants

1

By the time Dr Peter Watkins got out of the second feature, it was 5.30, dark and starting to snow. He always sidled off to the Circle Theatre to watch old films when he grew bored. Today it had been a James Bond double bill: *Dr No* and *From Russia with Love*. Having worked with the Subcommittee on Intelligence all these years, he knew perfectly well that the chief weapon in the Cold War was the file folder and the Xerox machine. There were never any naked blondes in Acapulco hotel beds. The few Soviet intelligence people he had encountered were short, dumpy men in outdated suits.

His first stop that evening was at his favourite bar – the Federalist Tavern, where he downed three Scotches and munched through a dish of peanuts as he listened to the election talk. The Scotch left him with a slight glow as he walked out into the cold night air. There was almost nobody else about on the streets as he plodded through the trodden slush. He loved Pennsylvania Avenue. It led, of course, to the White House, but there was always some derelict or other sleeping out on its pavements. Its six wide traffic lanes seemed to stretch from one end of the American dream to the other.

The neon light of Johnny's lurched out of the winter mist. Here was Peter Watkins's regular hangout: a tiny luncheonette left over from the

1930s. Just a few blocks from the Capitol, it served the city's best clam chowder. Justice Harmon of the Supreme Court had eaten lunch there daily for twenty-seven years, and it was a gathering spot for a handful of the most powerful Southern Congressmen. The menus – printed in 1946 – had the quality of parchment. Peter ate dinner there almost every night before heading back up to his office to work late on whatever project he was researching.

He came into the warmth of Johnny's, wiped his feet and headed for the small back room to take his usual table. As he removed his scarf, he noticed that someone was already actually sitting there – a woman, no less, hunched over a book, and not just any book, but *American Foreign Policy 1945–1975: The Strategic Collapse*! She never even looked up as he approached to claim his place.

'Excuse me, is this table free?'

'The table is free,' she said as she continued reading.

'That's great,' he said as he clumsily set down his damp scarf and briefcase. 'And you?'

She looked up – blonde, beautiful and sparking with anger. 'And me what?'

'Are you free as well? I mean like the table.' The Scotch had hit him rather harder than usual. How had he blundered into such a corny gambit? She was staring at him guardedly, obviously dreading a whole meal spent sitting across from him.

'Slavery ended with the Civil War. I guess I'm as free as anybody.'

She gave him a withering glare and looked back down at her page. It was now or never.

'I see you're brushing up on foreign policy,' he said. 'What do you think of that book?'

She stared at him for a minute, no doubt wondering whether or not to respond, and then she set the book down. He saw her face clearly for the first time. Her eyes were blue and startlingly direct. Her lips were full and slanted down at the corners. She wore a small touch of make-up, the effect of which lit up all the danger spots in his whirling brain.

She spoke cautiously, still watching him. 'Well, it's a very interesting analysis, but I've only read about half of it so far . . .'

'It's really quite a heavy work,' Peter Watkins said gravely.

'Well, yes, it's a very extensive –'

'I mean heavy . . .' he broke in, '. . . physically.'

'Physically?'

2

'Have you tried lifting it? Go ahead. Try. With one hand.'

He reached out and pulled her left wrist away from the book. She glanced up at him, startled, then she smiled, a broad lovely smile.

'OK, OK, you're right – it's really *heavy*.'

He released her, feeling a sudden joy at her unexpected smile. 'What I'm trying to say is it's a damned bore. I wanted to get rid of it while I was reading it, but it was too heavy even to throw away.'

She stifled a laugh and asked: 'So you don't enjoy reading?'

She took him for a wise-ass all right, he thought to himself. A charming one maybe, but a wise-ass nevertheless. 'No, what I mean is that his analysis of America's involvement in Vietnam is ridiculous. And then the section on the Cuban missile crisis is completely outdated. The footnotes are inaccurate and . . . Do you want me to go on?'

'Yes, yes. I'm fascinated. Please do.'

'Well, the overall viewpoint is . . .' He looked up and found her gazing into his eyes intently. She had to be really crazy about foreign policy. And she was beautiful beyond words!

'The overall viewpoint is . . .?' she prompted, staring at him.

'Uh, well, the overall viewpoint is . . . that you are the most gorgeous woman I have spoken to in a year.'

She smiled at him, brushed back a long, elegant wave of blonde hair over her shoulder. 'I'm flattered, really I am.'

'Can I buy you dinner?'

'With pleasure.'

It emerged that her name was Liza Samuels, she was twenty-nine years old and very bright. She seemed to be fascinated to discover that her host was with the Senate Subcommittee on Intelligence. He, on his part, was amused and delighted to find he had just bought dinner for the legislative liaison of the American Flower Growers Association. In other words, she was a lobbyist – for daisies.

Going on to Peter's favourite booth at the Federalist Tavern, they ordered two Brandy Alexanders. He grinned at her as she loosened her scarf.

'Where do you actually work for the flower people?'

'I spend most of my time over at the Department of Agriculture.'

'It's considered the sexiest part of government. Lots of sin and scandal.'

'You'd get turned on too if you spent all day with the hog-belly quotas and leafmoth blight,' she answered, laughing drily. Then, more seriously, she asked, 'Would you think it a bore to be asked about the election . . .? How do you reckon it'll turn out?'

'Looks like a pretty dull race. President Randall's been lame, but he may hang on. Then there's Willie Lamb – he's a dummy, but don't say I said it.'

'Not Governor Lamb of Texas? He's going to run?'

'Ah, it's still all behind the scenes, but he's getting a nice group of fat cats into his line-up.'

'And Senator Lerner?'

'Well, he's a fantastic guy. I've worked closely with him on the Subcommittee, him being our chairman now, you know. Extremely distinguished and able – but Jewish.'

'What's wrong with that? I'm Jewish.'

'My meaning was only that the country won't buy a Jewish President. Not even if he's Senator Lerner.'

She fell quiet as she sipped at her glass, giving Peter Watkins the chance to study her. She seemed more beautiful the more he looked at her.

He walked her back to a pretty townhouse on 3rd Street in the south-east. She asked him up to her apartment for a nightcap, fulfilling his hope that she might. There was, in the living room, an antique maple desk with an electric typewriter. He watched as she lit the gas jets in the fireplace. They sat across from each other in the fire's glow, listening to the dull hiss of the flames.

'You're tired of your job, from something you said . . .?'

'Yeah, I want out. It was OK for a while. I wouldn't mind being a foreign-policy adviser to one of the candidates.'

'So, which one – Senator Lerner?'

'I admire Lerner, but like I said, he can't be elected. If I decide to do this thing, I really want to go for it properly.' He took a sip of his drink and went on, 'I was thinking in terms of O'Donnell – Timothy O'Donnell . . .'

'Hm. He's a very dishy candidate. Bit on the young side, though. Do you really think he has a chance? Could he even get the nomination?'

'I've been watching that guy eight years. He's got something special for sure. Bright, articulate, presentable, lively . . .'

'But divorced.'

'That happened six years ago. If O'Donnell could get the vote of every divorced person in the States, he'd win a landslide. No, that won't be an issue. What's more, he's kept his romantic life very

4

low-key. I think if he can be nominated, there's no way for Randall to beat him.'

'So you'd go to work for him?'

'I don't know yet. If I go to work for anyone, he's the most likely. How does he strike you, dishiness apart?'

'Oh, I'm not really a political person. I don't know much about him. What's his stand on the Spanish geranium quota?'

'He hates Spanish geraniums. One of his first acts will be to abolish Spanish geraniums.'

She laughed, tilting back her head. 'Well, I think if you're tired of your job, you ought to contact O'Donnell. Seems like you've nothing to lose, and it could be interesting.'

'Maybe I'll do that.'

'But don't hang about. I think you've plenty to offer.'

She lay back now, stretched out in her ivory cashmere cardigan at the far end of the couch on which he sat, her feet tucked under a cushion. He knew he wanted her, but could hardly remember how you led into love-making.

'I guess I'd better be going,' he began, aware of a lameness in his voice. 'I've really enjoyed this talk tonight . . .'

But before he could finish, she delicately leaned forward into his arms and kissed him. Her lips drew back from his a moment, then she kissed him again. When they broke from the second kiss, their breathing was more urgent. He began to kiss her cheek, her ear, as she clenched the hair at the back of his head. Her cardigan had fallen open, and he could see her nipples hardening under her chiffon blouse. Then, all at once, she stood up and took him by the hand.

'This has been a wonderful evening, Peter.'

She led him to the front door. He reached down and picked up his scuffed-about briefcase. Again she embraced him. He felt the pressure of her warm slender body.

'Call me soon – won't you?' she said.

2

The O'Donnell-for-President Committee headquarters was only a little storefront office in an old building on New York Avenue. He would have missed it altogether if it hadn't been for the long blue and white O'Donnell banner in the window. When he went in, he found the makeshift beginnings of a campaign consisting of two tables of literature, buttons, bumper stickers, and a few young volunteers stuffing envelopes, typing letters and making calls.

It all brought back the Bobby Kennedy campaign of '68. Peter had organized the Stanford campus when he was there getting his Master's degree. Fifteen thousand students showed up to hear Bobby castigate the war in Vietnam. The crowd had been ecstatic, and Kennedy never more eloquent. Kennedy's advance people had said it was one of the best-planned rallies they'd seen. Then followed the fateful 5 June. Peter had drifted off into years of graduate school after Kennedy's death.

He stopped next to a brown-haired girl who was stuffing envelopes and asked: 'So what do *you* think of O'Donnell?'

She gave him a grin and said: 'I'm for Tim! He's great.'

'What do you base that on?'

'Well, he's right on all the issues, and I think he's also very compassionate. I don't know . . . He just has this something!'

She handed him one of the envelopes she was sealing and he wandered back down a hall, where he found a frantic receptionist taking three calls at once. He asked her where he could find Barney Shaw, and she pointed down the hall to a door at the end.

Peter peered round the door into the office of Barney Shaw, O'Donnell's campaign co-ordinator. 'Mr Shaw?'

'Yeah, pal?'

'I have an appointment . . . My name's Peter Watkins.'

Barney looked blank for a minute, then waved him in. He was on the phone. An unlit cigar stub was clenched between his fingers. He was a big, beefy red-headed fellow who wore a pair of bifocals perched on a flushed nose. He barked out a couple more 'Naahs' and 'OKs' before he hung up. Peter leaned forward and tentatively laid his résumé on the cluttered desk.

'Sorry, pal – I'm Barney Shaw . . . and you're, you say . . .?'

'Peter Watkins . . . I called about doing some –'

'Oh yeah, right. Lemme see your résumé . . . Let's see now, you worked for Bobby Kennedy. How old were you then? Three?' Shaw wheezed with laughter at his own jest, then read on: 'PhD International Relations at Stanford. Air Force two years. Hey, wait a minute – I thought you academic types hated the military.'

'I wanted to learn to fly . . .'

Shaw stared at him a moment, then tried to reignite his cigar stub. 'So, you're with the Intelligence Subcommittee now. Your references look top-notch. What you wanna do?'

'I'd like to work in the area of foreign policy.'

'Foreign policy, huh? I guess you know Tim's quite an expert in the field. He'll be making his own foreign policy. He's gonna be his own Secretary of State.'

'I've seen the Senator a lot in my work. I think my views and his are quite compatible. I think we could work well together.'

'I'd be lying if I said we need you. We've got stuff coming in from all the Ivy League boys. There's a lot of people after the Senator at this point.'

'I realize that, but I –'

'So whatya want to write about?'

'I'm interested in the Middle East situation.'

'The Middle East situation! The Middle East! Kid, lemme tell you something. The Middle East is poison. The public hates to hear about it. It's complicated, violent, disgusting. They'd rather hear about

7

radiation sickness when they're eating their cornflakes.'

'I thought maybe one should try and help clarify the issue.'

'Look, you know, the Senator's a strong supporter of Israel.'

'I'm aware of it. I'm sure we all support Israel. But there's a problem over there and it won't –'

'Look, there's only one problem, and it's not over there – it's right here. Lerner's the problem.'

'Senator Lerner?'

'You bet! He's a good liberal *and* he's a New York Jew. If Tim's to get nominated, he's going to have to win over the Jewish vote. Right now the Jews are 101 per cent behind Lerner. That dries up campaign funds as far as we're concerned.'

'And Lerner's been catching the New York media spotlight.'

'You said it. They may not really think he can win, but they want to wallow in his moral superiority, like Adlai Stevenson's supporters of old. But you're too young to remember all that.' Shaw spoke with the blunt disgust of the seasoned pro. His pragmatism grated on Peter's nerves, but as he well knew, ten Shaws surrounded every successful candidate.

Shaw's attention was drifting back to the other papers scattered over his desk, but Peter decided to make one last bid for attention. 'So, you'll be needing some strong pro-Israel speeches for Senator O'Donnell?'

Shaw looked up as if he had almost forgotten Peter was still there. 'Well, yeah, I guess a few good jolters for New York, LA, the B'nai B'rith convention, the usual junk. But, like I say, fella, we've got a lot of people here already who are giving us that input. And we're broke too. If you wanna volunteer, fine. Submit us a draft of some kind. I'll feed it to our policy people.'

'What about the Senator? I think if he saw my work he'd –'

'Look, here you can do one of two things: run for President or think. Tim O'Donnell is running for President. We'll do the thinking. OK, Dr Watkins?'

Peter shifted uncomfortably in his chair, an empty feeling flooding into the pit of his stomach. Shaw lifted Peter's résumé in his stubby fingers and handed it back, saying: 'So give us a call sometime . . . and here's your résumé. You may want to hang on to it.'

Shaw was already back on the phone as Peter rose. But before he left he set down a large manila envelope on Shaw's desk. It contained two essays on America's involvement in the Middle East and a short draft

8

for a speech. Shaw barely seemed to notice. Peter felt the sharp chill of rejection as he made his way out of the building.

There was no time to brood on his feelings as he hurried back to the Capitol for his meeting with the Intelligence Subcommittee. He quickly distributed copies of his three briefing manuals in black binders – one to each Senator. Dr Watkins was renowned on the hill for his clear, concise delivery and his meticulous reports. He had wrapped up his briefings with a survey of the world's various nuclear plants, the data-base employed, information on manufacturers and safety records. There were no questions following his presentation. The Committee adjourned for lunch as soon as the black binders had been locked in the Subcommittee's conference-room safe.

Peter headed at once for the basement cafeteria, matching his stride to Ronnie Montgomery's. Montgomery and Peter had gone to Stanford together, and once used to play tennis at night a lot. Montgomery was tall, athletic and freckled, and somehow never looked right in a suit. He had one of the driest wits in town and a smile that could break down the most determined defensiveness. He also enjoyed an unusually high level of access into the CIA. Peter had worked closely with him for three years now, and as far as he could trust anyone in Washington, Peter trusted Ronnie. They sat amid the noisy tables as each dug into the cafeteria's rendition of a cheeseburger.

'So what gives me this feeling there's something in the air today?' Peter asked as he bit into his burger.

'Ah. They're checking out the US government's role in the developing of Israeli nuclear power plants. That's why they needed your briefing.'

Peter looked up and frowned. 'I don't see it. Why get into all this Israeli stuff now? I thought Foreign Relations and Appropriations had already locked the whole thing up, the whole new aid package . . .'

'Well, sure, it's all set. The White House is happy and Israel is ecstatic. But Senator Shillings is not *happy*.'

'What's his beef?'

'Well, you know old "Evil Eyes", God's CPA on earth. The distinguished Senator claims to have sniffed a scent of some irregularities in the nuclear development expenditures.'

'It seems a waste of time to me. No one's yet even breathed a word about the Soviet–Iranian stuff, or the report just in from Nicaragua. What do you make of it?'

9

'Well, while I regard Shillings as a pain in the ass . . . I also try not to forget that the guy is usually right.'

The friends ate the rest of their burgers in silence and said nothing further as they headed back to the hearing room.

3

The Senators took their places around the long oak conference table as a heavy, white-haired gentleman with a healthy pink complexion was escorted in by Senator Lerner. Peter and Ronnie sat a little to one side, Peter's notebook open before him. As soon as everyone was settled, Senator Lerner brought the hearing to order. 'In pursuit of the inquiry initiated by our colleague, Senator Shillings, regarding Israeli nuclear power development, we are honoured to have with us today Dr Uri Eshkol of the Israeli Academy of Technology, current director of the Israeli Nuclear Authority. Dr Eshkol has overseen the projects we are examining – we have each received a copy of his report – and he'll be happy to answer questions.'

Dr Eshkol looked about sixty-five, and benevolent enough. He folded his hands and smiled calmly at the men about the table.

'So you feel you have some problems with us? Of what do these consist?' He spread his arms in a wide gesture.

Senator Shillings swooped like a hawk. 'Dr Eshkol, the development of the three reactors in line with the original agreement was budgeted at $2.9 billion. Is that correct?'

'That would be the figure, yes.'

'Yet is it not the case that, three years ago, you ran $100 million over budget, two years ago, $180 million over budget, and last year, $220 million over budget, to a total in excess of $400 million?'

'It was in fact $388 million, I believe. This represents an overrun of about 13 per cent, but I wonder, Senator, whether you are aware of what America's overruns are on its *own* nuclear plants?' Eshkol pressed his point home without pause. 'By your own government's records, overruns have averaged at least 50 to 60 per cent on every single American installation, some running as high as between 120 and 130 per cent!'

Yet, creasing his forehead as he tapped his pen against the table, Senator Shillings continued to stalk his prey. 'Dr Eshkol, I would quite like to get at a sense of the general efficiency of this thing. Now, looking at pages 29 to 37, I see a consistent pattern of personnel loss, subsequent slowdowns and general mismanagement at every level. Our original allocations strictly direct that all personnel trained at our expense remain at work on this project at least three years, or until equally qualified personnel can replace them. Now, my impression is that this has not been happening.' Shillings's voice had grown tense, his face red – always a bad sign with the Senator. 'You have, in fact, had people coming in and out of this project as though through some damn revolving door.'

Dr Eshkol sat back in his chair with a long sigh to indicate his patience. 'Senator Shillings, this has been a very complex project. It is not always easy to control –'

Shillings slapped his copy of the report against the palm of his hand. 'Dr Eshkol, you are being paid, and are given authority by our government and by your government, *to be in control.*'

'Look, now, Bill,' said Senator Lerner, stepping in nervously. 'Dr Eshkol is not here on trial. I am sure we all agree there are certain problems. I know as a member of this Committee and as a Jew that I would like to know what's the cause of these personnel problems, and I'm sure Dr Eshkol will be only too glad to enlighten us . . . Dr Eshkol?'

'We are a peaceful people, but God has not granted us the most peaceful place in which to live. Each of you knows the threat we face – a threat no less extreme than the one faced by six million Jews in Europe in 1939. They did not survive. We must, we shall . . .'

Shillings, glaring at the white-haired Israeli, showed no softening of approach. 'About the personnel, Doctor?'

'The point I was making before being interrupted is that it has been necessary to transfer a number of persons from the power plants to military installations and to areas more in need of immediate attention. We have a great shortage of advanced technical skills. These people will, of course, all be returning to the plants as soon as possible. But our defence requirements must remain a first priority.'

Shillings seemed unmoved. 'It seems to me essential that we, on the Committee, should receive a full accounting of the exact number of persons, their skills, and where and why they have been "temporarily" transferred. This whole thing has gotten quite out of hand.'

Senator Lerner turned towards Shillings as he said soothingly, 'Bill, Dr Eshkol will be back with us tomorrow and I'm sure he can provide us with all the relevant information then. I'd like to thank Dr Eshkol for coming here to answer our questions. And now, if there are no further comments . . .'

But there was one further comment. Senator Frank DeAntonio of Wyoming had served longer than any other Senator, and was known for his tactic in debate of applying a steady concentration of force at the point where links were weakest. He had actually turned down the position of Senate Majority Leader, saying it would ruin his mind for 'good calm fishing during recesses'. Now the tone of his voice was low and relaxed, as though his presence at the meeting was the merest coincidence.

'You've been most helpful, Dr Eshkol, and I'd like to add my personal thanks.'

The Israeli scientist smiled, relaxed a shade. 'You're kind, Senator.'

'And it looks like you've been trying real hard to iron the bugs out of this thing.' The Senator flipped casually through the massive Israeli report. 'What I want to know is, have there been any *special* problems along the way you'd like to tell us about which haven't come up?'

'Well, no, Senator. I think our discussion here today has been quite comprehensive,' replied Eshkol cordially.

'What I'm getting at is this. Is there any extra way we can help – from over here in the States?'

'But you have helped us already. You have given generously and the people of Israel acknowledge that gratefully.'

'Well, I enjoyed reading this report which you've filed with our Committee. It's a thorough piece of work, runs to about, ah, 600 . . .'

12

'To be precise, to 654 pages, Senator.'

'Thank you. Well, it's all so helpful that there's not much else we need to ask, I should think. There's only one little point . . . for my own clarification . . . see, down here on page 591, in this third footnote . . .' As he spoke, there was a rustling like the wind stirring leaves as everyone flipped through their copies. 'It's concerning this French consultant, this Dr André Longpré . . .'

Dr Eshkol's eyes were unblinking behind his spectacles. They looked like two goldfish observing an approaching cat. He coughed lightly and did not seem to notice that his pipe had gone out.

'This Dr Longpré's been doing a deal of consulting, it seems. He's been over your way seven times in the last year and a half.'

'Ah, yes, seven times maybe.'

'He must come pretty expensive, being a consultant. What would it cost to fly a nuclear physicist like him back and forth that often?'

Senator Shillings, returning to a peak of alertness, began to eye Dr Eshkol like a hawk.

'Well,' said Eshkol, 'as to the exact figure. We have so many people –'

'And how many of these are from France?' queried DeAntonio.

'Well, I believe . . . Dr Longpré's the only one. Yes, that is so.'

'You must be in pretty bad need of him – all this visiting going on. Can you go into Dr Longpré's work a little?'

Dr Eshkol began slowly to fiddle with the buttons on his tweed waistcoat. 'He's been advising us regarding the fuel rods – there we did run into a number of snags . . .'

'But I thought you just said there had been no special problems, Doctor?'

Eshkol's face seemed to have lost a little of its firm, confident outline as he pushed his glasses up on his forehead. 'It was no very serious problem. It did not come to mind when you asked about *special* problems.'

Senator DeAntonio stretched far back in his chair, linked his hands behind his head and glanced out of the window. A faint gleam of winter sunlight was penetrating the glass. The Senator seemed almost to be musing aloud as he continued, 'Well, I guess it couldn't really have been a serious problem, but then Dr Longpré needed to come all the way from France seven times to help out with the er, ah –'

'Fuel rods.'

'Sure. Now, I don't know a thing about fuel rods, but I would've

13

thought, this being a US government project, you might've hired an American physicist . . . That's why I asked you if you needed any help from America. We've lots of good physicists. Or does this Longpré fellow possess some special talent?'

Dr Eshkol fixed his gaze on the papers in front of him and kept his eyes down as he answered, 'This man is a generalist, able to handle virtually any technical problem. We felt he was the right one for . . .'

Senator DeAntonio, examining the nails at the tips of his long fingers, went on in his quiet, polite tone, 'Well, doubtless he is a most helpful individual, but unless I'm mistaken – perhaps Senator Shillings can correct – I understood this project was restricted to American and Israeli personnel . . .'

Senator Shillings's face had creased into a broad, tight smile. 'Indeed, Frank, that is one of the provisions . . .'

Dr Eshkol was nervously fumbling in his jacket pockets as though looking for some vital but mislaid piece of paper. Senator Lerner moved quickly to come to the aid of the old gentleman's discomfort.

'I think we'd all agree that Dr Eshkol has been most co-operative here today, gentlemen,' he said. 'I think we'll need to pursue this detail regarding Dr Longpré in another session – does Friday sound suitable to everyone?'

The Senators began to stuff their papers into their briefcases as Lerner continued: 'Before closing the session, I'd like to ask Mr Montgomery whether he has anything to add?'

Ronnie Montgomery, while following the entire exchange with keen interest, had not taken one note. He only said, 'Senator, I think I'd rather hold back my comments until we hear further from Dr Eshkol.'

The company was obviously glad to get up and start moving out of the stuffy room. Senator Lerner escorted Dr Eshkol from the table, and as the tall, double doors opened, Peter Watkins saw the familiar battery of network news cameras and the cluster of reporters waiting with their questions. As he and Ronnie slipped through the crowd, Senator DeAntonio was saying to the NBC reporter in his reassuring voice: 'Just a frank exchange of views on energy matters with our good Israeli friends . . .'

As Ronnie Montgomery dashed off to beat the traffic on the bridge to Virginia, Peter was left standing in the empty hall downstairs, feeling agitated and tense. He had already tried to ring Liza twice, but could raise no reply. As he wandered down back along the corridor, he became aware of the murmur of voices from one of the hearing rooms to the right. His curiosity and need for some diversion made him decide to see what was going on.

In the small interview room, which was not really a hearing room at all, a group of observers sat on chairs at the back and faced a young woman, speaking at the front. Peter could only just see her from where he stood, and he could hardly hear her voice at all. Her long, reddish brown hair had been gathered at the back with a ribbon. Her face structure was very delicate, and he noticed her enormous dark eyes. She was certainly delightful to watch, Peter thought, but he decided not to go into the room to listen. He did not particularly wish to hear what seemed, from her expression, to be a painful testimony. He preferred written reports in these matters. As he left the room, he gave a friendly nod to the nameless Senator from Delaware. No reporters, TV cameras or microphones lay in wait outside the empty doorway. These were not matters which anyone wished to hear about, especially over dinner. It was more heart-warming to have a quick glimpse of Dr Eshkol bringing friendly regards from Israel.

He hurried back to the hall phone and dialled the by now memorized number. Liza's answering service came on – she had gone to New York. When he left his name, the service girl said: 'Oh, Dr Watkins . . . she left a message. She'll be home sometime tomorrow afternoon, and is very anxious to hear from you.'

As he walked down the Capitol steps, oblivious of the snow and ice, a self-satisfied grin spread across his face and he felt in the pit of his stomach a lover's pleasurable lurch of anticipation.

4

At a quarter to eleven the next morning, Peter Watkins sat at his office
desk with half a dozen notebooks open in front of him, trying, without
luck, to piece together some snippets on Dr André Longpré. He felt
very on edge. He'd already called Liza's answering service twice and
was trying to restrain himself from calling again until noon. He began
to comb through the index of a fat notebook. When the phone started
to ring, it startled him into sitting back abruptly. She was calling him!
He would meet her immediately, anywhere. He tried to calm down as
the phone rang a second time.

'Hello . . .'

'Pete? Is this you?'

It was a gruff, male voice. Who in hell was it? No one ever called him
'Pete'.

'Barney Shaw speaking,' said the voice.

'Why – Mr Shaw. I didn't expect to hear –'

'Sorry I was busy the other day. Look, you still interested in
handling some work for us?'

Here was a sudden turnabout for you. Peter tried not to sound
over-eager as he replied, 'Sure. What did you have in mind?'

'Well, some of our people looked your stuff over and liked it. I don't

16

know the Middle East from a hole in the ground myself, but the long and short of it is we'd like to have you come in as assistant for Middle East policy . . . How does that sound?'

Peter's head reeled. 'It sounds fine. Yes, really great.'

'I'll give it you straight – the pay's lousy. But as we pick up momentum, there'll be more in the kitty. And the main thing is there'll be an important place for you in any future O'Donnell Administration.'

'Look, I'm not chasing the money here. It seems to me Senator O'Donnell's –'

'Sure, kid. Great. Listen, you'll be working under Dr Mattingly of Harvard. He's our chief foreign-policy guy right now. He'll have charge of most of Tim's speeches.'

'Right. I'm familiar with Mattingly's work.' Peter in fact loathed the man, saw him as an arrogant, conniving pedant.

'We'd like a basic draft for a policy speech on Israeli jurisdiction over Jerusalem – nothing too complex. Stress patriotism, friendship with Israel, the importance of keeping Jerusalem in a state of peace, open to all men of any faith, blah, blah, you know.'

'I'll see what I can come up with.'

'Thanks, Pete. Gimme a call next week. We'll arrange an office for you and so on.'

'Thanks for calling, Mr Shaw. I'll be in touch.'

Peter felt a sense of total amazement as he put the phone down. He slapped his notebook shut, grabbed up his muffler and overcoat and dashed out of the office. He wanted a drink and a long, lingering lunch at Rive Gauche.

As he went down the steps of the Senate, the snow was glittering in the sunlight. There was even a hint of warmth in the air – in December! He sauntered light-heartedly over to the kerb to wave down a cab. To his right a woman with her back to him was frantically signalling for a cab as well. She was wearing a white coat and hat and had a pair of the best legs ever. Maybe he'd actually offer to share a ride. He called out, 'Ah, Miss . . .'

Then came his next surprise. As she turned, he found himself looking into Liza's face as it broke into a radiant smile. Now was the moment for him to rush over to her, sweep her up in his arms and hug her and kiss her. He'd already acted out this meeting in his daydreams a hundred times during the last few days. But he hardly knew her really. Instead, he found himself just standing in front of her, smiling awkwardly.

17

'Peter Watkins! I got your messages . . . I really have been dying to hear from you.'

She gave him a little smile as prim as it was wickedly teasing.

'Well, let's not stand about freezing. Can I force you to take lunch at the Rive Gauche?' he asked.

He linked an arm in hers and pulled her close.

'No force will be necessary,' she said with a soft laugh.

With the Rive Gauche surprisingly empty, they got to sit at one of the better tables. Peter watched as Liza slipped her coat off her shoulders and admired the rounded beautiful slope of her breasts.

'OK. Tell me what's new,' she said.

'What do you mean?'

'You've been grinning like a Cheshire cat ever since I ran into you.'

'Have I? I'm just so happy to see you again.'

She looked at him mockingly. God, she was so utterly beautiful. He could barely speak.

'No, truly I'm just happy to see you. And on top of a surprise phone call. You remember I said I'd like to work for O'Donnell?'

'The Senator?'

'The same. Well, last week I went in for an interview and talked to this old hack who treated me like dirt. Then today he calls me and it turns out he wants me aboard – right away!'

'That's marvellous! To do what?'

'It's a bit on the vague side – Middle East policy mostly. They liked the material I turned in.'

'But such a complex subject. How can you start to study it?' Liza wrinkled her nose in mock distaste.

'Basically, I'll be working on some Israel stuff for the Senator, for the campaign.'

'It sounds exciting. I'm really pleased for you!' And she reached out with her warm hand, drew his head towards her mouth and kissed him gently with her moist lips, just as a forbidding waiter loomed above them with the wine.

When they emerged into the street, they were both shining with a warm and happy glow. Liza's hair was slightly disarranged, and its blonde wisps glowed in the sunlight. The snow shone like glass about them. It was still only two o'clock.

Having hailed a cab, they held hands as they drove to Liza's. When the car stopped outside her townhouse, Peter silently paid the fare and got out with her, clutching her close as she let them both in. They entered the house to find the living-room bathed in an orange sunlight which gave it a bizarre and magical glow. Liza did not switch on any lights, but turned at once towards Peter and began to kiss him. He pressed her against the door, and as he stroked her breasts he gently pinched her nipples. She murmured to show her arousal, while, still holding her against the door, he unzipped her skirt and slipped it down from her waist. Soon they both lay naked on the yellow rug near the front door, kissing and stroking in passionate concentration.

Two hours later, still dazed and happy from love-making, they were sitting in the kitchen with towels wrapped around them and the heating turned up high, drinking wine. Six white candles illuminated the room and made the beauty of Liza's face even more stunning. She smiled as he nuzzled her neck, and then, regaining a mock composure, asked very gravely, 'What are you going to write your speech about?'

'What speech?'

'Your speech for the Senator.'

'My mind's on other things right now,' he said, as he pulled the towel away from her breasts and discovered, to his great satisfaction, that she was as willing to return his kisses as he was to give them.

5

Senator Timothy O'Donnell sat in his swivel chair, looking down on New York Avenue from the window of his campaign headquarters office. The walls were covered with maps of the various states, showing precinct by precinct breakdowns of party registration, voter turnout, income levels. Three long tables were covered with computer printouts.

Tim O'Donnell had come a long way very fast. He had grown up in LA and had had a fairly middle-class background. He had gone to the University of Southern California, where he'd played quarterback for the Trojans and become something of a national sports hero. He just missed the Heisman trophy in 1964. He'd then gone on to Berkeley, where he got his law degree, graduating with honours.

When Nixon got into office, Tim raised the funds to establish a respected non-profit organization, the Institute for Social Justice. He was also lecturing at the UCLA School for Public Policy when he was approached to run for Congress. He was then only thirty. He took the offer seriously, but said he had to refuse because he felt an obligation to be with his family. He was so damned sincere about it that the Democratic Search Committee nearly fell over with surprise. They usually heard this excuse only when a guy's wife was an alcoholic or when he was about to be indicted.

20

Two years later, they came back with the same offer. This time they really went out of their way to put the pressure on. They told Tim again and again that he had to do it out of a sense of duty; the country needed men like him in the crisis in which it found itself. So, reluctantly, he finally accepted. He became popular very quickly, seeming to embody what people described as 'Californian' qualities: qualities of innovation, ease and energy. He'd gone on to a distinguished career in the Senate, but had maintained his interest in civil rights and had been one of the major supporters of national health insurance. Increasingly, he was a prominent figure on the national news, which was quite remarkable for a freshman Senator.

Three years into his first term, Tim and Allison were divorced. It had all been handled quietly and with dignity, though even the jaded Californian public was a little shocked. After that, he spent a lot more time working behind the scenes in the Senate. He became more interested in foreign policy. He was soon re-elected to a second term, and there was more and more talk about him being a good Vice-Presidential possibility in the coming election.

His personal staff was stunned when he called them together and told them he was planning to run for the Presidency itself. Now, as he sat there, he remembered what each of them had said at the time. Then his intercom buzzed: 'Mr Kovacs to see you, Senator.'

'Send him in, please.'

The day had been galloping by. He'd been on the phone half the morning to New York and LA. Already it was three o'clock. He'd been mentally poising himself all week for this meeting with Victor Kovacs, President of the United Federation of Labor, the biggest and most politically powerful union in the country. Kovacs was a brawny, aggressive operator, after whatever he could get for the rank and file. But he was also a fair man, and always willing to listen. Tim knew that his own record with organized labour had been good; an endorsement from Kovacs would boost his campaign immeasurably.

The large, red-faced man entered the room, his tie loose, his sports jacket wrinkled. 'Afternoon, Senator . . .'

'Come on in, Vic. Take a seat.'

Tim indicated a lounge chair beside a coffee table. He rose from his desk and went to a cupboard.

'Can I maybe fix you up with an early one?'

Kovacs beamed. 'I always like to see the working-man being served by his elected representatives.'

'Let's see now. If I remember, you're a Scotch drinker – on the rocks, am I right?'

Kovacs nodded and laughed as he took the glass. It was a good time to relax in a long day.

'Quite a set-up you got going here,' Kovacs said, looking around the room. 'So there's a fair bit of talk about you goin' for the big one.'

Tim flashed him a winning smile. 'Well, and hardly all talk. One of the reasons I wanted you to come here today –'

'Hold back a minute.' Kovacs lugged his heavy frame forward in an attempt to settle more comfortably. 'I think you know I like and respect you. So do a lot of the men I represent.'

Tim smiled appreciatively.

'And everyone knows you got a lot to offer. A whole lot. I say that sincerely. You *know* I do.' Kovacs cocked his big head up and fixed Tim O'Donnell with dark Hungarian eyes. 'But *you're young*. You've just about no money. And you're divorced. That would all be fine, but you're up against an incumbent President who isn't exactly a stooge, and you're up against Willie Lamb in your own party, who's running, as of today . . .' Kovacs fumbled a crumpled slip of paper from his coat pocket and unfolded it '. . . thirty points ahead of you in the polls.'

Tim felt stung into being more emphatic than ever.

'I'll tell you what I'm seeing when I look down that long road,' he said, pointing to the window. 'I'm seeing a big White House, and the man who lives there today is a Republican named Randall. I am of the eccentric notion that another man should be living in that house. And that man should be a Democrat! Willie Lamb's a decent guy, but he's not what this country needs, and people are going to realize it sooner or later.'

'Look, I didn't say Lamb was Mr Wonderful. What I'm saying is this – if you run, you might win a few primaries, you'll maybe even develop quite a following. By convention time, you could even have pulled mighty close to Lamb. That would be a long and bitter race, though, and who do you think will win it?'

'I'm going to win that race, Vic.'

'President Richard Randall is going to win it because an over-eager hot-shot muscled in and split his own party!'

Tim O'Donnell, more than a little steamed up, snatched up the glasses to pour out refills. Kovacs was cracking his big knuckles as he was handed another long one on ice.

'Vic,' said O'Donnell, 'I'm not a spoiler. I want to see Randall

22

knocked out just as much as you do. But I think I can run a stronger race against Randall than Lamb can manage.' He took three sips and then swallowed down the whole drink. 'There's just one thing I want you to tell me straight. If you had the choice between me or Willie Lamb for President, who would *you* pick?'

Kovacs looked at the Senator, gave a big sigh and took a drink. 'You, every time.'

It was what O'Donnell had been waiting to hear. 'I was hoping you'd say that, and I appreciate it, Vic. The Wisconsin Primary is six weeks today. Lamb will be in that race, and maybe Lerner. I'm going to be in it too, and I'm going to beat Lamb. If I don't beat him there, then you have my word, I'll get out.'

Kovacs rattled the ice about in his empty glass and stared down at the floor as Tim pressed on. 'If I beat Lamb in Wisconsin, I want to know, do I have your support?'

Kovacs rubbed a hand over his whiskers. 'Lemme put it this way . . . If you win in Wisconsin, I'll be putting in some very good words about you in plenty of the right places. You've got my word on it.'

He smiled broadly and held out his big hand. Tim shook it firmly. 'Thanks, Vic.'

O'Donnell sighed with relief as he saw Kovacs go. Victor Kovacs meant whatever he said.

6

As he left the campaign headquarters, Tim O'Donnell remembered
that his son Jeffrey's birthday present was still up at his Senate office.
He'd swing by there to pick it up, maybe catch a few minutes of
President Randall's press conference on the TV in his office. It was nine
o'clock when he went into the empty Senate building.

As he rounded the corner into his corridor, he saw a short man
hovering outside his door. Sprucely dressed in a large 1950s suit and
wearing a pair of gold wire-rims, here was a classic specimen of the
lobbyist – incessant, deferential, contemptuous. Nathan Pflug, despite
his modest appearance, was one of the most powerful men on the Hill.
As the head of IPAL, the Israel Political Action League, he held the key
to some of the richest coffers in America.

'How nice to see you this evening, Sen-a-tor . . .'

O'Donnell made an attempt at a smile.

'How do you do, Nathan.'

He put his key briskly in the lock, but as he went in at the door felt
Pflug stepping in directly behind him.

'I like this about you, Senator . . . that you work late.'

'I really just stopped by to pick up my son's birthday present.'

Pflug jingled his change in his pockets and moved closer as Tim

O'Donnell searched for the present.

'Let me come straight to the point, Senator. Now that the President's control is slipping . . . you're probably aware that a number of Jews believe Willie Lamb can help. We are naturally anxious to *concentrate* our support, so must choose the right man.'

'I understood the Jews were firmly behind Michael Lerner. He's been Israel's greatest friend in Washington, and he's running.'

'Senator Lerner is a great man, but Senator Lerner has a problem.'

'What would that be, Nathan?'

'He's Jewish. And no Jew can be elected President of the United States – not, at least, as yet.'

Pflug blinked his near-sighted eyes, then rubbed them. 'I am a realist, Senator, and so are the people I represent. We stay close to the possible, and *that* is where we push.'

'So where's the push to be this year?'

'Well, we've not told anyone *not* to give money to Lerner, but I think you'll agree that Willie Lamb is all set to be the next President of the United States.'

'He will be defeated.'

'Let me assure you, Senator, that President Randall will *not* be re-elected. We're already making it *very* difficult for him.'

'I'm not talking about Randall.' O'Donnell paused and realized that Pflug had never taken his eyes off him for an instant. '*I'm* going to beat Lamb and *I'm* going to beat Randall.'

Pflug smiled and took out a handkerchief to begin polishing his glasses. 'Senator, I had a feeling you might say something of the kind. But you are too young, and you have no funds. Without funds, you have no chance. And who do you think is going to give you funds?'

Pflug fixed the Senator with a strong glare, thrusting out his chin aggressively. Tim O'Donnell saw exactly what they intended. They were going to support Lamb, and they were going to squeeze him, O'Donnell, in with Lerner.

Pflug continued coldly: 'Senator, you are going to support Willie Lamb, and you are going to back Michael Lerner as his running-mate. You are not going to disrupt this campaign. To be perfectly frank, you really cannot afford to do otherwise. You see, Senator, you need us.'

Pflug had broken into a smile like that of a satisfied mortician. After he had left, Tim O'Donnell felt so furious that he flicked off the lights and was half-way along the hall before remembering that the birthday present he had called in for was still sitting up there on his desk. He would just have to come back for it at the weekend. For tonight, there was a quiet, relaxing dinner with a certain girl awaiting him. He had every confidence in her warmth and tenderness.

7

Peter Watkins ran into the Senate, thinking he must be late for the Subcommittee hearing. Under his arm he carried eight folders of material – one for each Senator plus one for Ronnie Montgomery. As he entered, he saw them all still getting settled. He handed out the folders, nodding to and greeting each one before heading for his usual seat.

Ronnie grinned in greeting. 'New boy in class today . . .'

'What do you mean?'

Ronnie inclined his head towards the top end of the hearing table. Beside Senator Lerner there sat a tall, gaunt young man with fair hair and large, pale-blue eyes. He looked detached and utterly in control.

'What became of Eshkol?'

'Unexpectedly called back to Israel – an urgent technical matter.'

'And your interpretation?'

Ronnie smiled confidently. 'I think they were flustered about this Longpré stuff, so wheeled in a tougher customer.'

Peter looked again. The young man was wearing a black jumper and carefully scrutinizing the Senators as they sorted their papers.

'Who is he?'

'Name's Shavinsky – Lerner says he'll soon be giving us a full introduction.'

At that point, Senator Lerner looked up, closed a notebook and cleared his throat. 'I'd like to bring this hearing to order. We shall be continuing our discussion of the Israeli nuclear-power programme. With us here today is Dr Lev Shavinsky.' The doctor smiled his acknowledgement. 'Dr Shavinsky is chief technical director to the Israeli Nuclear Authority, and chairman of the Physics Department at Hebrew University. He was educated at MIT and the Zürich Institute.'

In his usual style, Senator Shillings jumped in first. 'Dr Shavinsky, Senator DeAntonio brought a certain Longpré to the Committee's attention at our last meeting. Longpré, from France, has been called in repeatedly to consult with you. Can you fill us in with some background on this?'

Shavinsky stretched in his chair. He was very slender but had an athletic build. 'Dr Longpré,' he said, 'was called in to aid in the resolution of a series of technical problems centring on the fuel rods. With his assistance, we were able to bring the matter to a conclusion. The reactor is now operating at full capacity.'

He stared blankly at Senator Shillings, who seemed more than a little unnerved by the curt performance.

'Dr Shavinsky,' said the Senator, 'I'd like to remind you that this entire project – all three reactors – has been financed by the United States government. This Subcommittee has been given full authority to oversee the progress of that project.' His voice had begun to rise. 'Now, when I ask for information, I certainly expect a more detailed answer than the one just given. You show a disrespect for my intelligence and that of this Committee. I will not have it so. Is that understood?'

Senator Lerner cut in: 'I think that what Senator Shillings wishes to know is what exactly did Dr Longpré do? How was he picked and why was he there so often?'

Shavinsky contemplated the table top. 'These are simple matters. I shall be happy to respond. Dr Longpré's area of expertise is the installation and removal of fuel rods – which are the heart of the reactor, its very fuel supply. These rods are, of course, made from a special enriched uranium. They must be handled extremely carefully and must be positioned with extreme precision.'

Shillings continued to stare at Shavinsky, never once blinking as

27

Shavinsky went on in perfect calm. 'As you know, the reactors we have were designed and built by Vendewerke of Frankfurt, West Germany. These three reactors are the first of their kind, so not a lot is known regarding their special – I believe you use the word "quirks" – especially in the assembly of the reactor. Dr Longpré was brought in as a result of initial difficulties with the implementation of this fuel rod assembly.'

Shavinsky looked about the room. The Senators seemed satisfied with his answer. Senator Lerner was putting aside the notes he'd been making as he said, 'Thank you for your helpful response, Doctor. Now, could you relate how Dr Longpré was selected for the project?'

Shavinsky stretched out his long lean arms on the table. 'We had made an inquiry with your Atomic Energy Agency, but were told America lacked experience with this type of reactor. We contacted the technical director of Vendewerke, and he supplied us with a list of European physicists who might be of help. We contacted all those on the list, but only Dr Longpré was immediately available.'

Shillings shielded his eyes from the overhead lights and stared directly at Shavinsky. 'The Committee would like to obtain copies of all your correspondence with both the AEA and Vendewerke. Is that possible, Doctor?'

Shavinsky smiled back tightly. 'Oh yes, I'm sure I can have it sent for your inspection, Senator. Our project is open to all inquiries. We share all our records with you.'

Senator DeAntonio, who had been practising tying some flies for his fishing during the next recess, looked up and held an elaborate, colourful fly between his fingers, admiring it cheerfully. He barely glanced at Shavinsky as, speaking softly, almost to himself, he asked: 'Doctor, I'm really just a country lawyer from Jasper, Wyoming. You must forgive my ignorance, but I have to confess I don't really understand this nuclear-energy thing. Now, we've heard about rods, and Dr Watkins here has already given us a briefing on something called processed plutonium – some kind of stuff that gets stolen, it seems. Can you run over all this a little for me, please?'

Shavinsky smiled patiently at DeAntonio. 'Senator, it is really most simple. The uranium rods are the fuel of the reactor. After a certain period of generation, the uranium rods become used up, depleted. But they can then be rehabilitated, as it were, at a nuclear fuel reprocessing centre.'

'So it's kind of a big circle, and you can just keep the thing running for ever?'

'Just about.'

Senator Shillings cut back into the centre of the arena. 'In light of this process, can you explain in more detail the problems Dr Longpré encountered, the problems which delayed the reactor being put into operation by almost . . .' he flipped through the report, '. . . almost seven months?'

'We found that the injection chambers, the lattices in which the rods are inserted, were not properly aligned – perhaps a result of faulty machining. Dr Longpré first consulted with us on reconstructing these lattices.'

'And did that require seven visits?'

'It was a highly complex problem, Senator Shillings. Dr Longpré had other projects that he was also working on in Europe at the time.'

'So what of the spillage incident described on page 87 of the report?'

'As we were trying to align the lattices – and this is an operation which requires almost microscopic precision – one of the rods being inserted cracked, so releasing a number of pellets into the immersion tanks. The rod was removed, the pellets were collected and both were disposed of at our El Zevon disposal facility near the Dead Sea.'

By now Senator Shillings had dug firmly back into the report. 'And as a result of that incident, there was a slowdown, while our government, as I understand it, authorized the shipment of additional enriched uranium. This is very expensive stuff, Dr Shavinsky, and time is also money.'

'Yet we had the plant in full operation within ninety days. We were not far off schedule.'

Senator Devereux, a veteran in his late seventies, set down his long cigar in a big ash tray and looked up, as though coming out of coma, as he asked, 'How are you today, Dr Shavinsky?'

'Very well, Senator. Enjoying our discussion a great deal.' Shavinsky's grin flashed like a knife-blade.

'I'm glad to hear it. Washington isn't at its purtiest this time of year. You come up sometime in April, see the cherry blossoms . . . a most lovely sight.'

'I should be happy to return.'

'What I was going to ask is probably just because I'm an old man and don't always follow these things so good. On the chart I got confused where you requested a shipment of uranium – the shipment of 24 September. That shipment was to help you all get the second reactor going. Am I on course?'

'Yes, sir.'

'But, now, that second reactor, according to what we've heard, has never been put into operation. So I was wondering why that uranium got shipped over if you weren't ready to use it?'

'Well, the shipment of 24 September was, technically, to have been for Phase One of the second reactor, but then we found it necessary to use these additional rods in the first reactor, the one Dr Longpré had helped us with.'

A number of heads had begun to turn. Peter caught Ronnie's eye, then glanced back at Shavinsky. Senator Lerner looked up sharply from the chart, and said: 'Dr Shavinsky, I must say, like Senator Devereux, that I assumed, when I read the chart, that the 24 September shipment was for the second reactor. Now you tell us it was used for the first reactor. This seems to me to be highly irresponsible documentation which could most unfortunately be seen as a deliberate attempt to mislead this Committee.'

Peter Watkins sensed behind the rapid glances that Shavinsky threw around the room a realization of having underestimated these old buffers of the American Senate. Meanwhile, Senator DeAntonio was looking mildly up from his fly-tying. 'Well, I'd like to get sorted out on where all this uranium was going, but we seem to keep circling back round to this Longpré fellow. He's evidently a brilliant genius, yet we've seen nothing but problems everywhere we look. I think it might be worth the Committee's time to request that Dr Longpré appear before us on behalf of the Israeli government. Might that be arranged, Dr Shavinsky?'

Shavinsky leaned forward, pressing his white hands down hard on the table's edge. 'Dr Longpré cannot appear before this Subcommittee . . .'

'Now listen here,' said Senator Shillings, breaking in angrily, 'Shavinsky, if you think –'

'I'm afraid, gentlemen, Dr Longpré's dead. He died six weeks ago in Lyon, from heart failure. Sadly he was only fifty-three.'

The whole room stared at Shavinsky, who calmly turned his gaze out of the window.

'Dr Shavinsky,' said Senator Lerner, agitatedly shuffling his report, 'I think it would have been helpful for you to have made this clear to us earlier.'

'The question did not come up,' Shavinsky replied as he propped his chin on his fists, coolly awaiting the next question.

'Perhaps, gentlemen, at this point I might make a contribution.' All the Senators looked over as Ronnie Montgomery stood up, put on his glasses and slipped a sheet of paper out of the back of a folder.

'Ah, Mr Montgomery,' Senator Lerner nodded to him amiably. 'We're always glad to hear from you.'

Ronnie wore his studious, academic look as he faced the hearing table. 'I have some information on Dr Longpré that should be brought to the Committee's attention.' Shavinsky was sitting up very straight and watching Ronnie intently as he continued, 'Dr Longpré's expertise must have been highly regarded, for he has been sought out as a consultant by countries all around the globe. He made five trips to China during the last four years alone. He did extensive work in Argentina, and there is evidence that he also undertook an assignment in Iran prior to the fall of the Shah.'

Senator Devereux's bushy white eyebrows had shot up high on his forehead. 'You mean to tell us that we had someone working on one of our reactors who was also working for the Communist Chinese?'

'I must say that that represents a remarkable list, Mr Montgomery,' said Senator Lerner, scratching the back of his head. 'Is it a typical itinerary for a nuclear consultant?'

'I'm afraid not, Senator Lerner. Dr Longpré, you see, was no typical consultant. His particular area of expertise was not reactor technology at all.' Ronnie set the paper down in front of him as, for a few seconds, he kept them hanging on his words. 'Gentlemen, André Longpré's speciality was the design and construction of nuclear warheads.'

For a moment it seemed as though the Senators were frozen wax-works. The only movement came from Shavinsky, who leapt to his feet, his eyes flashing with bitter anger as he shouted, 'Mr Montgomery, I protest that you have no documentation whatever to back this ludicrous charge! His work for us was directed solely to nuclear power – nothing more!'

'Perhaps I can usefully supplement Mr Montgomery's remarks here,' Peter's voice quickly slipped in in the wake of the outburst. 'If you'll be so kind as to look at the reports I distributed as I came in . . .' There was a pause as stacks of documents were reshuffled. 'My department has obtained much the same information as Mr Montgomery regarding Longpré's travels. All the approximate dates are listed on pages 7 to 9. What I'd especially like to draw your attention to is the emergence of a certain pattern . . .' He walked to the front of the room and unrolled a long stack of computer printout on the hearing table. 'My staff has been working on correlating the approximate dates of plutonium thefts and losses, as derived from various American intelligence sources, with the dates when Dr Longpré was evidently in consultation in the respective countries where such thefts were noticed. I think you'll perceive a striking set of coincidences, if that is the apt term.'

Shavinsky's face looked almost drained of blood as he said, his jaw rigid, 'This is utterly slanderous, Dr Watkins . . . You imply –'

But Senator Shillings cut swiftly across Shavinsky's attempts to cover his confusion: 'Dr Watkins, correct me if I misinterpret on what has been, of necessity, a rapid reading of your excellent résumé, but do I take it you suggest that, during certain periods of time when Dr Longpré was active as consultant in certain countries, plutonium "disappeared" in significant quantity?'

'Damnation take it!' Senator Hartley had slammed down the palm of his hand flat on the table. 'We're all pussy-footing round the main point here. What's the point of getting bogged down in all this data about this guy Longpré's trips? What we're really talking about, and thinking about, but don't want to say, is that Israel has the darn bomb! Isn't that so? Isn't that what we're saying?'

Senator DeAntonio set down a fly he had just finished tying as he said quietly, 'Exactly so.'

Senator Lerner glanced at his watch nervously before speaking up, his face set in rigid lines. 'Gentlemen, we have reached a most serious juncture in all this. We'd all hoped to see these hearings finish on schedule, but now, Dr Shavinsky, I have to say we'll be requiring your presence here for some time yet. I'll have the Senate communicate this fact to your Prime Minister. We have no choice but to begin at once with a full inquiry into the Longpré matter. The election campaign's coming along, I know, but here we have a matter of the utmost gravity. I hardly need to point out to you all, gentlemen, that should the press get the tiniest whiff of what has passed here today, we'll find ourselves sitting on a hornets' nest.'

Ronnie Montgomery and Peter Watkins gazed after the figure of the lanky Israeli as he left the room. His stance conveyed all the tension of a coiled spring as he fixed a smile on his face for the benefit of the network news teams gathered outside the door. There he submitted to a few pictures as he told them: 'We are making excellent progress in our partnership. A strong Israel means a strong America. The Senators and I are agreed on that.'

8

The moment Peter was back in his office, he phoned Liza and she suggested he drop by for dinner. He went home, showered, shaved and hurried over. When she answered the door, she was looking stunning in a black silk jump suit. Before he was half in at the door, she had flung her arms round him and begun a long passionate kiss. As he caressed her slender body, he enjoyed the sensation of his hands running over the sensuous black silk. Her hands were already up under his shirt when a bell sounded in the kitchen.

'Dinner's ready,' she said, promptly disappearing with a laugh.

He tucked his shirt tail back inside his belt, feeling hot and slightly flushed.

'Smells good,' he called.

In the dining room the table had been elegantly set. A spectacular arrangement of wild flowers stood in the centre, while six candles burned in a pair of silver candelabra. Liza carried in two plates of steaming lasagne.

'Can I do something?'

'Sure. Get the wine. There, on the counter. And the salad.'

He sat as she leaned over to pour the wine into their glasses, and found his eyes looking down the front of her loosely buttoned blouse.

He put an arm about her waist and pulled her into his lap. She laughed as he began to try to kiss her.

'You don't wish to sample my cooking?'

'I'd rather sample your –'

'Now, now . . .' She slipped off his lap and took her seat opposite.

There was nothing he could do to stop himself staring into her eyes. They were almond-shaped and blue. She made him think of a graceful lynx, or a leopard perhaps. As she met his gaze she smiled. He lifted a large forkful of lasagne, fragrant with herbs, to his mouth. 'Mmm – fantastic.'

'You like lasagne?'

'My favourite food – always excepting . . .'

'Don't worry. There's something for dessert.'

Both ate hungrily. Home-made Italian bread and a miraculously crisp salad went with the lasagne. It was all beginning to be like a dream for Peter, whose life had seemed so dim and narrow so long.

'Did your day go well?'

Peter frowned at having even to think about it. 'More hearings.'

'Something exciting?'

'A whole heap of boring testimony.'

'I'd like to sit in on a hearing sometime.'

'Well, sometime maybe. There's seldom much to see . . . How did your day go?'

'I spent it discussing wild flowers with the Canadian export board. The centrepiece there is what might be termed a bribe. There's one thing about this job. I always have my house full of flowers.'

'And you're the most lovely of them.' What was coming over him? He'd never said such things before in his life.

She smiled and reached out a hand gently to touch his cheek. 'I thought you Washington bureaucrats were all dull dogs by repute.'

'Well, a week ago maybe. This happens to be the new me,' he said.

He kissed the palm of her hand as she lifted her glass. 'Let's toast the new you,' she said. 'I think you're probably just as excited by this O'Donnell offer as you are with me.'

'O'Donnell? Who's O'Donnell?'

'Come on, Peter. Oh, come on, do tell me about it. I know you've been up to something.'

'To be honest, I'd completely forgotten about it until you brought it up.'

It seemed he had taken her in as she leaned forward agitatedly.

34

'Peter, don't you see it's your big chance? Don't you realize the opportunity it could mean for you? You've got to get in there, you've got to push, I mean –'

He began to roar with laughter. 'For someone not into politics, you seem to carry more than a glint of the old power lust in your eyes. Liza, you have my assurance I've been working my ass off on this O'Donnell thing. I dropped off a rough draft for a new Israel speech yesterday. I think it's the best thing I've ever done.'

'On Israel?'

'Yes. A policy speech on jurisdiction over Jerusalem. It's more or less something I've had at the back of my mind a long time, but now it should help to swing the Jewish vote O'Donnell's way a bit.'

'Why does O'Donnell have to chase the Jewish vote? I thought he'd always been popular with Jews.'

'You're right. But he's up against Michael Lerner. He's got to make sure the Jews support him and not Lerner in the end.'

'The way you talk, you'd think the whole election hinged on the Jewish vote.'

'Look, there are a lot of factors in an election: labour, business, the media, the Catholic vote, the women's vote, all of that. The Jewish vote is just one among those factors, but very important nevertheless.'

'When there aren't even that many Jews, why worry so much about their votes? I still don't understand.'

'The Jews have money, Liza. They're highly organized socially. They're politically motivated. They're super-active. You should know what I'm talking about – they're your people.'

She sat back, looking a little startled. ' "My people"? You make it sound like I belong to an Indian tribe or something.'

Quietly he topped up their wine glasses. 'Let's not talk about politics any more.'

'I thought we were talking about religion.'

'Politics. Religion. OK, OK. So, with the Jews, it all gets a little confused.'

'Anyway, I *do* want to talk about politics. I've never met anyone quite as close as you are to it all. It's really fascinating.'

'Truly, I'm no expert. I've never worked in a campaign. I'm really just a guy who's slightly nuts on foreign policy.'

'But only think, if O'Donnell gets elected, you'll be one of those helping to guide American foreign policy. You'll be making a real mark.'

'I'm just a small fish in a big pond. O'Donnell's got plenty of advisers. I've never even met him. I just have a hunch that if he saw my work he'd sense I could make a contribution.'

After supper it seemed they only wanted to relax. They settled in the dimly lit living room on one of the big white couches, Liza stretching out with her head in his lap. It was enjoyment just to be together, quiet and close. Peter kept on touching and stroking Liza's hair, to reassure himself she was real.

Liza was reluctant to speak about previous lovers. She said that recently she'd been giving herself completely to her work. She couldn't stand the Washington bar scene, and hated going out with someone for the sake of going out. She needed to be with someone she cared for. It took a lot of waiting sometimes. He smiled understandingly. They'd both been waiting a long time.

Gazing back into his eyes, Liza calmly began to unbutton her black silk blouse. She wore no bra and her breasts, half-revealed, were firm and full, their whiteness contrasting with the black silk. As he began to stroke them she closed her eyes and her breathing deepened. She reached to undo the two bottom buttons of Peter's shirt and, as he continued to caress her, began lightly to kiss his stomach and run her hands up his abdomen to his nipples. Then the phone rang. Without getting up from his lap, Liza reached for it on the table.

'Hello? Yes, he's here.' She handed Peter the receiver. 'Your answering service.'

'Yes? How long ago was that? Fine. Thanks.' He hung up and began to redial. 'Dr Mattingly, O'Donnell's chief foreign-policy guru. Wants me to ring back. Probably read my draft.'

Peter shifted himself upright but Liza stayed put in his lap, languorous, her bare breasts rising and falling to the rhythm of her breathing. 'Is that Dr Mattingly? Yes? Watkins here.' As he was speaking so Liza began to occupy herself with unbuckling his belt. Peter smiled and wriggled a bit, but went on fixing his concentration on the call.

'Did you have a chance to look at my Israel piece?'

Mattingly's voice was harsh and gravelly. 'Yes, Dr Watkins, I looked it over. You write very nicely, but I can't see any new ideas there. We've already been working out a comprehensive Middle East policy for the Senator, you know, and I'm afraid you've come aboard a bit late.'

'Ah, well, it was only that Barney Shaw told me someone was interested in the work I submitted earlier.'

Liza had meanwhile tugged his zipper down. Gently he pushed her away, but gently she persisted.

'Well,' said Mattingly, 'I quite understand that Barney never wants to turn anyone away from helping in the campaign. I'm sure we can find something to occupy your talents . . .'

Liza had by now loosened the waist of his trousers and begun to fondle him intimately. He swallowed, breathing hard as he kept after Mattingly. 'But what about the Israel speech? Won't he . . . ah . . . be needing, uh . . .' Peter's distraction became harder to control as he felt a sexual urge begin to gather in his loins.

'Let me be frank with you, Dr Watkins. We have no desire to focus on the Middle East. I intend to place the Soviet Union at the centre of the Senator's foreign policy. Israel is perhaps important for an election campaign – for all the obvious reasons – but has very little strategic significance at this time –'

A loud sigh escaped from Peter. Liza had begun to suck on him. He was trying to hold her head away, even as he wanted her to go on.

'Dr Watkins?'

'Ah . . . yes . . . I'm sorry . . . just moving the phone.'

'Therefore none of our broad objectives entail specific attention being given to Israel. As for the Arabs –'

Peter gasped and shuddered as Liza brought him to a sudden but total climax deep inside her mouth.

'Dr Watkins?'

'Sorry . . .' Peter managed to say. 'Seems like a bad connection.'

'As for the Arabs, I was saying, they are easily controlled by our government. I think the Senator fully understands the importance and nature of that control. Thus we do not expect to see any great changes in the Middle East just now.'

'Yes . . . well, it was good of you to call, Dr Mattingly.'

'I'm sure you see the way of it. Good night, Dr Watkins.'

Peter hung up and fell back on the couch with Liza standing naked before him. As he reached out for her, she jumped clear.

'So what was that call all about?' she asked.

'Oh, that bastard Mattingly's trying to cut me out of the campaign. Says they have their Middle East policy worked out. They're not interested in Israel any more.'

Liza came forward and pressed her warm naked body to him. She kissed him, as though to ease the disappointment of the call. 'Don't you worry. You just have to try a bit harder to get to the Senator. Don't give up. Bypass Mattingly.' She had begun to stroke his back. 'I'm sure that if the Senator knew all you had to offer . . .' He pulled her down on top of him. Politics could wait till tomorrow. Or till next year. All he wanted was for Liza to take complete control over his body and to pour the balm of oblivion over his bruised mind. And that was precisely what she did.

9

The next three days passed glumly. Liza was out of town at a convention of the American Flower Growers Association in Chicago. He found he spent half the time daydreaming about her body. Never had he felt such an intense desire for a woman. On top of that, the O'Donnell thing depressed him. Liza had kept on encouraging him, telling him he'd get there somehow. Just hang about headquarters, she'd said, and wait around for the Senator to come through. Then he could buttonhole him for a few minutes and hand him some of his work. She made it all sound so simple, but Peter hadn't the nerve to try it. It seemed too pushy for his style. He guessed he really wasn't the political type, he told her, sensing a little of her disappointment as he said it. Even so, she kept on trying to boost his spirits. Perhaps, in any case, he should just settle for keeping his job with the Subcommittee. He felt defeated, and empty inside.

Nevertheless he kept on watching the news on TV and reading a clutch of the national dailies. Whatever happened, he was going to follow this campaign carefully, try to get behind how an election really worked. President Randall had begun to campaign a little, running unopposed for the Republican nomination. He'd appeared several times in New Hampshire before the primary there. The crowds seemed unenthused, though Randall always managed to project a certain Presidential dignity. He was respected if not loved.

Willie Lamb was also running unopposed in the New Hampshire primary. Between Lamb and Randall, the media were calling it the most boring primary campaign in living memory. An exceptionally low voter turnout was expected. Peter felt concerned that O'Donnell might have already blown it. Wouldn't it have been better for him to have run in New Hampshire against Lamb? By the time Wisconsin rolled around, Lamb could have built up so much momentum that O'Donnell would be forgotten.

But even as Lamb was devoting attention to New Hampshire, O'Donnell had been making frequent trips to Wisconsin. He'd laid the base for a strong grass-roots movement up there, got a lot of students working for him, even some housewives. It brought him up a bit in the polls against Lamb. It was about the only good news Peter had all week.

Peter had stayed home from work, the Subcommittee having adjourned for the moment. He sat looking through books, making notes about the Middle East. The more he read, the more bewildering that whole situation became. Maybe Mattingly's rejection had saved him from getting into a real mess. Still he itched to be in on the campaign, and felt in his bones that O'Donnell would be going places, and going places without him if he didn't do something soon.

The phone rang from the next room, and he went to answer it.

'Is this Peter Watkins?' The voice seemed vaguely familiar.

'Yes, Watkins speaking.'

'Senator O'Donnell here.'

'Ah, yes, Senator.'

'I've been looking over some of your work. Seems like fine stuff.'

For an instant, Peter felt his head reel. Just a few minutes earlier he'd been thinking his career in politics was all washed up. Now this. Washington was a crazier place than even he'd imagined.

The Senator continued, 'I'm sorry I'm only just getting back to you. The pace has been a mite hectic. I've been out of town a lot – up in

39

Wisconsin.'

'Yes, Senator, I heard. Thanks for getting round to it so quickly.'

He felt his heart sink at the subservient words which emerged from his mouth when he knew he should be using this chance to sink his hooks into O'Donnell. He ought to be sounding more confident, more aggressive . . . He should be pressing for a meeting. How was he going to look with Liza if he blew it at this point?

But the Senator said, 'I'd like us to get together to discuss your ideas . . .'

'Sure, I can fit in any time it's convenient. I know you're so busy . . .'

'Well, tomorrow's out. Then I've got the kids over the weekend. Monday, I'm back up in Madison. Tuesday, I'll be busy all day at the Senate.' The Senator sighed. 'How about today, an hour from now? If you can get out to my place in McClean, we'll have a late lunch.'

'I'm at your disposal, Senator.'

'Good man. You come to 420 Greenfield Road, off the old highway. You familiar with that neck of the woods?'

'Sure thing. I can be there about 12.30 or 1.00.'

'I'll look forward to that, Dr Watkins. Bye for now.'

The moment he put the phone down, Peter found himself shaking nervously as he hurried to scramble a few papers together into his briefcase. Should he dress up to look like the aggressive senate aide, or play it cool, dress casual? He figured he might as well just put on some slacks and a sweater. One of the things he'd always liked about reports on O'Donnell was the Senator's reputed lack of pretence. Hell, the guy had called up out of the blue and invited him for lunch at a moment's notice.

He drove like a madman over the bridge into Virginia. The traffic was light, thank God. It wasn't snowing. The sun had even begun to poke through. He kept glancing at a crumpled slip of paper on the passenger seat – 420 Greenfield Road. He felt as if he already had an appointment with the President himself. What topics should he raise? Maybe he ought to talk about his work with other Senators on the Subcommittee, play the old hand. No, better to let O'Donnell take a lead and respond accordingly.

He tried to slow down his racing thoughts as he stepped up and rang the bell. The door swung open promptly, opened by Timothy O'Donnell in a faded old USC sweatshirt.

'Dr Watkins, or Peter may I call you? Come along in.' The Senator gripped his hand firmly and offered a warm smile. Peter followed him into his den. There was a fire going in the fireplace, while the room was wood-panelled and there were some stunning Indian rugs on the floor.

'Have a seat. Take off your shoes and pull up to the fire, if you want . . . I'll only be a minute in the kitchen.'

Peter sat alone, looking about the room, hardly believing where he was. The panelled walls carried stuffed deerheads, and there was an oil painting of Lincoln. The Senator reappeared, carrying a tray and beaming relaxedly.

'You know, divorce is a horrible thing, but it's the fastest way in the world to learn to cook.'

The Senator set down the tray, revealing toasted cheese sandwiches, two large bowls of tomato soup and cups of hot coffee.

'This soup's the real thing! A constituent of mine, down in the San Joaquin Valley, always sends my office a crate or two of tomatoes. As we never know what to do with them, I decided to learn how you use them in soup. I'm hoping next to crack the secret of tuna casserole. That should impress the White House chef . . .'

Although the Senator had said it with a robust laugh, just hearing the White House mentioned sent a cold chill up Peter's spine. He sat back a moment, then said to the Senator: 'I'll have to be honest and tell you, your call surprised me.'

'How so?'

'Well, several days ago, after I submitted my Israel draft, Dr Mattingly called me. He said you wouldn't be needing my stuff, that my ideas were no use to you.'

The Senator chuckled dismissively. 'So, old Howard got to you? He can be one pain in the ass. He has this way of talking to you like you're one of his Harvard undergraduates who's just handed in a term paper with chocolate syrup spilled over it.'

Peter found himself liking the Senator more every minute.

'Sure, I know Howard wasn't too happy with your work, the papers and the Israel draft. It interested me, though. You write well, your ideas are clear, your approach balanced. And what's more, I've been hearing some good things about you.'

Peter had hardly expected this to turn into such an ego trip. 'About me? Whoever from?'

'Oh, people on the Hill – people worth paying attention to. The thing I liked in one paper of yours was the idea of examining the roots of an ancient conflict, getting back to the origins of the dilemma.'

The Senator fixed him with a serious look. 'You know, I've always been a strong supporter of Israel. They can be a stubborn lot of bastards, but you've gotta give them credit for all they've accomplished. And they've been damned good allies.'

'That's why I've placed such emphasis on Israel in my papers.'

'Right. I liked it. But you're a little critical of them at the same time, and that's something we haven't seen enough of. I'm concerned to look at the whole thing a little more deeply, with a deeper sense of history, perhaps. I think our relationship with Israel would be strengthened if we understood them better and if we understood the Arabs a little more, too. I sense that's the kind of feeling you have as well.'

Peter nodded. 'I guess I've grown a little sceptical about reporting of Middle East news in this country. I don't see how our people can ever really understand what's going on over there.'

The Senator started to gather up the dishes with Peter's help, who figured he'd better make a move towards leaving. But before he could say anything more, the Senator suddenly asked: 'Say, you know, we can use all kinds of help in this campaign. How would you like to come in and assist on a secret project I'm involved with . . .?'

Peter looked at the Senator, who stared back at him with a slight but assessing smile. What was all this about now? 'Well, sure – if I can.'

'Come along, I'll show you.'

He followed the Senator down a dark hallway and into a room where the Senator switched on the light. It had the look of a small boy's room, the furniture in disarray. The walls had been stripped of wallpaper. There were buckets and brushes and a tarpaulin on the floor.

'It's my son Jeffrey's room – when he stays. It's his birthday this weekend. I decided to put up new wallpaper.' The Senator picked up a roll and unrolled the end. The design was blue, covered with space capsules and astronauts floating on the ends of their umbilical cords.

'Official NASA wallpaper,' the Senator said with a wink. 'What do you think? Can you assist with my space programme here?'

They set to work, two bureaucrats rendered inept in the face of genuine physical labour. They struggled with rolls of wallpaper, with paste and brushes, talking all the while as they worked.

'You work a great deal with Lerner on the Subcommittee . . .' said the Senator.

'Yeah.'

'What do you make of him?'

'I'm very impressed. He's decent, astute, and he has this moral seriousness. You could even call it wisdom.'

42

'And as a politician?'

'Well, I'm no politician, but I do know the Senator is widely respected. The people in New York love him. He's got the Jews behind him all the way – and Israel.'

'But can he be elected?' The Senator's observation of Peter's reaction became very close.

'The guy's Jewish. The people won't vote for a Jew – not yet, at least.'

'How about as Vice-Presidential material?'

'Well, could be . . . He's a good man and people know it. He's honest. He could probably deliver New York State. I guess that'd be important.'

'Now you're into my game – politics. New York State is second only to California in electoral votes. Swinging New York is one of the major goals of every campaign. If Lerner could deliver New York, then you'd say he'd make a good Vice-Presidential running-mate?'

'Well . . . yes, I would.'

'So what about the anti-Jewish vote? I mean those people who'd vote against the Presidential candidate because he has a Jewish running-mate?'

'I don't know. That one needs some thought. I do think, though, that prejudice against Jews is fading – the same sort of thing that happened when Kennedy beat the Catholic Issue in 1960.'

'But it still could be a liability?'

'Yes, maybe so.'

'Especially if the Presidential candidate also needed to overcome a few other liabilities . . . such as being young, divorced and without a great deal of financial backing.'

The two men smiled in mutual understanding. Peter was enjoying this sudden closeness with a man he had admired for some time. For once, someone he had liked from a distance seemed even more likeable close to.

The Senator pressed on. 'So how about Willie Lamb?'

'Not at all my kind of candidate. I just can't accept that the American voter could elect him President of this country.'

'No? But they went for Nixon and Carter. How do you ever know what the voters really want? No doubt about it. Lamb can deliver Texas and a good portion of the deep South – Louisiana, Mississippi, Alabama, Arkansas. He may just do well in the West too. That's a lot of votes.'

'So you're suggesting Lamb could be valuable as a running-mate?'
'Yes, indeed.'
'But wouldn't Lerner make a better running-mate, and one more compatible with your views?'
'There's something to which I've been giving a lot of thought. Lerner or Lamb – which should I take? Either one of them could pull me over the top, while together they could sink me. How does it strike you?'

It was a new concept for Peter to think of an election as one big, calculated poker game. He was receiving a quick education.

'Well, Lamb's front runner. He's been a Vice-Presidential candidate twice. He has a good record in the Senate.'
'OK, so that's his résumé. What of the man?'
'He's a good man, but not one who's particularly dynamic or ambitious. And he's got a nice family.'
'Yep, and he's probably never had herpes. What I want to know is, whether you think he can be elected?'
'I think he'll run a weak race.'
'But can I beat him for the nomination?' The Senator studied Peter intently.
'Yes, yes, I think you could. Once people look at the both of you, compare the two of you, they'll see you've something he's never had.'
'Such as?'
'Leadership.'

The Senator smiled. 'Thanks. Now how about a beer?'

They dumped the equipment among the debris on the tarpaulin and headed for the kitchen. Sitting at the breakfast table, drinking beer and looking out at the snow-filled yard, both men fell momentarily silent, lost in their thoughts.

'What you just said about people comparing us – Lamb and me. Could that be the key?' the Senator asked eventually.
'Absolutely! Once they see the difference, Lamb will be left standing in the dust.'
'I've been toying with the idea of challenging him to a debate. It's a risk. He talks fairly well and the people up in Wisconsin may not like all I have to say. They may think I'm just some flake from California. I could stumble. He's way ahead of me, so can afford to take the gamble.'
'Debate him! You'll win. You could really knock him sideways that way. You couldn't lose!'

The Senator broke into a wide grin as he gazed out of the window.

44

'Well, now, that makes two of us of the same opinion. Peter, I must say I like your way of thinking and I'm sure we'd work OK together. Would you consider coming in full-time as a foreign-policy aide?'

'It would be an honour to work for you, Senator.'

Driving back towards Washington, Peter Watkins felt as though his life was starting over a second time. O'Donnell was surely an amazing guy. He felt in his guts that here was a man destined to be the one in the right place at the right time, and now the chance had opened out for him to share a little in the making of that destiny.

10

It took two days and nine trips to get all Liza's stuff over from her place to his. As Peter pulled up with the last carload in front of his townhouse on M Street, he looked over at Liza. They were both exhausted but jubilant.

'I'm glad you're here,' he said. 'It's been a very lonely home.'

Liza leaned towards him and gave him a long kiss. 'I want to be with you. It's that simple.'

For the past two weeks, Peter had been spending each night with Liza, then getting up early in the morning to hurry back to his place to change and grab up his papers for work. It only took a few days to establish a regular routine, and each night he spent with Liza seemed more passionate than the previous one. He knew how much he wanted her to move in with him, daydreaming half his time away at the office about how it would be, living together. But he sensed on her part a slight reluctance, was aware of a streak of independence and self-sufficiency that might stop her short of saying yes. She had her own handsome apartment, in which she took a great pride. It made him too nervous to ask. In any case, they were having such a terrific time together that he didn't want to upset the balance by raising the wrong questions. And there remained a certain mystery about Liza, a hidden part that he couldn't see into.

And then she *pushed* him, made him attempt things he'd never done before – and not only in bed. Her encouragement over the O'Donnell job had been a life-saver. She would read his drafts and then suggest small changes here and there, but her criticism was always gently offered and he agreed with most of what she said. But still he didn't really *know* her, know who she was inside. That would all take time.

At last one night, as they lay in each other's arms after love-making, watching the full moon through the open curtains, Peter said softly, 'I want us to be together every night from here on.' Liza looked at him gravely and kissed him. She never said a word, but he knew he had her agreement – she would live with him. Two days later, on a Saturday, they began the move.

Peter couldn't get over how much stuff Liza possessed. There was a ton of clothes! She always dressed exquisitely, being the kind of woman who made other women look in her direction. How had she bought all this stuff on a lobbyist's salary, he asked. She replied that she was the sharpest-eyed bargain-hunter in Washington. For her part, Liza was overwhelmed by the number of books on Peter's shelves. Nearly every room was lined with them. He'd long since overflowed his library. Now all of Liza's books added to the confusion. As she went around the house, she admired his antiques, the small, enclosed back yard, the big kitchen.

They got her things unpacked, arranged a few of them around the house, got her clothes hung up. They sent out to a local Chinese takeaway for their supper. After a whole weekend of moving, they were both exhausted. They sat, Scotches in hand, watching the fire. A great feeling of contentment came over Peter as he looked across at this woman who had just entered his home and his life. It occurred to him that tonight would be the first time they had made love at his place.

On Monday Liza had arranged to take a day off work to give her a chance to recover from the move. It was strange for Peter to wake up in his own bed for a change, and a little disorienting to kiss Liza goodbye as he left for work, as though they were already married. Before he left the house, he had told her to feel free to treat it as her own, explore it from top to bottom if she liked. That evening, when he arrived back, she was already at the front door to greet him before he could get it open himself.

'Welcome home.' She gave him a big kiss as he set down his briefcase.

He brushed back one of her long blonde curls. 'You look more beautiful than ever.'

'I don't. I look horrible. I've been working all day like a mad housewife.'

'Hey, what smells so good?'

'How does asparagus soup sound, followed by Cornish game hens with wild rice and mushrooms? Come on, take a shower while I finish getting dinner ready.'

'You mean, you won't take a shower with me?'

'It could delay dinner three hours,' said Liza with a laugh.

They walked up the stairs, holding hands. A few minutes later, Liza was busy back at work when Peter, his tie off, his shirt untucked, came stamping into the kitchen.

'Liza, what in hell have you done to my study?'

Calmly Liza went on preparing the meal, never looking up once.

'I mean, you could have asked. That room is my favourite in the whole damned house.'

Liza slammed down a large spoon. 'I'm sorry, Peter – I thought I also lived here now . . .'

'You do, but you've taken over the room I work in, moved out all the furniture, and never even asked.'

'How could I know you'd be so mad? You've still got all that space in the library downstairs.'

'Oh yes, but the light's lousy down there – and that's a cold room. What'd you do with my desk and other stuff?'

'It's all in the attic.'

'What's this about anyway?'

'Well, I need space to work in, too. My office at work is small and noisy. I do a lot of correspondence at night. I got the storage people to bring some of my furniture over and asked them to move your stuff into the attic at the same time. We don't need antiques in every room, do we?'

'That's hardly the point.'

'So tell me what is.'

'You should've asked me . . . You could've called me at work. If you'd just explained, I'd have said yes.'

'I see. I have to ask permission every time I turn around in here?'

'Jesus Christ, Liza, stop being so stupid. I'm only asking for a little consideration.'

'Consideration? Consideration! – I've only been here a day and already you're telling me what to do. The next thing –' Liza jerked her head towards the oven. 'Oh, God, the meat!'

She ran over and pulled out the pan with the Cornish game hens, then banged it down on the counter, with its charred contents, and sighed wearily, 'Dinner's ready.' As Liza angrily put the food on the table, Peter mixed them a couple of drinks. His own anger still simmered, but now he also felt badly that he'd upset Liza and ruined their first dinner at home together.

Peter turned on the TV so they could watch the network news while they ate. They avoided meeting each other's eyes as they struggled with the dried-out, tough meat. The soup had gone cold before being served. The rice had been overdone. Peter battled unsuccessfully to suppress the feeling that it was all his fault.

The first item on the news was a spot on President Randall's poll ratings – which had slipped again. Willie Lamb remained the Democratic front-runner and was now running a good eighteen points ahead of the President in the polls. His election looked more and more a sure thing. There was a brief item on Tim O'Donnell, campaigning hard in Wisconsin. Few commentators gave him much of a chance, though some people up in Wisconsin had begun to show enthusiasm as he toured their state, criss-crossing its many snowbound towns. Peter couldn't keep down a faint smile when they showed the Senator speaking at an old people's home in Milwaukee. He looked up at Liza. She glared back.

After the stream of commercials, the news continued with reports from the Middle East. President Randall's negotiator had been making little progress in the peace talks. Israel apparently refused further discussion of withdrawal from the occupied territories of Gaza and the West Bank. The Israelis claimed that no further constructive steps could be taken while the Arabs continued with their military build-up of recent weeks. The White House and the Pentagon would neither confirm nor deny that such a build-up had taken place, though the network correspondent in Damascus said there were few signs of any large-scale military movements in Syria or Jordan.

Meanwhile, on the West Bank, violence had erupted once more when a twelve-year-old Palestinian boy had been shot by Israeli police during a series of house-to-house searches for terrorists. The boy had darted from his home as two officers attempted to enter. Fearing an attack, one of the officers shot the boy in the head. The neighbourhood broke into a riot as word of the killing spread, and a squad of nearly a hundred police had to be called in to restore order to the scene. One American Palestinian spokesman who was interviewed called the act 'another senseless slaughter committed by the true terrorists of the Middle East'.

Liza stood up and snapped the set off.

'Hey, come on, I was watching.' Peter glared at her.

She sat down again. 'This dinner has already been bad enough without having to listen to a load of anti-Israeli crap from some Palestinian who no doubt spends his time blowing up school buses.'

'Liza, they shot a twelve-year-old boy, for Christsakes!'

'It was an accident. No one denies it.'

'An accident? My God, Liza, the Israeli police are the best-trained in the world – at least, if we take *their* word for it.'

'Don't you see, Peter, it's just like Vietnam . . . Remember how it was when our troops entered villages friendly with the Vietcong? American soldiers shot twelve-year-olds, ten-year-olds – sometimes accidentally, sometimes not. Sometimes those kids carried hand-grenades. You never knew then and you never know today.'

'So, are you saying Vietnam was right, that America should have been there? Is that your justification for Israeli treatment of the West Bank? I wasn't aware that Israel had declared war on the West Bank.'

'Israel is trying to bring some kind of order to a very backward area. Those people live like animals. They're dirty, uneducated. Even though they hate Israel, Israel still tries to help them. The Arabs who live in Israel and on the West Bank live better lives than most Arabs in the Middle East.'

'You make it sound like they should be giving heartfelt thanks to Israel for –'

'They should. They *will* in the end.'

'It's a military occupation, Liza. Whatever Israel does is done directly to improve its military position.'

'Can you blame them? Each time they've turned their back in the last

49

thirty years, they've been attacked by fanatics who want to drive them into the sea.'

'It's not so simple, Liza.'

Liza got up, walked over to the bar and made herself another drink – a double. She did not offer Peter one, but turned around and took a couple of big gulps before smiling weakly. 'There's enough fighting in the Middle East without us going at it too, OK?'

Peter nodded and pushed his plate away.

'Besides,' she said, 'you should be thinking about your future . . . *Now.*'

Peter looked up. 'My future?'

'This is your moment. You should be up in Wisconsin right now – with Senator O'Donnell. He's nobody as yet, but the moment he wins, as he may, everyone in the country will be after him. You should be working to get as close to him as possible.'

'We had a good meeting at his house. I'm writing up some things for him this moment.'

'My God, Peter, he meets dozens of people each day. You know how many people are probably writing up something for him right now?'

'But I can't go to Wisconsin at this instant. I've got my work with the Subcommittee to finish.'

'Quit your job. Tomorrow.'

'How can I do that?'

'Why not?'

'There's a most important hearing coming up, and I've done a lot of the groundwork for it . . . I can't just quit.'

'Do you think the Subcommittee will give a damn about Peter Watkins the day after the hearing?'

'Liza, I've been working alongside these men for years. They're fine people. Many of them I consider to be my friends.'

'In that case, what I want to know is this – which one of them is going to be President? Are any of them going to get you into a better job? No!'

'OK, OK. I know the O'Donnell thing's important, but I can't leave before the next hearing.'

'Why not?'

'It's an important hearing.'

'Peter, you've attended a million hearings on the Hill. So you miss one. What's so important about it?'

'We're dealing with sensitive issues. I'm their chief research analyst.

50

They need me to supply a lot of the data and interpretation.'

'So what's so sensitive about the issues you work with?'

'Liza, the Subcommittee's work is, by nature, highly confidential. I can't just tell –'

'OK, OK. If you don't trust me – fine.' She drank her glass empty and poured another refill before looking at Peter defiantly. 'First you ask me to move in. Then you bitch because I shift a few things around. You treat me like I'm a child of ten or something, and when I ask you a bit about your work, you act like I'm some kind of Russian spy. I thought loving also meant having to do with respect – and *trust*.' She banged down her glass and rushed out of the room. There was the sound of her running on the stairs and of a door slamming.

Peter reflected that it had turned into one of the most miserable evenings he'd ever spent. His life had begun to change at a great speed during the past few weeks. Before that, it had changed very little in ten years. The pace of it was leaving him feeling exhausted. He felt he'd certainly over-reacted to Liza's moving the furniture around. He'd been living alone for so long that he'd grown used to having everything just as he wanted it. Maybe she had been a little pushy in the way she went about it, but didn't he like her for her aggressiveness? And maybe her remarks about Israel had been a little surprising. She'd sounded harsh and bitter, but then she'd been in a bad mood while they were watching the news. It could be she was right that he ought to quit the Subcommittee pronto. And why was he being so cautious in talking to her about the hearings? In future, he'd try to be more open with Liza, try to make her feel more a part of his work. As he had reason to know, her suggestions were usually excellent. She was bound to have a lot of good ideas to feed into his work with Senator O'Donnell.

Peter sat there for several hours, watching the fire, sipping his drink, pondering on the melancholy of the evening. There was the faint click of a door opening upstairs, and quiet footsteps approached the head of the staircase.

'Peter?' Her voice echoed down, timidly and softly, as if she'd been crying.

'Uh-huh?'

'Will you come up – *please*?' She spoke pleadingly, like a hurt child.

'I'll be up directly,' Peter said softly, happy she seemed as ready to make up as he felt himself to be. He switched off the lights and picked up his shoes.

11

Three weeks before the Wisconsin primary, a certain flurry of excitement began to be noticeable in the American political landscape. The Republicans, unenthused with the President, had been able to come up with no better alternative, with the result that Lamb's Democratic campaign had grown remarkably bland and complacent. There had been talk of Senator Lerner running in New Hampshire, but he failed to get organized quickly enough and, it was rumoured, was very tied up in the Senate. With the Wisconsin primary approaching, however, Senator Timothy O'Donnell's uphill battle had begun to draw increasing attention. Day by day, more of the press arrived in Wisconsin as increasing news coverage came to be given to the primary competition in the state. O'Donnell was showing all the irresistible charm of a spirited underdog, and the media could scent a good story when they came across one.

Timothy O'Donnell had spent virtually the whole of the last few weeks in Wisconsin. Each night he would stay at the house of a different supporter, have dinner with them and a group of their friends and neighbours. He had come to know the people of dozens of small towns and cities. It was a good tactic and Tim loved every minute.

Each night, Tim checked back on the phone to Barney Shaw. Their coffers were almost empty, and he was running at 28 per cent to Lamb's 57 per cent in the polls – with 15 per cent of voters undecided. It had him turning and tossing in his sleep, wondering whether he'd made some terrible blunder getting into this race in the first place.

The odds against him were certainly long. Tim could meet a few hundred people in a day, might reach several thousand with a speech. He could get a minute or two's exposure on the evening news. But, the fact remained, he was being steam-rollered by Willie Lamb's extremely well-oiled campaign machine, one of the slickest in American election history. Lamb suffered from no shortage of funds. His staff was huge and well-paid. Every detail of his campaign was carefully planned far in advance. Lamb's people conveyed a sense of their man having already won, of Lamb already *being* President. 'A President You Can Be Proud Of' ran their campaign slogan.

Lamb had access to a powerful series of TV spots, produced by the best political promoters in the country. He was also putting in an appearance at a few carefully organized fund-raising dinners, attended by all the biggest contributors in Wisconsin at $1,000 a plate. But the most effective aspect of Lamb's campaign was probably his use of televised 'town hall' meetings, during which he would field questions and answers on a variety of topics. The questions would be fired at him by a perfect cross-section of Wisconsin voters: farmers and factory workers, housewives and businessmen, blacks and women, storeowners and pensioners. Lamb could be seen to be deftly handling their questions, some pretty tough ones among them. Then, at the end, the crowd would break into spontaneous applause, followed by a television narrator's soft voice-over: 'Willie Lamb . . . a President you can be proud of.' What the promotion never said was that here was no spontaneous community meeting, but a carefully orchestrated and staged political event, the questioners all carefully pre-sifted, and Lamb's responses planned down to the last syllable.

One tactic of the Lamb campaign was to avoid almost all mention of Timothy O'Donnell, as though his campaign had already run out of steam. There was only one sly, indirect reference to Tim in the Lamb campaign ads. It was a line which struck at Tim's youth and lack of experience: a barb which carried a particular sting. Didn't Jack Kennedy beat down that phoney age-and-experience issue back in the 1960 campaign, and now here he was, having to do it all over, with his record in the Senate better than Lamb's, even if he hadn't got his seniority. The emphasis of O'Donnell's campaign was on a fresh dynamic: 'For the 80s . . . a New Energy'.

There were eighteen degrees of frost the night Barney Shaw and Peter Watkins flew into Madison to meet the Senator. At his hotel Tim O'Donnell greeted them warmly and sent for room service to bring up some steaks and drinks. Time was running out. A number of important decisions needed making quickly. Barney Shaw downed two Scotches in succession as he unwound from the journey, and sat rubbing his big red nose. He tended to play the cranky Irish uncle with Tim, having been with him ten years now: 'Timothy, my boy, I trust you are having a helluva nice vacation up here in this godforsaken region.'

Tim smiled indulgently. 'Look, Barney, I'm meeting plenty of people. I'm gaining more support each day. The people here are beginning to wake up to Willie Lamb's slick packaging and canned town hall meetings. Our volunteers are working day and night in every corner of the state. They believe in me, Barney. That's what winning an election has to be all about.'

Barney replenished his glass from a bottle he pulled from his beat-up suitcase. 'Senator, I am well aware of "the little people". In Ireland, they call them leprechauns. In Wisconsin, they call them campaign volunteers. Somehow I had been imagining you were after the Presidency, not running a heart-warming crusade.'

Tim's voice grew sharp: 'Barney, I have to let these people see me, get to know me. I'm a Californian. They don't know me in Wisconsin.'

'They'll know you're from California, all right, if you keep wandering all over the state like some hippie throw-back. And this staying at people's homes every night. Really touching . . . just like Johnny Appleseed! Jesus!'

'Barney, that side of it's important!'

'Important, my ass. I'm working my butt off in Washington trying to hold the show together, and where the hell are you? You've three weeks in which to overtake Lamb – and he's way, *way* in front of you.'

'So what are *your* suggestions?'

'Well, for starters, get your ass on the next plane to New York. Do you realize that at this moment Willie Lamb is at a fund-raising dinner in the Waldorf Astoria which will net him a good $150,000? You know what that means? Fifteen more minutes of TV time in Milwaukee and Madison and Racine and Sheboygan and Osh Kosh and every rotten little town in Wisconsin which it will take Tim O'Donnell five hundred years to reach in person.'

The Senator stood up and looked out of the suite window at the snow-speckled night air. 'Barney, I realize TV's important. We've got our TV budget . . .'

'We've got about enough of a TV budget for a thirty-second spot running at three in the morning. I'm telling you, money's in New York and Washington.'

'But I can't not campaign here in –'

'Look, I'm not saying ignore Wisconsin. What I'm saying is, use your time effectively. Don't spend *all* your time here. You need to be building a national base. This very instant, you should be doing it.'

The three men ate into their steaks and the conversation lulled until the Senator asked about Peter's Subcommittee work, and was told there would only be one more hearing. After that, he'd be with them full-time.

'Now, Barney,' said the Senator, 'I'm going to tell you why I wanted to bring Peter up here tonight.'

Barney was finishing a last piece of potato and was dribbling butter down his chin. He looked up with his usual expression of perpetual annoyance. 'I must say, I've been wondering. But one thing I will tell you, Mattingly is pissed as hell.' He ran a hunk of bread around his plate to mop up the last of the juices.

The Senator only laughed. 'Every time I ask anybody for a little foreign-policy advice, Howard blows six fuses. The reason, Barney, is that I want Peter to tell you about an idea he has that he and I discussed . . .'

Peter sat back, feeling the slight shock of being put on the spot. Barney Shaw was staring penetratingly at him, his buttery chin thrust forward, his glass half-way to his lips. It took Peter only an instant to realize how cleverly the Senator was manoeuvring: testing out an idea on Barney without drawing the fire.

Peter Watkins swiftly gathered his resources: 'I was thinking if only people could be made to see the real difference between O'Donnell and Lamb, could see them debating, then there would be an automatic shift of support for –'

Barney gave him a withering look. 'Sure, kid. If my aunt had balls, she'd be my uncle.'

The ready-made sarcasm stung Peter into anger. 'Listen, you old hacks are all alike. No one can tell you a thing. Well, perhaps you don't realize it, but Willie Lamb consists of nothing but pomposity and hot air. He's never had to take a real decision in his life. Sure, people have been fooled by that smooth manner, but I'll tell you right now, if you could get him and Senator O'Donnell together on the same platform, it would be all over in minutes. Maybe you're too wrapped up in all this New York money stuff to see what could be in the idea.'

'Well, young feller,' said Barney, no more visibly ruffled than usual, 'if you'd care to hear a thing or two from an old hack, maybe you'd like to consider some of the disadvantages. First of all, if Timothy debates with Lamb and he loses, that's it. Finis. No more campaign. But if Lamb loses, he can go on, he's still front-runner. The next thing is, Lamb speaks well, along with being older than Tim, more experienced. That's something else people will see as they compare the two of them. On balance, it all adds up to trouble.'

'But think of the exposure, Barney,' said Tim O'Donnell. 'Far more than we could afford in paid TV ads.'

'In any case,' said Peter, 'how do we know that Lamb will play ball? Will he agree to debate, when his whole strategy has been to avoid any mention of Tim, to play the Presidential role to the end?'

The Senator frowned and nodded agreement, but Barney suddenly brightened up as he took a noisy gulp from his glass of Scotch. 'OK, then. So who says Willie Lamb gets to *choose* anything? We're going to *make* him debate, whether he wants it or not. We'll do it if we have to chase his ass across Wisconsin.' The gruff Irishman rose from the table. 'Well, one old hack's ready for bed. See you in the morning, gentlemen.'

'Thanks for coming up here, Peter,' said Tim O'Donnell as soon as they were alone.

'My pleasure, Senator.'

'I appreciate what you said to Barney . . . He talks tough, but he knows his stuff. He's been very loyal.'

The phone beside the bed began to ring, and Tim walked over to answer it. He looked at his watch and exchanged a few words before hanging up and returning to the table. 'Jesus, they never leave you alone in this game. There's a visitor coming up. You're welcome to stay . . .'

'Oh, I don't want to get in the way.'

'As a matter of fact, I'd like you to stay. You ought to meet Marty, see him in action.'

'Marty?'

'Marty Rifkin – head of the New American Israel League, better known as "NAILs". And that describes perfectly what Marty does . . . he nails you. Marty's all right. I've known him ever since I entered

56

Congress. But he's a hard man . . .'

As he spoke, there was a knock at the door. Tim opened it to Marty Rifkin, and Peter found himself being introduced to a short, wiry man with curly hair, aggressive, but not at all bad-looking. Rifkin spoke to the Senator as though they were close friends. 'How are Laney and Jeffrey?' he asked.

'Both just great. Jeffrey had his tenth birthday.'

'My God. You don't say, ten years old already! I'll bet they enjoy watching their Dad on TV. See you're picking up a little in the polls. I saw some good shots on the news – that NBC correspondent seems to have the hots for you.'

'Responding to my charisma,' the Senator said good-naturedly.

Marty looked in Peter's direction. 'How does it feel to be working for the best Senator in Washington?'

'It feels just fine,' said Peter.

'So, Senator, it seems you're in for a tough time against Lamb.'

'Well, Marty, I guess Willie *needs* a big lead. He's so far behind me in every other respect that if he didn't have that poll rating in his pocket each morning, he'd never get out of bed. Care for a drink, Marty?'

'Thanks, no. I'm short on time right now. I guess you heard the talk about Lamb taking Michael Lerner as running-mate?'

The Senator inclined his head slightly.

'Michael Lerner as Vice-President. That would mean a great deal to the Jews of America.' Rifkin was not taking his eyes off the Senator. 'It's important he be given every chance of reaching that position.'

'Marty, I have much respect for Michael.'

'Your backing for a Lamb–Lerner ticket is very important . . .'

'Marty, Willie Lamb hasn't yet been nominated, and here you already have him in the White House. There's one problem with that . . .'

'A problem?' Rifkin looked back at O'Donnell hard, letting all pretence at humour drop from his face.

'You're leaving out of account the fact that I'm going to beat Willie here in Wisconsin a couple weeks from now, and that I'm going to beat him everywhere else, too.'

'Hm. It doesn't seem too likely. What you may do is hurt Lamb's chances – and, by extension, Michael Lerner's. That is an eventuality which the Jews I represent would not forgive, Senator.'

'So you'd like to see me disappear in a puff of smoke?'

'All we ask is that you withdraw from the race once you're beaten in

57

Wisconsin, and then support a Lamb–Lerner ticket. It could mean a lot to your future.'

'Listen, Marty, Nathan has already got to me with this line.'

'Nathan? Nathan?'

'Come off it, Marty. I speak of Nathan Pflug. If you two haven't been colluding on the phone for two hours earlier today, I'll eat this chair.'

'I haven't spoken to Nathan in weeks. The fact that we both represent concerned Jewish voters . . .'

'And I'm on record as a good friend to the Jews and to Israel. You know that's so, Marty.'

'Sure, Senator. It's our wish to ensure the friendship continues.'

'Well then, you can tell Nathan and your friends at NAILs that I'm sticking in the race and I'm out to win.'

Marty Rifkin stood up slowly. 'Senator, I am sorry that you make things so difficult for yourself and for me. Remember the influence I have over Jewish campaign contributions in this country.'

'Jesus Christ, Marty, I've not had a dime from the Jews since I entered this race. I know damned well that you and Nathan and the others have turned off the tap. Even so, I intend to keep running, and maybe I'll just get by with a handful of supporters mailing me a few dollars every now and again.'

Rifkin buttoned up his greatcoat, looking coldly at the Senator. 'You've never run in a Presidential election before. You'll find things can get very out of hand suddenly. Give it some thought, Senator . . . I'll be here in Madison, at the Sheraton, at your disposal any time you change your mind.'

Rifkin turned and walked out without saying goodbye. The Senator smiled grimly as he looked after him. 'Well, Peter, welcome to the major leagues.'

As Peter walked down the corridor to find his own room, he began to wonder what it was that made a man want to be President. It was like choosing to fight your battle on quicksand.

12

The next day, Timothy O'Donnell threw down the gauntlet. He kicked off his campaign appearances with a public proposal to Willie Lamb that they join in debate. He goaded his adversary with running a 'long-distance campaign', realizing that the public had by now had enough of it. He described how a similar campaign had been conducted in the recent past – with staged meetings, carefully rehearsed give and take, the candidate's isolation from the public. To which campaign was he referring? The campaign of 1968. And who was then the candidate? Richard Nixon.

Tim's audience lustily applauded their approval of his attack as he closed with, 'And do we want another Richard Nixon in the White House?'

The crowd roared, 'No!'

And Tim responded, 'Do you want Willie Lamb to come out of hiding?'

And the crowd shouted, 'Yes!'

It was all great theatre, and he repeated the act at every location. Tim's energy came to life as he went on to the offensive. He was picking up a few more seconds' news coverage with each day that passed. He revealed a dry wit and a gift for mockery that the public had rarely glimpsed before, and as he went after Lamb, he began to unleash the gift to ever greater effect – and quickly won the hearts of half Wisconsin. He would gaze out across every large crowd with the beginnings of a smile on his face and say, 'You know, I've seen these signs plastered up all over this state. What is it they say? "Willie Lamb – A President You Can Be Proud Of . . ." Forgive me, I didn't know Willie Lamb *was* President. I thought he was just another Senator like me . . . But if Willie Lamb says he's President, then he must be, because I've known him twelve years and I sure know he always tells the truth. If he's President, then it would explain one thing – why he's never in Wisconsin!'

After a week and a half of it, Willie Lamb descended on Wisconsin and began making ten to fifteen appearances a day. He scrapped his televised town hall meetings, realizing they had become a ripe topic for humour. Meanwhile, virtually every newspaper and TV editorial in the state had begun to join in the clamour for a debate between Lamb and O'Donnell. At first, Willie Lamb had tried to dodge the issue, but this only added fuel to the flames. In the public perception, he was beginning to show he was afraid of a challenge. The press grew more and more impatient to see a confrontation.

Then, at last, word reached the O'Donnell camp that Lamb had agreed to a debate two days before the primary. This looked risky for Tim, for if he put a foot wrong then, it would leave him no time to recover. He summoned Peter Watkins back to Wisconsin to coach him in foreign-policy areas. Each day, all day, he would campaign, driving himself on to near exhaustion, before returning to his hotel suite at night to face a thorough grilling by Peter. Peter then took on the role of the press, throwing at him all kinds of tough questions. In general, the Senator handled these very well, but when he faltered in areas where he was fuzzy or confused, Peter quickly interrupted and gave him additional information or suggested a fresh line of approach.

Peter grew more and more impressed with the Senator as he worked closely with him, night after night. He showed an excellent sense of delivery and of timing. He spoke economically and never stopped striving for greater conciseness. Above all, he exuded a confidence which could be the decisive factor in a debate.

Tim, for his part, found these sessions intellectually stimulating and began to look forward to them. He would question Peter over various rather minor points, searching out more and more details. Where Peter was not able to give an immediate answer, the Senator always asked the next night whether he had tracked down the information. And Peter would have conscientiously and diligently gone about digging up whatever had been required. Increasingly, he was amazed by the intensity of the Senator's curiosity, by his powers of retention. Each day he grew steadily more certain that the Senator was going to shine in debate against Lamb.

As the primary came nearer, the Senator spent increasing amounts of time on foreign policy. He felt confident on the domestic issues, but was keen to work hard to project an image of experience and competence as a potential world leader. He was well-read and well-informed, knew all the basic issues and where he stood on them. But he wanted to master each nuance of every trouble spot in the world, and to this end drove himself harder and harder and Peter with him.

Both men realized that the Middle East would be an issue, what with the reported Arab military build-up, Israel's foot-dragging in the peace negotiations, and the new eruption of violence on the West Bank. The Senator felt himself to be weak in the area of the Middle East – one of the things that had drawn Peter to him in the first place. He wanted to be sure he understood how the problems had arisen initially, what historical and social factors were involved, why the Arab nations were so hostile to Israel, a nation that had clearly achieved much. The demands it put on Peter were immense. He spent most of each day reading at the library of the University of Wisconsin or calling his Washington office to get material sent out. He, too, was learning along with the Senator.

The pace began to heat up during the closing week of the campaign. Timothy O'Donnell was narrowing the gap between him and Willie Lamb, but he still lagged far behind. The money problem was becoming critical. Although Tim had a steady stream of small contributions coming in – envelopes containing $5, $10 or $20 – it was nothing to match Lamb's multi-million-dollar effort. The Lamb promotion had a whole new series of TV ads prepared in New York, which showed the Senator with his family, in the Senate and on campaign. These flashed on once every thirty minutes throughout the day and all night too. Lamb's media blitzkrieg was certainly doing damage to O'Donnell's chances.

Tim kept touring the state from dawn to dusk, speaking at university campuses, at factory gates, at farmers' meetings in rural areas. He had felt that he was carrying the momentum, that people were finally seeing him for what he was, when a darker note began to slip in. Stories of his divorce appeared in several papers, which rehashed and distorted events from six years earlier. A malicious rumour was put about that he had dodged the draft during Vietnam. To top it all, a notorious TV starlet appeared in a national tabloid, relating details of her romance with Timothy O'Donnell and claiming that he drank heavily and ignored his children. The truth was that he had been out with her on only two occasions and nothing had taken place. Yet a picture of Tim, arm in arm with a bleached blonde with dazzling white teeth as they stepped out of a cab together in front of the Twenty-One Club in New York City, appeared on the front page of every tabloid paper and hence beside every cash register in every American supermarket.

Peter, depressed by these events, complained about it that night to the Senator, who only said, 'Well, Peter, I guess it's all part of the game. Certain very popular forces have decided that Lamb will be the next President, and two days before a primary, you start to play hardball. Most of these people are dedicated to making Michael Lerner Vice-President. In that stake, Lamb is really just a vehicle. On paper, Lamb looks like a sure-fire winner. Maybe they're not so wrong about it, after all.'

Tim looked pensively away, his eyes clouding with a sudden fit of self-doubt such as he had not allowed himself in weeks. Peter felt disturbed, but commented, 'I've heard about mudslinging, but this is my first sight of it close up, and it's pretty damned disgusting. Who the hell does it? Lamb himself?'

'Well, I'm sure Willie isn't directly involved. In fact, he called me yesterday to say how personally sorry he was about this sort of thing. At the same time, he's aware it does him no harm.'

'But someone obviously orchestrates the dirt.'

'Who knows who they are? They hover round the fringes of nearly every campaign.'

'What about Marty Rifkin? He threatened you that night, said things could get ugly if you didn't co-operate . . .'

'Marty? He'd cut his mother's throat with a broken bottle if she opposed him politically. Sure, he's a powerful, determined man. It would be a fair guess that he had something to do with the tabloid story appearing when it did, and if he wasn't behind the draft-dodging rumours and the stuff on my divorce, he could tell you who was.'

'Yet you were friendly towards him the other night.'

'You know the old saw, "politics makes strange bedfellows"? Maybe I despise some of the things Marty represents, but at the same time I need him. We get along OK, on the whole.'

'All this dirt and rumour just seems unnecessary with Lamb already so far ahead. What makes them think they need to resort to that sort of stuff?'

'You're missing the real crunch point, Peter.'

'Crunch point?'

'Money. Backing. Campaign funds. They can call me names and spread rumours, but a rumour gets to be passé in two or three days. Without money, on the other hand, you're nobody and you're stuck where you are.'

'So that's where Rifkin comes in.'

'That's precisely where, and Nathan Pflug with his Israeli Political Action League. It's through such organizations that you have access to a political community with a great deal of money at its disposal.'

Peter wished the Senator good night and returned to his room. The intense preparation for the debate was keying him up so hard he could hardly sleep these nights. He poured himself a Scotch on the rocks, before lying down on the bed. The Wisconsin primary campaign had opened up a whole new world – and it was a world that was far from beautiful. He tried to reach Liza on the phone, but there was no reply. Maybe she was working late, or maybe she'd gone to New York. Thoughts of her began to invade his mind and fill him with a terrible longing for her soft voice, for her silky body. It was no good. Despite his utter tiredness, he twisted about between the sheets all night as sleep evaded him.

13

The night of the debate had all the anticipatory tension of a heavyweight boxing match between a vaunted, older champion and a rapidly rising young unknown. The Civic Auditorium in Madison, with its 1,500 seats, was filled to capacity a good hour and a half before the debate was scheduled to start. The debate – sponsored by the League of Women Voters – was to be televised live throughout Wisconsin, as well as parts of Michigan, Illinois, Indiana and Minnesota. A whole region was lined up to get a glimpse of the candidates, the proceedings having even sparked something off of world-wide interest, attracting newspaper and TV crews from Europe and Japan. Willie Lamb had spent a lot of time in Europe and was well known in European banking and financial circles, but now the world was also waking up to Timothy O'Donnell, a young, new phenomenon running a remarkable underdog campaign. The word had gone round to expect a gladitorial contest that could make or break O'Donnell.

Backstage, in the inevitable pale green dressing room, Tim was being made up for the cameras. As two make-up artists danced around him with comb and powder, he and Peter kept up a rapid-fire question-and-answer review. They had covered every conceivable topic at least five times – from grain exports to steel quotas, from the stability of NATO to Japanese defence spending. Now, as a halo of hair spray floated about his head, Tim was asking Peter about the present régime in Guinea-Bissau. The Senator gave every impression of being calm and confident and eager for the confrontation. His concentration was heightened, there was a lively glint in his eye. Peter, however, felt like a nervous wreck. His hands were shaking as he flipped through his many pages of notes. It was Tim who was telling *him* to calm down.

A technician announced that airtime was in five minutes. Both the candidates backstage now, please. Tim put on his jacket, straightened his tie, appraised himself in the mirror. He was exuding a kind of emotional charge that was tangible to everyone in the room. 'How about wishing me luck?' he said.

Peter stepped closer to shake his hand. 'Senator, there's no need for luck. If you're one tenth as sharp as you've been during our sessions, you'll tear him to shreds . . .'

Along the corridor, Tim opened the door to Willie Lamb's dressing room and found his adversary sitting with three supporters – well-heeled New York types – all with glasses in hand. Willie was looking as glossy and self-satisfied as a stroked tomcat. His hair had been lacquered back and his cheeks were flushed. He rose quickly and greeted Tim, making some general introductions before saying, 'So, Tim, they tell me you've been getting your teeth into a lot of homework before our little fray.'

'Well, Willie. It takes a deal of study for us grade C students to catch up with you grade As.'

The harassed face of a stage director came round the door. 'On stage please, Senators.'

Lamb glanced at Tim. 'A quick one before battle.' He was already reaching for the Scotch bottle.

Tim smiled back. 'No, no, Willie. Those too young to be President should stick to milk.' Lamb and his group laughed as they moved off. Peter Watkins settled himself wearily into a backstage chair from which he had a clear view of a TV monitor screen.

The crowd fell quiet as the Senators appeared at their respective podiums and had microphones hooked about their collars. Red lights came on on a battery of TV cameras, and a moderator explained the ground rules: a question directed to one Senator, then a follow-up response by the second Senator, who was allowed to comment on his opponent's answer. Questions would be given by three prominent members of the national press corps.

65

O'Donnell came across looking even younger on TV than he did in person, but he gave an impression of being vital and eager and well poised. Lamb, on the other hand, looked on the gaunt side, as though he had been on a grapefruit diet for two weeks and was nearly fainting from hunger. He seemed dapper enough, though, in an expensive black silk suit – and very establishment.

The debate began with a flat question concerning what each candidate intended to do about unemployment. Lamb kicked off with a typical expression of dismay about the plight of the jobless, recommending that the private sector be encouraged to hire more people, set training programmes in motion. He believed the problem could be solved under his leadership. Tim followed, moving in vigorously as he spoke of his years of work in civil rights, the horrifying poverty he had seen, the despair marking the lives of millions. He pointed to the dismal failure of private enterprise in helping the disadvantaged. He attacked the inadequacy of earlier government efforts. The problem had always been dealt with as *a* problem, he said, when it should be dealt with as *the* problem, the unacceptable, intolerable blight on the American dream. Senator Lamb, he commented, had said how 'he "hoped" the problem could be solved under his leadership'. But the time for *hoping* was over. The time had come for effective action. Lamb was shown blinking a little at the strength of Tim's response.

For a couple of questions about defence spending and trade agreements, the two men differed little in their reactions. Then followed a question on environmental policy. Lamb told the meeting how he had been a supporter of several Bills in the Senate to protect the environment. Existing laws were, he felt, adequate to handle the problem, while a certain excessive zeal on the part of many so-called conservationists needed to be cooled down. Tim saw his opening, knowing there to be much pro-environmental sentiment in Wisconsin, and attacked Lamb's record, including a failure to support several wildlife-protection Bills. He wondered whether Lamb's caution, his protest against what he termed 'excessive zeal', could be linked to his supporters' interests. Hadn't nearly a third of Lamb's support in Wisconsin come from the big oil companies, to a total of almost $3.5 million? You could be sure the oil companies weren't interested in Wisconsin . . . A friend in the White House was what they were after. A murmur ran through the audience.

Questions followed on the economy, on nuclear disarmament, on immigration. Lamb voiced vague generalities in a monotonous tone. He seemed less and less able to mount any kind of effective counter-attack against Tim O'Donnell. Everything which he said seemed to belong with last year's fallen leaves. By contrast, Tim spoke with a vivid sense of emotional commitment to the issues. He seemed to be relishing this, projecting an air of obvious self-confidence.

During one of the later station breaks, a cluster of Lamb's advisers hovered nervously about their sagging front-runner, reading him scribbled notes, frantically gesticulating. O'Donnell sat a little way off, calm and alone, writing something on the pad provided.

The next main part of the programme focused more on foreign-policy issues, allowing O'Donnell's mastery of world affairs to take off into an impressive display. Lamb muttered on uncertainly, evasive and contradictory. When a question came up about the Middle East, Lamb emphasized how he had supported Israel for twenty years in Congress, regarding Israel as second to none among America's allies. He charged President Randall with undermining the chance of peace in the Middle East by his recent pressures on Israel at the peace negotiations. Any Arab military build-up, Lamb warned, would result in American action, and he personally would request a significant boost in aid to Israel if elected President.

O'Donnell approached the question in a more roundabout way. He appeared reflective, as if measuring his words precisely. After noting that he had always been a firm supporter of Israel, having been there twice on fact-finding missions, Tim O'Donnell blasted Lamb's pledge for an aid increase to the country, emphasizing that Israel was quite strong enough at present. As for an Arab build-up, O'Donnell said, there was little credible evidence to support such a contention. He approved of the peace negotiations, but warned that many Americans were growing impatient, that a just, fair and lasting settlement to the problem was becoming imperative. The Israelis should promptly clarify their long-term position and offer a precise timetable for withdrawal from the occupied territories, in conjunction with suitable security agreements and national recognition from their Arab neighbours. O'Donnell said that he would, if elected, go directly to the Middle East and offer a detailed, comprehensive peace proposal. All in all, the O'Donnell answers had seemed more considered and judicious, more diplomatic and more balanced than Lamb's somewhat stereo-typed responses.

The closing question was on the issue of age and experience – and

67

clearly directed at O'Donnell. He answered it calmly and forcefully: 'Much has been made of this issue, but I think there's really very little to it. I served three terms in the House; Senator Lamb served three terms in the House. I've been a Senator eight years; Willie Lamb's been a Senator fourteen years. But I challenge anyone to make an adverse comparison between my record in the Senate and Senator Lamb's. I have supported or co-sponsored more legislation than he. I have spoken on more issues than he, served more actively on Committees and Subcommittees than he. Even my attendance record is better than Willie Lamb's. If this merely concerns a question of age – and I'm forty-four this year – I'd like to point out that both Teddy Roosevelt and John F. Kennedy were younger than me when they became President. And I think you could say they made pretty good Presidents.'

The auditorium had fallen remarkably quiet as O'Donnell eloquently continued: 'We are a youthful country. Our Declaration of Independence was written by a rather competent twenty-seven-year-old named Thomas Jefferson. Our Constitution's primary author was a thirty-year-old legislator named James Madison. But I don't consider age to be an issue with which the American public will be greatly concerning itself. They will be looking much more for qualities of leadership, energy and courage. *These* are the qualities which I hope to bring to my Administration if elected.' The room broke into applause, even though applause had been prohibited by the ground rules.

Willie Lamb was at an obvious disadvantage trying to follow such an act. He assumed his most statesman-like pose: 'The problems which confront us today are highly complex. The situation before us is perilous. As the American people decide who shall lead them, who is *most* qualified to lead them, they may find themselves faced with a choice between the wisdom of experience and the ambition of youth. I have served proudly in the US Senate for fourteen years. I have served as Majority Whip for my party in the Senate. I have headed Congressional delegations that have met with virtually every world leader of our day. I have twice been a candidate for the Vice-Presidency. The American people know me. They know what I stand for. The Presidency today demands the level of experience which I can offer – as a Senate leader, as a figure on the world scene, as an active participant in national political life for more than two decades.'

Lamb paused, as if to put a sharper cutting edge on his words as he continued: 'I'm also a family man. My wife of twenty-eight years –

Edith – has distinguished herself in two national campaigns. We lead a quiet life. We're close to our children. We're the kind of family I think most Americans can be proud to belong to. It's a family which reflects the kind of values I would hope to bring to the Presidency: decency, stability, maturity. That, in the last resort, is what it comes down to: maturity. I, for one, do not think the American people are ready to turn over the White House to be a spring training ground for a President who still has gains to make in that direction.'

It had to be admitted: Lamb's rebuttal had not gone too badly, even if the audience showed little enthusiasm. The closing ten minutes of the debate were reserved for questions direct from the audience. There was one brief one about veterans' benefits, then one on the death penalty. There was a sense of things winding down, with time for one last question, for Senator Lamb in this case. He looked out into the auditorium, squinting against the bright lights and pointing to a man who was waving his hand in great determination. The man stood up quickly, showing himself to be wearing a long black coat and a black hat. He had a thick, square beard and long sideburns, seemed in his late fifties and looked foreign.

'Senator Lamb,' he said, 'you say you strongly support Israel. Do you really *know* anything of Israel? Do you realize that the state of Israel was created against the will of its own people, the Jews who have lived there for 2,000 years? That this so-called nation of peace has led to a state of constant warfare and bloodshed? That the state of Israel represents violence, spiritual bankruptcy –'

Lamb responded hotly and sharply, cutting in on the questioner: 'Mister, I don't know who you are or where you're from, but I will tell you one thing – you have no right to say such things about Israel. The American people support Israel and will continue to support Israel against its enemies . . . I think, now, we could make time for one last *serious* question . . .'

Lamb looked at the audience, satisfied with his brisk putdown of a troublemaker, sure he had scored a few points. He looked for another question. But the man in black was not letting himself be dismissed. He yelled at Lamb as two ushers began to struggle with him: 'Senator, I am a *Jew*! I was born in Israel, as was my father, and his father before him. I know my country far better than you ever could. Now, here, you try to stop me speaking out, just as my own country does. What do you know of the Jews?'

Every TV camera was now aimed squarely at Senator Lamb. He sat confused, shaken and surprised, his mouth hanging open. For a minute, he had no idea what to say, the flashbulbs mercilessly catching him in his moment of indecision. He blinked, gave a slight shrug and spoke nervously as he said, 'Now then . . . so you're an Israeli. Well, we all know these are complex questions, and so, ah –'

As Lamb floundered, O'Donnell broke in again, speaking directly to the man in black. 'Sir, unless I'm mistaken, you're a member of the Neturei Karta?'

The man beamed, pleased at the recognition, and gave a courteous bow. 'Yes, Senator. That is so.'

'Your people believe the creation of the political state of Israel to have been an act against God, a substitution of earthly power for true spirituality . . .'

'We believe,' the man answered, 'that becoming a nation has crushed our faith, that this has nothing to do with the divine message our people have been given.'

O'Donnell's response was measured, even warm. 'Allow me to say that although I cannot share your viewpoint on the state of Israel, I admire the strength of your faith and your beliefs, and I welcome their being expressed here tonight.'

The man replied calmly, 'Thank you, sir, for your patience in stopping to listen.' He held up his palm. '*Shalom.*'

The Senator returned the gesture. '*Shalom.*'

At this point the mediator swiftly interrupted to say that time was up and he must thank the candidates for their participation. The closing camera shot showed Senator Lamb at his podium, looking on passively, his face empty of expression.

The moment Tim O'Donnell was backstage again, he was besieged by a cluster of well-wishers. He made no pretence about his elation at his own performance. Peter Watkins managed to break through the crowd to shake his hand, and the Senator at once took him aside. 'Well?' he asked.

'You did it! You annihilated him. And as for that guy in the audience –'

'Surely you didn't think I'd forget about the Neturei Karta? But I wouldn't have known the first thing about them without your help and all that crazy homework.'

A wave of network reporters and cameramen came surging down the corridor towards them. Peter extricated himself from the mob as the victorious Senator began to answer questions from the press. The buzz of excitement at O'Donnell's success seemed to be running through the entire building.

14

That night and throughout the next day, the topic was discussed over and over: of how Lamb lost control with the Israeli religious nut and O'Donnell gathered up the situation into an engaging dialogue. Lamb had at first come off as blustering, then as confused and hopelessly off course. Every morning paper in Wisconsin gave the palm to Timothy O'Donnell. He had managed to make an indelible impression as a forceful, sharp-witted and attractive candidate. The national media picked up the shot of Lamb standing with his mouth open, a desperate look of confusion on his face. And the same newspapers and magazines ran a second picture: O'Donnell with his hand raised, smiling as he said, '*Shalom*'.

It was rumoured that a cloud hung over the Lamb headquarters, that they were floundering about, trying to decide on new tactics, since any further personal appearances would, for the time being, be counter-productive. Tim O'Donnell, on the other hand, began to race around the state, attending a series of rallies at which the crowds were larger and more excited than ever. He had become overnight a media sensation, and Barney Shaw's pollsters showed him beginning to outstrip Lamb, though the running was still very close.

Shaw's great worry had been the lack of support among Jews, since he had never heard of a Democrat winning a Presidential race without their backing. Now the tables had been turned by Tim's handling of the religious fanatic. The papers recorded how shocked many Jews had been by the protester, most American Jews having had no idea that such opposition groups existed in Israel. One thing they now saw clearly was that Timothy O'Donnell knew a little more about Israel than they did, and it made a powerful impression. By sheer good fortune, O'Donnell had walked away from the debate enjoying support from a lot of Jews around the country as soon as the networks ran a clip of the stubborn questioner on their national evening news. No Jew could forget the image of O'Donnell with his hand raised and saying, '*Shalom*'.

Then all the weeks of work, the gruelling schedule, the speeches, briefings and appearances came to a momentary halt, with the day of the Wisconsin primary. There was nothing to do now but wait. Upstairs, in his suite at the Madison Sheraton, amid a handful of aides, O'Donnell watched the returns come in. He showed little emotion and constantly urged caution on those around him. But then, as the hours passed and the vote tabulations mounted, the margin of Tim O'Donnell's victory became apparent. By eleven that evening he had passed Lamb by over 70,000 votes. When the totals were finally in, O'Donnell could be seen to have taken 57 per cent of the vote to Lamb's 41 per cent.

It took for ever to get Tim out of the tumultuous hotel lobby and down the street towards a waiting limousine. He and his weary staff were setting out to fly back to Washington at once. As he and Peter approached their waiting car, they saw a familiar figure standing on the kerb, bag in hand, trying to flag down a cab amid the traffic. Marty Rifkin spun around as if he had eyes in the back of his head, gave the Senator a beaming smile and gripped his hand. 'Hey, Senator. Congratulations. You ran a great primary.'

'Thanks, Marty,' said the Senator.

Rifkin stood there grinning. 'Oh, and I almost forgot – *Shalom*.' Marty raised the palm of his hand to accompany his laugh.

Tim joined in before glancing down at Marty's bag. 'Can we offer you a lift? We're heading for the airport.'

'Great. I'm due on a flight for New York.'

They loaded their baggage into the boot before being whisked off through the icy night.

Marty took out a pack of Winstons. 'Mind if I smoke?'

The Senator shrugged. 'Marty, I'm objecting to nothing tonight.'

Marty lit his cigarette and took a long drag. 'You really went to town against poor old Willie. That debate . . . I've never seen the likes of it!'

The Senator let a smile play over his face as Marty eyed him closely. 'So, what comes next?' asked Marty.

The Senator looked out of the window as they sped through the dark outskirts of Madison. 'Well, in the short term, I'm broke . . . But I suppose we can expect contributions to start to come in from now on.'

Marty exhaled. 'You're damned right they will. Look, I talked to Arnie Weiss. He's out here for *Time* magazine. He said they'll probably use you as their next cover story . . . I suppose,' he continued, 'you'll be gearing yourself up for all the other primaries now?'

Tim reflected. 'I don't have much of a national campaign organization assembled yet, so I'm thinking of taking on only the key primaries, the big ones – Illinois, New York, Texas, California.'

'What of Michael Lerner?'

'He's never going to win, but he could cause me a lot of problems. If he runs a good race, he can pull away the Jews and a lot of liberals, especially in California and New York.'

Marty stuffed out his cigarette in the ash tray. 'Oh, yes, Michael has some very strong support. I don't see any way you can beat him in New York. You ought by now to know how hard the going can be when you don't have any Jewish money at the back of you.' He smiled grimly.

O'Donnell's face suddenly flushed with anger. 'Look here, Marty, if you intend to play cat and mouse with me from here to November, lemme tell you just one thing – go screw yourself!' He twisted about in his seat to fix Rifkin with a glare.

'Senator, Senator. Please now, don't let's get so excited here. You've had my support for years.'

'And you've gotten back precisely what you were after – right?'

Marty lit another cigarette, took his time waving out the match. 'I'm trying to be of some help . . .'

'Help, my ass, Marty. I'd rather you came straight to the point.'

'What point? I didn't hitch a lift to argue with you.'

Tim folded his arms and stared out at the passing night as Marty calmly smoked, briefly looking at his watch from time to time. 'I'll be seeing plenty of people in New York in the next couple of weeks,' he said. 'Mostly admirers of your career, Senator . . .'

73

Tim sat on, silent and motionless. Peter Watkins admired his reserve when he himself felt like stopping the car and heaving Marty out on to the expressway.

'I consider you could run a very strong campaign,' Marty continued. 'With the right running-mate, you'd be practically unbeatable. Of course, you'll need some balance on the ticket. You're young, and from California, so you'll need someone from the East, someone older. You'll want someone who shares your liberal outlook, to give you a compatible team. You're Presbyterian, so you'll need someone of another persuasion to pick up the ethnic vote.'

Tim stared back with no trace of emotion. 'The ethnic vote?'

'Sure. The Italian Catholic vote, the Jewish vote . . . whatever.'

'Come on, Marty, don't play so coy. Why not come out and say it? You want me to pick Michael Lerner as a running-mate.'

Marty stubbed out his cigarette defiantly. 'Did I mention the name of Michael Lerner? Did I? You were the one who brought him up. But I will tell you from my point of view, from the point of view of the organization I represent and a lot of similar organizations, that an O'Donnell–Lerner ticket looks an unbeatable combination.'

'So?'

'So many people could happily support you if they knew you shared their view that Michael Lerner would make a good Vice-President.'

'My admiration for Michael is widely known. He has my highest respect. He seems eminently suited to national office.'

'Well, I'm so glad to hear you say so. Many people would like to hear those very words from your lips . . . But I quite understand it's too early for you to be announcing any running-mate. That wouldn't be good politics.'

The limousine swung on to the airport's perimeter roadway. Marty looked anxiously at his watch again. 'On the other hand,' he said, 'if I had some kind of word from you – a small and harmless understanding between us, maybe – I could make sure that a lot of the help you'll be needing comes your way.'

'If you think you can squeeze a guarantee out of me about Michael Lerner, you can think some more. I'm not saying I'll take him as running-mate, I'm not saying I won't. It's too early for any kind of decision . . . Besides, I don't care for the way you're handling this, Marty, I don't care for it at all.'

The limousine pulled up before the main terminal. Peter lifted out his and the Senator's bags. Marty snatched up his own. As Tim

O'Donnell turned to walk off, Marty gripped his arm. 'You looked great in Wisconsin,' he said. 'I mean that sincerely. No hard feelings, huh?' He stuck out his hand and the Senator gave him a brief handshake. As they parted from him, Marty called after them, 'Hey! Give my best to the kids!'

The entire car journey had left Peter Watkins feeling chilled to the bone. After witnessing Marty's performance at the hotel earlier, his veiled threats and everything that had gone on in Wisconsin, he felt shocked that the Senator could even have spoken to him, much less offered him a ride. And here it had happened all over again. Following the moments of triumph, it left a bitter after-taste. Before they went aboard, a very weary Peter tried to give Liza one last call, but there was still no reply. Then he and the Senator headed for the plane, where both dropped off into an instant sleep. The campaign had been a rugged enough business but the long haul itself was only just beginning.

15

It was 2.30 in the morning before Peter arrived home, feeling more tired than ever before in his life. As he reached the top of the staircase and flipped on the light, he could hardly believe what he saw. Glasses were clustered on every table, on the mantel, and on the floor. There were overflowing ash trays everywhere, bowls of stale snacks, plates carrying the remains of *hors d'oeuvres*. The kitchen looked like a pigstye; the waste bins overflowing with bottles and garbage, food spilling across all the surfaces, a mountain of dirty dishes, the oven stacked with used pots and pans. It was too grim a prospect, and he turned his back on it. So, Liza must've had a party. Perhaps she never even heard the phone ring with all the racket. What the hell. In a few moments he'd be upstairs in her arms.

He got undressed before tiptoeing into the bedroom, but when he reached down to pull back the covers, he found the bed still made. He turned on the light. No sign of Liza. Annoyed and perplexed, but much too exhausted to think about it, he fell into bed and dropped off to sleep within minutes.

He awoke at noon next day, still feeling hungover with fatigue. Going down to the foyer, he picked up the *Washington Post*. Its headline read: 'O'Donnell Pulls Surprise Upset – Debate Turning-Point'. The article had an assessment of the Wisconsin primary and Tim's performance in the debate.

Picking his way through the dirty dishes, Peter managed to salvage some toast, coffee and fruit juice for breakfast. Then he went downstairs to his library, where he'd set up a table as a temporary desk. He still felt vexed by Liza having taken over his upstairs study. And where the hell *was* she? She might at least have left a note.

He settled down to work. Tomorrow was the last of the Subcommittee hearings on the Israeli nuclear plants, and since he had formally submitted his resignation it would be his last day on the job. They had certainly been a remarkable three years, and the experience had taught him much.

He worked hard throughout that afternoon and evening. While he had finished most of the essentials before leaving for Wisconsin, he wanted every detail to be perfect. After taking a light evening snack, he began to review several classified documents which he took from a high-security safe in the library. For the most part, they contained tedious technical detail on nuclear power-plant operations around the world. He worked till midnight before locking his files away again.

The hearing, which began at 10 a.m., was scheduled to run all day, and into the evening if necessary. What had begun as a routine inquiry had turned into a security nightmare, and just at the worst possible time, with every Senator on the Committee desperate to get away to start on campaigning, either on behalf of himself or another. It was essential to have it all wrapped up today as efficiently as possible, though with the information he carried in his locked briefcase, Peter knew the picture could get messy. More than messy. He felt he would give his eye teeth to know what Ronnie Montgomery might have up his sleeve. For years the two of them had been running in an unspoken, amiable competition, each pumping his own resources to try and outdo the other. Naturally, Ronnie had a big head start, being with the CIA, but Peter was no mean amateur when it came to contacts. And even Ronnie had to admit in Peter a real genius for digging up controversial data from seemingly innocent documents.

As Peter entered the corridor, he saw the members of the Sub-committee filing in at the door ahead of him. Senator Lerner was holding the door open and greeting each Senator in turn. Beside him stood Shavinsky, lean in a black turtleneck. The look of icy arrogance on his face was not in any way diminished.

Lerner greeted Peter warmly, smiling paternally as they shook hands. 'Looks like you didn't do a bad job in Wisconsin.'

Peter smiled back diffidently. 'When you've got a candidate that good, you stand back and let him get on with it.'

The Senator laughed. 'I've always had a soft spot for Tim. He's got a big future, and I know you'll do a great job for him. I only wish I had you working for me . . .'

Peter could tell from the Senator's voice that the compliment was sincere. 'Well, Senator,' he said, 'you would've been my first choice. I didn't know you were looking for anyone.'

Senator Lerner put his hand on Peter's shoulder. 'No worry. It's the way the game goes. I'll always value your friendship and I'm glad you work with Tim – a fine young man. Let's go in.'

The Committee sat in their familiar places, and Peter could sense a certain rested quality about the meeting. The Senators were fresh for action, fully prepared with notes and questions and ready to dig their way under every stone. Such days conveyed a certain patriotic pride and excitement. These men, with their individual flaws and weaknesses, were all, when it came to it, reasonably intelligent, decent and hard-working. When called on, they worked well together as a body, despite their party differences.

Senator Lerner offered a general welcome and complimented Senator Devereux on his flowery hand-painted necktie before bringing the hearing briskly to order. 'We will be continuing our inquiry into the question of the Israeli nuclear plants. Today has been stated as being our last hearing date on this matter, but if it proves necessary, I shall be requesting additional meetings. Dr Shavinsky joins us again today.'

Shavinsky allowed a hawk-like glance to swing around the table at each Senator in turn, ignoring Ronnie and Peter at the back. Senator Lerner handed round copies of a document. 'This letter, from Prime Minister Peritzsky, was communicated to the Subcommittee in response to our letter of two weeks back, to the Israeli government regarding the Longpré matter. Mr Peritzsky specifically denies the charge of Dr Longpré's involvement in nuclear activities, and insists that his duties consisted only in those of consultant. There is also a letter attached from Dr Eshkol, providing a detailed chronology of Dr Longpré's involvement at the power plants in Israel.'

The Senators began to examine the papers closely, but Shavinsky never even picked up his copies. He only allowed himself a brief but sharp glance at Ronnie and Peter as they began to whisper together, took out his silver pen and set it neatly on the surface in front of him.

As soon as Senator Lerner saw that most had read the letters, he asked: 'Are there any comments arising from our previous session before we move on?'

'Senator,' Ronnie spoke up, 'I have obtained information from French intelligence sources confirming André Longpré's various world travels in his capacity as an expert in the area of nuclear warhead assembly. With your permission, I'll distribute copies.'

Senator Lerner inclined his head as he went on, 'As I recollect it, we reached, last session, a discussion of the September 24th shipment of uranium which, the report indicated, was to be used for the second reactor, although this never went into operation. Dr Shavinsky has testified that this uranium was, in fact, used for the first reactor.'

Senator DeAntonio smiled cordially. 'Seems like we have all this uranium going in all directions! The rods didn't fit right. Then some of the stuff got spilled and had to be tossed out. So we sent over more uranium. Then there was a whole second shipment of uranium, and all for the same reactor. Sounds to me like we got a machine that eats the stuff, Dr Shavinsky.'

Shavinsky managed a wary smile. He was clearly treating Senator DeAntonio with a degree of respect and was not to be taken in twice by his backwoods manner as he replied, 'Senator DeAntonio, the picture is very confusing, and perhaps I haven't done too good a job at explaining. I'm more accustomed to the environment of physics classrooms or laboratories than I am to Senate hearing rooms . . .'

An amused murmur went round the table, and Shavinsky's smile became positively charming as the Senators began to warm up a little.

Senator DeAntonio smiled back. 'Young man, don't you concern yourself about us. We may seem like a bunch of rattlesnakes, but we don't intend any harm. Now, to come to all that crazy uranium. You must have rooms full of it.'

Shavinsky gave a light wave of his hand. 'I only wish that were so. After the spillage, fuel rods were injected and the plant began operation as we continued work on the second reactor on schedule. Eventually, however, the fuel rods became depleted and required reprocessing.'

Senator DeAntonio nodded. 'You're talking of the plutonium reprocessing, where they take the used-up rods and treat them, so you can use them all over?'

'Exactly, Senator. It was this reprocessing stage that gave us difficulties on this occasion. We had the depleted uranium rods transported to the reprocessing centre outside Beersheba, which does not come under Israeli control as it is run by the International Atomic Energy Agency. As soon as we received back the reprocessed plutonium fuel rods, we once again put the first reactor into operation. It greatly surprised us to find that the new rods showed yield levels far below normal, and this we put down to a technical misunderstanding on our part. It was at this point that Dr Longpré was called in for his third consultation. His conclusion was that no malfunction existed in the reactor – that the fuel rods themselves had been incorrectly processed at the treatment plant.'

Senator Devereux sat up, blew his nose and set down a seven-inch cigar. 'So what you're saying, son, is that everything was fine until these International Agency people somehow messed things up?'

'Yes, Senator.'

'Well, I've always admired Israel's technical abilities and think your people have done right well. But that being so, why do we have to have a lot of foreign international types horning in on the deal?'

Shavinsky gave the Senator a look of grateful relief. 'Well, I'm afraid it's not up to us to decide. You see, the International Atomic Energy Agency, headquartered in Vienna, oversees all reprocessing of nuclear fuel. They carefully supervise every step of the recycling process, at every reprocessing plant throughout the world. You might call it a form of "quality control".'

Senator Shillings, as alert and irascible as ever, had begun to wrinkle up his brow as he prepared to move in on the conversation. 'Dr

Shavinsky, does not your explanation of the IAEA leave out some most important points . . .'

Shavinsky frowned. 'I only sought to clarify its function –'

'But you have avoided any mention of the basic reason for the Agency's existence. As you and I know full well, the Agency was established specifically to maintain tight control in the light of the concern that reprocessed plutonium may be readily and simply employed by virtually any nation on earth to construct a nuclear bomb. Is not that the case?'

Before Shavinsky could respond, Senator Devereux had raised his bushy eyebrows. 'So, those folks make sure that whatever comes in goes back to the reactor concerned, for fuel purposes only?'

'Correct,' said Shillings. 'Now what I think we need next from Dr Shavinsky is some explanation for this apparent lower yield of the reprocessed plutonium.'

Shavinsky leaned forward, interlocking his long fingers. 'We are still in dispute with the IAEA on this particular matter. I have with me copies of all correspondence, records of the fuel-rod transfer, back and forth, and our final evaluation of the fuel-rod deficiency.' Shavinsky passed round his copies as he spoke. 'In agreement with our own conclusions, they found the rods functioning at 20 to 25 per cent below capacity, although they were unable to provide any explanation. This was the stage when we requested further enriched uranium from the US government so we could bring the plant back to its proper level of output.'

All at once, Senator Shillings brought a fist crashing down on the table top as he said, red-faced, 'I'm mystified that we sit here discussing these damned fuel rods and never get to the obvious points. First, this entire nuclear power programme in Israel has been riddled with irregularities from the start. Second, every question we try to answer turns up two more that don't get answered. Third, there's been an unusual demand for extra amounts of enriched uranium – whatever the reasons. Fourth, the central figure in all this was a shady international agent who specialized in nuclear weapon design and was linked with plutonium thefts right around the damned world. Now, you tell me, doesn't all this add up to something? How much more circumstantial evidence is needed? There are too many "smoking guns" on the floor to even walk on it, and don't forget for one moment that we're talking about a country – Israel – which has for years been after its own nuclear deterrent.'

Shavinsky was on his feet as he shouted, 'That's an evil lie!' He looked ready to spring across the table.

Shillings glared at Shavinsky level and hard. 'We're grown men here, Shavinsky, not a bunch of school kids hoping to be told fairy stories.'

Senator Lerner took a sip of water before speaking calmly. 'Gentlemen, we are discussing a most complex and highly sensitive matter. I think it best for the purposes of this inquiry for all concerned to maintain a gentlemanly demeanour . . .' He let his glance play between Shillings and Shavinsky. 'I think we need to stick to the facts and to proceed accordingly.'

Senator DeAntonio linked his hands behind his head and sighed. 'Well, it's quite a puzzler, this one. No doubt about it. Bill's right – an awful lot of things don't look good, not at all. As I always say, if you find a trout in the hayloft, that's circumstantial evidence. On the other hand, suppose there's been some hanky-panky, some secret bomb-building. In that case, this Longpré fellow would've needed to sneak a good bit of plutonium into Israel – and Israel is a long ways from any plutonium.'

'No stolen plutonium need have been necessary.'

Every head in the room turned to look at Peter Watkins, and Senator Lerner acknowledged him, 'Ah yes, Dr Watkins, can you throw some light at this point?'

Peter surveyed the Senators calmly. 'In theory, it could be possible for a nuclear bomb to be constructed in Israel without any plutonium coming from outside.'

Shavinsky broke into a great roar of laughter. 'Can Dr Watkins be suggesting that Israelis have developed a nuclear bomb that requires no plutonium? An amazing feat! But one beyond even our ingenuity, I think.'

'Perhaps I rate your people too highly. Perhaps I overestimate their ingenuity.' Peter paused and gazed out the window as he asked his next question. 'Did you ever hear of the "Patagonian Switchback", Dr Shavinsky?'

There was a moment's hesitation before Shavinsky replied. It was this almost imperceptible gap for which Peter had been listening and which told him precisely what he needed to know. And now he could see from the look in Shavinsky's eyes that Shavinsky knew that he knew. But the Israeli's stare was calm as he said, 'No, I don't believe I've ever heard the term . . .'

81

'Sounds like some kind of road up in the Mississippi hill country,' drawled Senator Devereux.

Peter smiled good-naturedly amid the Senators' laughter. 'Well, it doesn't go on up in your hill country, but it did go on in the hills of Argentina – in Patagonia, to be exact.'

Shavinsky sat back. 'I fail to see what any of this has to do with Israel. I understood we were here to discuss our reactor development.'

'Exactly,' said Peter, crisply and coldly. 'That is our precise subject.'

'So, this "Patagonian Switchback" – how does it relate to plutonium theft?' Senator Shillings asked, alertly interested.

Peter slipped his notes away into a folder and began to speak in a quiet, measured tone. 'The establishment of the IAEA was an attempt to control the world's available reprocessed plutonium. To steal enough plutonium to make a nuclear bomb is extremely difficult. It would require elaborate planning, complex transport logistics and immense expense. Few nations in the world could even contemplate doing it. Our intelligence sources, however, indicate that there is good reason to believe that Argentina today possesses secret nuclear armaments. The country currently has eight nuclear power plants in operation and the IAEA maintains a reprocessing plant in Rio Gallegos.'

'So how could they get plutonium for bombs with the IAEA supervising?' asked Senator Shillings.

'By a clever procedure, which one might even call *ingenious*.' Shavinsky pointedly ignored the emphasis which Peter put on the word. 'The IAEA does a very thorough job of reprocessing all the depleted fuel rods brought in. Each stage of this recycling process is meticulously supervised. When it is complete, their personal representatives accompany the reprocessed fuel rods back to the reactor and verify they are back into use. The entire procedure takes place under extreme high-security conditions to prevent any kind of theft.'

'So,' Senator Lerner interrupted, 'you imply that these safeguards have not been rigorous enough, that somewhere along the line it has been possible to breach the IAEA's control.'

'The weak link, Senator, was not actually in the IAEA reprocessing centre. The key lay in the original shipment *to* the plant from the reactor – in this case, from a reactor in Patagonia.'

Shillings had been following every word with increased intensity. 'Then what you're saying is that somehow plutonium was removed on its way to the reprocessing plant? Yet the IAEA has a record of the

82

exact amount of plutonium in transit. Would it not become obvious as soon as some was missing?'

Peter nodded. 'Just so. The IAEA knows precisely how much is coming in and, just as precisely, how much is sent back to the power plant.'

'So please come to the point on this, Peter,' said Senator Lerner impatiently.

'The point is that the shipment sent to the reprocessing plant did not entirely consist of depleted uranium fuel rods. Certain of the fuel rods – the cells containing the depleted uranium pellets – had been removed.'

'But wouldn't that have been detected?' demanded Senator Shillings.

'Certainly it would, if the reprocessing plant discovered it hadn't received the correct number of depleted rods . . .'

'But you say they'd removed some of them.'

'Yes, Senator, but then dummy rods had been carefully substituted.'

Shillings looked at him quizzically. 'Dummy rods?'

'Yes, fuel rods not containing the original depleted uranium which had been in them.'

'But couldn't such rods have been detected during the reprocessing?'

'There's the clever part. They did put *uranium* inside those dummy fuel rods, but not *enriched* uranium, only easily obtained industrial-grade uranium. The industrial uranium hoodwinked the IAEA since it correctly registered radioactivity. It was also, in fact, mixed with a quite large proportion of actual enriched uranium. The Argentinians had taken out only a certain percentage of the depleted fuel.'

Senator Lerner looked up from his rapid note-taking. 'So they took a certain quantity of enriched uranium from the depleted fuel rods and substituted industrial uranium, no one being the wiser.'

Peter nodded. 'Not as yet, anyway. Of course, once all of this had been through the reprocessing treatment, the dummy rods included, the net result was reprocessed plutonium of a slightly lower quality than usual.'

'And what exactly does that imply?' asked Senator Shillings.

'It means that after the fuel rods were returned to the reactor, there would have been substandard performance and a loss of power output.'

'How much of a loss?'

'Well, the Argentinians were very cute. They removed only a small proportion of enriched uranium from their first shipment to the reprocessing plant, and so substituted only a small amount of industrial uranium. When this "hybrid" was reprocessed and returned, the power loss was small enough to be easily covered up. What made the Patagonian switchback so effective was that it was done over a period of years, with each shipment of depleted fuel having only a small amount of industrial uranium switched to replace the enriched uranium removed.'

Senator Lerner looked at him gravely. 'The net result being that the Argentinians secretly and methodically obtained enough plutonium or enriched uranium to make a nuclear bomb?'

Peter stared at the Senator. '*A* nuclear bomb? Eight nuclear bombs.'

As Senator DeAntonio hunched forward, his face seemed to have lost its customary relaxed appearance. 'Very interesting, I must say, this switching technique. And so you end up with a power loss at the reactor . . . just like we have heard about at this Israeli plant.'

The others looked at their fellow-Senator, who had been the first among them to leap forward to voice the alarming conclusion to Peter's dissertation.

Shavinsky scowled, seemed speechless for a moment before thundering out, 'I will not tolerate this kind of innuendo. I came here for a technical discussion, not to be smeared by a CIA lackey who hasn't –'

'I am not yet finished speaking, Dr Shavinsky,' said Peter in a tone of complete neutrality.

'Surely, Dr Watkins,' Shillings broke in, 'if this kind of thing had gone on before, then the IAEA would have spotted it if it happened again in Israel.'

'In fact, the IAEA never did spot it. My information comes from classified documents of the National Security Council, who maintain a special unit to monitor the movement of industrial-grade uranium around the world. One of their people just happened to propose this explanation for events in Argentina.'

'So why wasn't the IAEA informed?'

'If it had been publicly revealed, that would have shaken confidence in the IAEA, which would have been very bad. If they had been privately informed, there was a fear that a leak might make the technique even more widely known.'

Shillings grunted with dissatisfaction. 'So, what did the IAEA ever conclude about the gradual power loss in the Argentinian reactor?'

'They held a long-drawn-out investigation. No one knew what to make of the altered performance. There was evidence of technical incompetence at the plant – it was being supervised by Argentina's Air Force – and various reports of corruption. The whole thing became quite an embarrassment to the Argentine government – and to the IAEA.'

Senator Hartley spotted an opening. 'Therefore you had all the usual screw-ups at this reactor, and you had an investigation which got nowhere, with no blame being registered, no –'

Peter cut in on him. 'No, Senator. Blame was assigned. The investigation came to centre on one man, Humberto Sequieros, formerly director of the power plant facility.'

'Did he face any kind of questioning?'

Peter opened one of his folders. 'Humberto Sequieros committed suicide during the course of the investigation. The case was closed. This is a photograph of Sequieros taken just before his death.'

Peter passed around copies, and Senator Devereux lowered his old-fashioned bifocals, squinted at the print and then looked up. 'Now,' he asked, 'is Sequieros the man on the left or the man on the right?'

'The man on the right, Senator.'

'And who is this gentleman on the left?'

Peter took a deep breath, as if about to plunge into a swimming pool. 'This is Dr André Longpré . . .'

It was as though a jolt of electricity had simultaneously run through everyone seated at the hearing table, while Shavinsky himself sprang from his seat and stalked across the room towards Peter, crumpling the photograph in his hand.

'Is this what you call evidence?' he bellowed. 'Is this what you call an investigation?' He tore the print to bits and scattered them over the floor. 'It is a travesty. Smear, rumour, innuendo and guilt by association. You tell a most interesting tale, Dr Watkins, but you have yet to demonstrate an ounce of wrongdoing by my government or myself. You do not alarm me in the least!'

Senator Lerner pounded the table with his small mahogany gavel, an event almost without precedent. 'Could we bring this hearing to order, gentlemen, please?'

Shavinsky, trembling, returned to his seat and sat down, folding his arms tightly across his chest.

Senator Lerner sounded shaken as he spoke. 'We have heard a number of very serious charges being made here this morning, which will require further discussion. I suggest we adjourn for lunch and

85

return in ninety minutes.'

Everyone rose slowly. There was a sense of relief at leaving the tension-filled room. Shavinsky had gone out first, slamming the door behind him. Ronnie and Peter exchanged grim glances. It was going to be a long afternoon.

16

Peter was so wrung out from his confrontation with Shavinsky that he could barely eat at lunchtime. He and Ronnie had a great deal to talk about in a very short time. Peter's last day on the Subcommittee was turning into the most demanding afternoon of his working life. But he was beginning to relish the thought of the coming battle – knowing Shavinsky could not win.

As the members of the Subcommittee filed back into the hearing room, Shavinsky gave Peter and Ronnie a small grin that bespoke an arrogant confidence. Peter nodded back in his most cordial manner. Then Ronnie surprised Shavinsky by going across to speak to him. 'So, Doctor, I hope your stay in the States has been interesting.'

Shavinsky looked at him with detached, pale blue eyes. 'Quite . . . but a little *longer* than I intended . . .'

Ronnie gave Shavinsky one of his most charming smiles. 'Well, I am sure that when we're through with this afternoon, your work can be wound up here.'

As the meeting began, there was none of the usual after-lunch jokes and gossip around the table. Senator Lerner called on Peter to speak first. 'Dr Watkins, you have introduced a photograph of this Humberto Sequieros with Dr André Longpré. In view of all we have heard about Longpré and his long-term involvement with the Israeli project, this link seems a most troubling one – especially if the hypothesis of the Argentine situation is correct. Now, let us be clear. Are you making a direct accusation that Dr André Longpré was present in Israel to build a nuclear bomb?'

This was the moment for which Peter had been waiting. 'Senator, I put it to the Subcommittee that some very persuasive evidence exists for this being the case.' He was aware of Shavinsky leaning forward and setting his pen down on the table, never blinking an eye and clearly playing it very cool. 'I believe that André Longpré was brought in by the Israeli government for the specific purpose of constructing a small number of nuclear warheads. We have seen that Dr Longpré had extensive experience in this field. He also acted as a consultant in Argentina, and was, I suggest, the originator of the Patagonian switchback – an almost fool-proof method for obtaining the enriched uranium required for a bomb, without any of the problems of theft.'

'You're saying, Dr Watkins,' cut in Senator Shillings, 'that the power loss at the Israeli plant was a result of this same switchback technique, the one Longpré pioneered in Argentina?'

Peter licked his dry lips. 'Yes, but I think, first, we should look at the whole sequence involved.' Shillings nodded approvingly as he went on, 'I would suggest that the story we were told of the spillage – the pellets spilling from the rods into the immersion tanks – was fabrication.'

Shavinsky sat up very straight and said indignantly, 'Then this Subcommittee is being told that I have lied . . . that I have misled –'

Peter continued calmly and evenly, 'I am merely sketching in what I believe to have been the most probable sequence of events.'

'Please continue, Dr Watkins,' Senator Lerner said, ignoring Shavinsky's interjection.

'The spillage was no more than a cover for Longpré to obtain a small quantity of uranium so he could begin work on a bomb. He had intended to use the Patagonian switchback method, as he did in Argentina over a period of several years, gradually accumulating more and more enriched uranium. But here he ran into a particular problem.'

'A problem?' Senator Shillings was hanging on every word.

'Longpré's method took time. Too much time. Here someone wanted a lot of uranium, and wanted it fast. Longpré was obliged to remove a great deal more enriched uranium from the first shipment to the Beersheba reprocessing plant than he could have felt was advisable. He had to put in so many dummy fuel rods containing industrial-grade uranium that the result was a large loss of power output after the reprocessed rods were returned to the plant – a loss, as we have seen, in the region of 20 to 25 per cent. Someone was bound to notice such a significant drop in output, so Longpré utilized the enriched uranium shipped over for the second reactor in the first reactor. And he probably took the reprocessed material from the first reactor and used that for his bomb project. At a rough estimate, one more switch of dummy for real rods in the next shipment to the reprocessing plant would have gained Longpré enough enriched uranium to construct perhaps six medium-sized nuclear warheads.'

Shavinsky pounded the table with his fists. 'It is the most incredible pack of lies I ever heard. Perhaps others enjoy Dr Watkins's speculations and fantasies, but I have to warn you that I and my country are being subjected to the grossest of insults and this is not something to be tolerated.' Shavinsky was trembling. He gripped the edge of the table with shaking hands.

The Senators looked over at Peter, whose head was bowed, whose chin was on his fist. Slowly he looked up as he continued: 'I have a great interest in proof, Dr Shavinsky, in whatever proof I can find. But one thing I have noticed is that you have not been entirely helpful in this regard.'

'I?' Shavinsky's eyes seemed starting out of his head.

'Yes, during our previous hearing, we discussed with you why you hired Longpré. You stated that you had faced certain technical problems with the new reactors. Senator DeAntonio wondered why, in that case, no American physicist had been called in. You claimed that a letter was written to the American Atomic Energy Agency, and they replied that none of the Americans available had experience with this new type of reactor. You then requested assistance from Vendewerke, the reactor's manufacturer, who supplied you with a list of consultants, André Longpré among them. You stated that he was the only name on the list who was immediately available. Do I accurately summarize your statements, Doctor?'

Shavinsky shrugged as he began idly doodling with a pencil.

'At the time you told us of all this,' Peter continued, 'the Subcommittee requested copies of your correspondence with the IAEA and Vendewerke. That was over two weeks ago, Doctor. I was wondering whether you had those documents with you here today?'

Shavinsky looked up, irritated. 'I called the IAEA just after the hearing, requesting that a copy of their letter be sent here to me in Washington. As of today, I have not received it. I am not accountable for American bureaucratic inefficiency. Likewise, I contacted Vendewerke. They were unable to locate the particular person who would have a copy of the list. In no way have I attempted to avoid providing –'

'Then perhaps this is one thing we could clear up right now,' Peter said. 'I suggest we have some phones brought in, and have Senator Lerner lead a conference call to the IAEA regarding your correspondence. Then, tonight, we could call Vendewerke in Germany and verify that you contacted them two weeks ago, requesting the list.'

The Senators all gazed at Shavinsky intently. With the ball squarely in his court, he squirmed slightly in his chair as he almost hissed between his teeth, 'Why, you're suggesting I never even called, that there was never any correspondence.' He had a tone of frantic incredulity in his voice.

'Prove me wrong, Dr Shavinsky,' Peter invited him. 'Shall we get the phone?'

Shavinsky stared at Peter but remained silent as the Senators all looked at one another nervously.

Peter went on, 'And while we're making conference calls, I suggest we also contact the Coroner's office in Lyon, France.'

'Lyon?' asked Senator Lerner.

'Where Longpré suffered his heart attack . . .'

Shavinsky's face was by now contorted with rage. He shot up from his seat, glaring at Peter. 'You imply that Longpré's death was –'

Peter responded calmly, never even looking at Shavinsky. 'I think that Dr Longpré realized the switch of the uranium rods was going to be detected. He had been forced to act too fast. His position was becoming precarious. In all likelihood, he fled Israel, fearing disclosure. What happened next was . . .'

Shavinsky turned as pale as stone. He walked back to the table, swept up his briefcase and papers and strode swiftly to the door as the Senators watched in helpless silence. It was Senator Devereux who cleared his throat and called out to Shavinsky, 'Come on, son, don't you be in such a hurry now. We're here to help Israel . . .'

Shavinsky turned and looked at the old man, a long-time ally of his country, as the Senator went on, 'Please, now, sit back down and tell us how you see it. We've listened to Dr Watkins. We want your side of it.'

Shavinsky pondered for a moment, then, very warily, reapproached the hearing table and returned to his seat. He looked Senator Devereux full in the face as he adopted an open, candid and hurt tone. 'I can assure you, Senator, that there is not the slightest shred of truth attached to anything Dr Watkins has claimed. His entire story is speculative, and he has deliberately left out the most obvious point. If uranium was being removed on its way to the reprocessing plant in the manner in which Dr Watkins has suggested, then the fuel rods would have been depleted. The only way in which uranium can be employed in a nuclear explosive device is if it is reprocessed. Obviously, the IAEA stringently controls all reprocessing in Israel. What would be the point of going through all these subterfuges, this so-called "Patagonian switchback", if there was then no way to use the uranium once it had been obtained?'

Senator Lerner, thinking carefully, made some notes and looked back at Peter. 'Do you have a response to that, Dr Watkins?'

It was a point which Peter had been considering ever since he read the file on the Patagonian switchback in the night. Everything fitted perfectly, except the very point which Shavinsky had just raised. He was right, of course – depleted fuel rods were useless without reprocessing. Even as Peter had arrived at the hearings, the point had been troubling him. Lacking an answer, his whole argument, persuasive as it was, seemed immeasurably weakened. It was a relief to be able to say, 'Senator Lerner, I think Mr Montgomery is more equipped to deal with this point than I am at this time.'

Shavinsky's eyes darted towards Ronnie, as Senator Lerner went on, 'Thank you, Dr Watkins. Now, Mr Montgomery, would you take this up, please?'

Ronnie offered the Senators his most charming smile. If they were looking to him to create some kind of ultimate coherence out of this tangled mess, he was not about to disappoint them. 'I'm afraid that what I have to say here today more or less confirms the scenario presented by Dr Watkins. Longpré did, in all likelihood, mastermind a uranium theft for purposes of constructing a nuclear bomb.'

Ronnie paused, reached down and snapped open the catches on his briefcase. He removed a large bundle of photographs, which he distributed about the hearing table. Shavinsky shuffled through several nervously as the Senators quietly passed them back and forth.

'These,' Ronnie continued, 'are satellite reconnaissance photos taken over Israel during the past year. The building which you see is located about twenty-five miles south of Masada, close to the Jordanian border. From the exterior, it appears to be a water desalination plant – the Dead Sea is close by. However, if you'll take a look at these other photographs . . .' Ronnie handed around some curiously coloured prints, which the Senators examined with fascination. 'These, as some of you may know, are infra-red reconnaissance photographs taken during various U-2 surveys. The red wavy lines which you see almost vibrating around that water treatment plant are indications of such radioactive substances as uranium or plutonium.'

The Senators quietly whispered as they examined the photos. Senator Shillings looked up in agitation. 'Then what you're saying is that this is no water treatment plant . . .'

'I'm saying it is a plutonium reprocessing plant, carefully masked by the Israeli government to conceal its true purposes.' There was a deep silence, the only sound the dim hum of the overhead fluorescent lights, as the Senators stared at Ronnie, as amazed as they were dismayed. He continued, 'And it is probable that, by using the so-called Patagonian switchback, under the supervision of Dr Longpré, the Israelis could, over a period of several years, have amassed quite a formidable nuclear arsenal.'

Senator Lerner looked at Ronnie, then across at Peter. His face was ashen. 'If this is true, then we are facing a most serious breach of treaty provisions between the United States government and Israel!'

Senator Hartley, who had kept quiet all afternoon, now looked up and spoke in an obviously distressed voice. 'I entirely agree with Senator Lerner that this is a most frightening development, and one which I find shocking and depressing. But the anger I feel now, Dr Shavinsky . . .' They had almost forgotten about Shavinsky, and suddenly all eyes were turned on him. 'Here we've sat, battling with you for almost two full hearings. You've shouted at us, bullied us, threatened to walk out. And now, with all that Dr Watkins and Mr Montgomery have told us, it's pretty damned clear that you have been lying, and lying from virtually the minute you arrived here.'

Senator DeAntonio looked up mildly from fiddling with various fly-tying materials in his lap. 'David here considers you're a damned liar, Shavinsky. I pretty much agree with the sentiment. What do you say?'

It was about as harsh as DeAntonio had ever been known to grow. The impact was instant – as it usually was when he spoke out. Shavinsky looked around the table at each of the Senators, as the Senators, in turn, watched him attentively. It seemed as though he was gathering some fresh resources as a smile of curious detachment played about his lips. When he spoke, he did so forcefully, but with no trace of emotion: 'I did not expect to receive an objective hearing here –'

'Now, one minute, Doctor,' interjected Senator Lerner.

'May I please continue?' Shavinsky said in an exaggeratedly flat tone.

Senator Lerner nodded grimly.

'*I* can put up with your crude treatment. The thing which concerns me more is the hatred for Israel which has been witnessed in this hearing room. Each question, each charge, each innuendo has been voiced specifically to discredit Israel. My conscience is clear, gentlemen, on all I have said and done in these hearings . . . I only hope that yours may be equally so.'

'Doctor Shavinsky, my conscience is as clear as cut glass,' said Senator Shillings, his eyes flashing. 'I consider you've had a fair hearing and have been treated with quite remarkable patience in the circumstances. Your little tirade on Israel rang more than hollow, but I reckon you fancy yourself in a bit of play-acting every now and then. However, I note that, amid all your denunciations, you never once addressed yourself to Mr Montgomery's implication – that Israel has built a secret reprocessing plant which could be used for nothing except obtaining illegal plutonium.'

Shavinsky sat bolt upright as he unsnapped his briefcase. 'That's the trouble with Americans . . . they never know when to leave a thing alone. Yes, I have lied here today – and lied earlier. If you want truth, I will give you truth, gentlemen. But after that, *you* will have to live with it.'

A tremor of unease ran round the table as Shavinsky took a stack of documents from his briefcase and laid them out systematically in front of him.

'Putting a nuclear power plant into operation certainly presented us with no difficulty,' he began. 'We did just that – were even ahead of schedule. All ran smoothly until about seventeen months ago, the date of the first shipment of depleted fuel rods to Beersheba for reprocessing –'

'After the spillage incident?' asked Senator Hartley.

'There never was a spillage, Senator. I'll come to that shortly. Meanwhile, on the night of 19 July, a convoy of two trucks under guard left the reactor facility with the depleted rods. The trucks in fact carried a high percentage of our fuel cells. They then headed across the Negev Desert for Beersheba. At about three o'clock in the morning, they halted. In the roadway ahead there stood a large flatbed truck, half-filled with produce, smashed head-on into a VW bus. The bus was on fire and two bodies lay in the roadway. The driver of the truck, apparently bleeding profusely, waved for help as he stood in the glare of the convoy's headlights. Our men instantly ran forward with first-aid equipment, and at that moment the truck driver took up an automatic weapon from the shadows and opened fire. The bodies on the roadway, assumed to be victims of the accident, also opened fire from where they lay, before scattering to take up battle positions. Our crew was caught completely off-guard. Most were killed or immobilized within seconds. It was a brilliantly planned and executed operation.'

'How did you come by this account?' asked Peter Watkins.

'My informant is one of our men, who suffered only a shoulder wound. He was able to observe everything that happened. The three men dragged out the drivers' bodies and drove the two trucks off into the darkness. When the convoy failed to make its routine radio contact call forty minutes later, security people immediately checked the route. The scene of the ambush was discovered and my informant, the only man to survive, was flown out by helicopter.'

'And the trucks?' Ronnie asked.

'They were found abandoned in the desert next day, following a very thorough air search.'

'And what of the uranium, the depleted fuel rods?' asked Senator Lerner, his voice hard as rock.

Shavinsky paused a moment, then looked towards the window. 'They were gone . . .' He again fell silent, seemed to become almost vague. 'Perhaps they were removed by truck . . . but our belief is that they were flown out in a cargo plane which took off from somewhere in the desert close by. That seems the most reasonable assumption. Trucks filled with uranium would never have made it out of Israel.'

'So explain to us precisely what you mean by *out* of Israel,' said Senator Lerner.

'Those who set the ambush were Palestinians,' Shavinsky stated, his voice dead.

Senator Devereux flung down his smouldering cigar into an ash tray. 'You sit there and tell us that a bunch of goddamned Palestinians hijacked American uranium from right under the noses of you bungling Israelis!'

Senator Devereux was mopping his brow with a big white handkerchief. 'In that case, the Palestinians could have a darn hydrogen bomb rigged up this very moment!'

The atmosphere in the room had grown even more electric as the Senators turned back their incredulous attention to Shavinsky, who looked by now as grey and pale as a shadow. 'Yes, it is true, they may have the bomb . . .'

Peter Watkins stared at the subdued Shavinsky. 'Shavinsky, I presume you have some more solid evidence to offer than suppositions?'

'Yes, Dr Watkins, I can furnish you with quite a bit of solid evidence, but permit me first to finish my story.'

'I am sure we'd all like you to continue,' Peter answered calmly.

'The man who survived the attack – his name was Yigal – had caught a good look at two of the men, and was later able to identify their photographs. They were Hasan Ahmad and Ali Nasr, both known to be members of a Palestinian terrorist group. Hasan has a background in chemistry and physics, while Ali is considered something of an expert with Soviet surface-to-air missiles. Here are our Israeli intelligence dossiers on the two men, if I may pass them round.' Shavinsky quietly distributed the documents, and Peter and Ronnie at once began to examine them carefully. The reports were certainly remarkably detailed.

Shavinsky sat back down again as he continued to speak. 'As soon as he had positively identified these two, our deepest fears were confirmed. It had been a brilliantly executed guerrilla operation, designed to seize the fuel cells for their potential as the basis for a nuclear bomb. There has subsequently been some speculation that the Palestinians must have had a contact inside the power plant, but this has not so far been confirmed.'

'So where does Dr Longpré fit into this pretty picture?' asked Senator Shillings, looking more and more lost in the confusion.

Shavinsky sighed and shrugged his shoulders. 'The moment our government realized the Arabs had their hands on this uranium, our military people naturally became alarmed. With nuclear weapons at their disposal, the Arabs could destroy our country in an instant. It was therefore decided that Israel had no choice except to embark on a crash programme to develop a credible nuclear counterforce as a deterrent to whatever threat the Arabs might be preparing.'

'But this uranium they hijacked was depleted fuel, wasn't it? It needed reprocessing, didn't it? So where in hell can an Arab reprocess plutonium in the middle of nowhere?' demanded Senator Shillings, getting back into his more abrasive stride.

'Senator, the Palestinians enjoy excellent relations with the Soviet Union. It is our belief that they would have no difficulty in getting the uranium reprocessed.'

Ronnie Montgomery tapped out a staccato rhythm with his pen on the table top. 'Therefore exactly what were you saying about a crash programme to develop a nuclear deterrent?'

'We concluded that it was imperative for us to begin construction of a nuclear bomb without delay. At that point, we approached Dr Longpré, who suggested we utilize the switchback technique, though he warned us that it required a period of years if it was to escape detection by the monitoring authorities.'

'So Longpré initiated this switchback technique,' said Senator Hartley, 'but your government pushed him for over-fast results. And now, just how far has this crash programme to build a bomb gone, Dr Shavinsky?'

Shavinsky folded his hands meekly. 'From our point of view, not far enough. We have not yet been able to assemble a weapon. Dr Longpré did, in fact, come to fear disclosure, and so departed unexpectedly for France. He was the key to the project.'

'And as to your solid evidence, Doctor?' Ronnie pressed Shavinsky relentlessly.

Shavinsky began to pass round further items from the thick stack of documents in front of him. 'Here you see photographs of the two abandoned transport trucks, of the site of the faked accident on the Beersheba highway. There is also a full transcript of Yigal's testimony and dossiers on the two Palestinians, with copies of their fingerprints. We do, moreover, submit to you a report on the construction and operation of our clandestine reprocessing plant, as well as a detailed accounting of Dr Longpré's work.'

As the Senators passed the material back and forth between themselves, the occasional low murmur of the voices created a background sound as Shavinsky took out a sealed envelope, which he handed to Senator Lerner.

'Prime Minister Peritzsky has additionally instructed me to convey this communication to the Subcommittee,' he said.

Senator Lerner opened the envelope and silently read its contents with careful attention. Then he passed the document to Senator DeAntonio, giving a weary look at his fellow-Senators. 'Prime Minister Peritzsky has requested that we maintain silence in this matter – on the hijacking and Israel's plan to establish a nuclear deterrent. He requests this in the interests of Israel's national security.'

'Maintain silence?' asked Senator Shillings in great agitation. 'My God! At least twenty major treaty violations are involved. A concerted effort has been made to mislead the American government. There has been theft, negligence, a major breach of security, the illegal development of a reprocessing plant. I never saw a more appalling set of circumstances in all my twenty-eight years in the US Senate. And now, in all likelihood, this incredible blundering by Israel has led to the nuclear arming of one of the most politically erratic groups in the world – the Palestinians. The President should be informed this minute, and a broad range of investigations be opened up here in Congress, including a full-scale review of our relations with Israel.'

'I'm concerned that we are witnessing here the birth of a nuclear nightmare,' said Senator Hartley, thudding the table with his fist. 'Look at what we've been told today. It's like the opening of a radioactive Pandora's box.'

'I'm sure,' said Senator Lerner, 'that none of us here disagrees with your assessment. It is truly a horrible situation. I feel personally outraged. But what we must now consider is the action which this committee is ready to take . . .'

'What we need to do,' said Senator Devereux, 'is hand Israel six or seven nuclear warheads here and now. If Israel had possessed nuclear weapons in the first place, we'd never have seen any of those senseless Middle East wars.'

'Chauncey,' said Senator Lerner calmly, 'I think everyone here would agree with you that our first concern has to be the continued security of Israel.'

'Permit me to disagree with you, Senator,' Peter interrupted gently. 'Surely our primary concern ought to be the proper exercise of *American* foreign policy. Israel has committed a most serious mistake, embarking on a unilateral course of action involving a criminal cover-up and making a mockery of this Subcommittee. It may even be a situation which requires the judgement of the American people and as thorough an inquiry as this Congress can bring to bear.'

'Then you suggest we go public, Dr Watkins?' Senator Lerner asked, thoroughly alarmed.

'I suggest that could be your obligation, Senator.'

Senator Lerner looked pleadingly across at Ronnie. 'And from an intelligence angle, what is your view, Mr Montgomery?'

Ronnie folded his arms, sighed and allowed himself a few moments' thought. 'I have to agree that the situation is most serious. It seems to be one which strains the capacities and responsibilities of this committee. The documents Dr Shavinsky has provided look to me to be pretty much in order, but I am still troubled by many of the circumstances surrounding the whole thing. There's a great deal we still don't know that we need to know. The kind of investigation which the situation requires lies beyond the scope of this Subcommittee. The matter should, at the very least, be referred at once to the Foreign Relations Committee and the Military Affairs Committee.'

'What's needed,' said Senator Shillings explosively, 'is an immediate vote of the full Senate on a resolution halting all aid to Israel, pending a full inquiry, in addition to a forthright statement of condemnation by the President.'

'Well, Bill,' Senator DeAntonio finally spoke up, 'considering all that the Israelis have been up to, they probably deserve that and a good bit more. But we'd better not let this thing go off half-cocked. We'd better be damned sure of ourselves. There's a lot to be considered. Exactly what will be the result if we do go public?'

At this point, Shavinsky came back to life. A glint returned to his eyes, which even contained a bizarre trace of triumph. 'Allow me to tell the Committee what "going public" would mean. The action would provoke an international crisis of the first magnitude. You would destroy every chance of the current peace negotiations making progress. Apart from that, you would discredit the development of peaceful use of nuclear power for at least the next fifty years anywhere in the world.'

'Nevertheless, Doctor,' Shillings replied grimly, 'we of the Committee must act in a way which is right, regardless of consequences.'

'Yes,' agreed Shavinsky, 'but you must ask yourselves of what "right" truly consists in these circumstances. You have, I hardly need to point out, a Presidential election almost upon you. You are dealing with the most sensitive issues. Will the Jews of America accept a Senate rebuke that could hazard Israel's future? Will the Jews of America be able to come to terms with the idea that you five men here unleashed fear and panic in Israel?'

Shavinsky's voice, as he spoke, had grown steadily more resonant. His glare had all of its former hawk-like arrogance as he continued: 'You will be remembered as the men who blocked Israel from obtaining her own bomb, stopped her defending herself against a deadly threat by terrorist gangs. That is how the Jews of America will remember you. That is how *history* will remember you . . . The decision, of course, is yours.'

Each man in the room was aware of having reached the tensest moment since the hearings began, and Peter Watkins, looking drained and exhausted, spoke up with determined severity: 'I had expected that Dr Shavinsky would by now have gone beyond the bullying tactics and blackmail threats that he threw in the face of this Committee at an earlier stage. It is the duty of this Committee to act for the long-range good of American foreign policy. No decision which is made should be made as a form of bargain with any particular group or with an eye on any election.'

'As designated chairman of this Subcommittee on Intelligence,' said Senator Lerner solemnly and evenly, 'I hereby put forward for vote the question of whether this report shall, at this time, be made known outside this Committee. Those who favour making known our findings here, please say "Ay". Those who favour withholding our findings at this time, please say "Nay".' Slowly he looked around the table. 'Senator Hartley?'

'Ay,' replied Senator Hartley loudly.

'Senator Devereux?'

'Nay.'

'Senator Shillings?'

'Ay.'

'Senator DeAntonio?'

But DeAntonio seemed lost and brooding within himself. When he finally spoke up, his voice was sombre. 'This,' he said, 'is the most difficult vote I have ever cast, and I've been through some rough ones. With due deliberation, and the gravest of reservations, my vote must be "Nay".'

Two ayes and two nays. Senator Lerner had noted each response on a scrap of paper. He looked up. 'The chairman's vote, gentlemen, is "Nay". The nays have it.'

17

Standing in the draughty Capitol corridor, Peter Watkins suddenly felt defeated and alone. The whole world seemed to be shattering into splinters before his eyes. He looked back towards the door of the hearing room, where the network news people waited with their cameras and lights. Correspondents with microphones, reporters with pads and pens, all clustered competitively just outside, ready to fall on and devour whatever fictitious scraps of news were tossed in their direction.

Then, as the door swung open, old Senator Devereux emerged with his arm round the shoulders of a beaming Shavinsky. The two men stopped for pictures and a few words, as the other Senators filed out behind them. Peter had been part of this team for three years. Now it was over. He could not have imagined a worse ending. Wanting to avoid meeting a soul, he made for the stair-head rather than the elevators. He would head for the Federalist Tavern for three or four stiff drinks. As he went down the corridor an open door caught his eye. It was the cubbyhole where they were holding the refugee hearings where he had paused once before. He stopped again and peered in.

The new young Senator from Delaware, Senator Daniels, was there again, still with his two earnest young aides beside him. A low voice was speaking from the far end of the room. In a chair, giving testimony, sat the same dark-haired young woman whom Peter had seen last time. She spoke with the directness and carefulness of a child relating an important story. But he had arrived too late to overhear any of it. Senator Daniels was already thanking her for her assistance and adjourning the session until next week.

Peter stalked away from the Capitol through the freezing night air. He decided he would, after all, go home, take a hot bath, get some dinner and try to put the whole dismal conclusion to the hearing out of his mind. It seemed to make a mockery of all his three years' work. He tried to block out the memory of the broad but thin smile on the face of the triumphant Shavinsky as he had emerged with Senator Devereux. He wanted to be home and warm, in Liza's arms. They had been apart too long.

As he approached his townhouse, he was perturbed to see that the windows were still in darkness. He fumbled impatiently for his key. When he got into the hallway, he found the post piled on the mat. Where in hell was Liza? He flipped on the living room lights as he reached the top of the stairs. The mess from the big party was still scattered about. It seemed a most unwelcoming homecoming.

Upstairs in the cold bedroom he undressed, took a quick shower and put on a wrap before going back down to the kitchen. The garbage smelled even worse. The dirty dishes were still as dirty. He felt he needed a drink right away. He couldn't find a single clean glass, so washed one of those on the table. He went to get some ice, but there weren't any ice trays in the freezer. They'd all been left out empty. Feeling highly irritated by now, Peter grabbed a bottle and poured himself a straight Scotch which he drank in one gulp as he stood over the sink of dirty dishes.

He decided to plunge straight in and start the cleaning up as he watched the national news. He had got to a big stained baking dish at the point when Senator Tim O'Donnell came on the screen. Tim was speaking modestly of his big win in Wisconsin, even complimenting Lamb on running a good race. Had he had any thoughts about a possible running-mate, he was asked. The Senator smiled boyishly, saying he never thought that far ahead. He emphasized that President Randall, despite his Administration's many failures, would be a tough nut to beat in November. As the news clip ended, he announced he would be going on in two weeks to the upcoming Maryland primary.

Laying the last of the dishes on the draining board, Peter turned to start preparing for himself a turkey sandwich and some soup. At that point, Israel's Foreign Minister, Sol Goldblatt, came on the news, warning how Israel would stand firm against what he termed 'the rapid Arab military build-up we have witnessed during the last few weeks'. There had, Goldblatt said, been little progress at the peace talks, and he blamed President Randall for making unreasonable demands on Israel.

Peter felt in no mood to hear complaints from Israel, especially not tonight. He began to eat his sandwich, poised to snap off the TV as another story caught his interest: the final day of hearings on the Israeli nuclear power programme. The network commentator, standing in front of the Capitol, solemnly noted how the Intelligence Subcommittee's hearings on Israel's nuclear plants had gone on far longer than expected, so sparking rumours that the Subcommittee had found irregularities in the plants' development. The rumours had ended today with the Committee's joint statement praising Israeli co-operation in the vital area of energy conservation and giving high marks to their efficient development of the plants. Then they ran a live interview with Senator Devereux out in the corridor, the very scene from which Peter had turned away only a few hours before. Senator Devereux, smiling good-naturedly, reaffirmed the long-standing good relations which existed between the United States and Israel. He said the United States could learn much in the field of nuclear power development from Israel.

Peter felt an anger beyond words. That old Southern windbag of a hypocrite! Then there was Shavinsky on the screen, grinning like a cordial wolf and shaking hands with Devereux. The commentator noted how Senator Lerner, the Subcommittee's chairman, did not wish to make any personal statement at this stage.

Peter finally snapped off the set. He felt in a state of high agitation, and hoped never to see Shavinsky's face again. There were 60 million people sitting in their homes tonight who would feel as strongly as ever that Israel deserved every bit of support she could get from America. If only the Subcommittee could have gone public with their findings, with the truth! Peter stamped downstairs to his library.

'What is good for Israel is good for America.' How many times had Peter heard that in Congress? That was the one unshakeable belief to grip American political life. He sat at his desk and began to look at the notes he had been making on the Middle East. No wonder most Americans didn't wish to hear or read about it. Every book on the

101

subject which he opened said something different from the one before. Peter had come to be convinced that a clear understanding of the problem rested on an understanding of the problem's origins, no matter how tangled or obscure they seemed to be.

Every event could be traced back to a preceding one – where the hell was one to start? He looked down at the opening page of a thick volume. The first sentence read: 'The origins of the repeated crises in the modern Middle East lie in the crumbling of the Turkish Ottoman Empire at the end of World War I.' He yawned wearily and shut the book. All at once, there came the sound of the front door opening. It could only be Liza!

He sat there silently, wanting to surprise her. From the sounds, he knew she had set down her suitcase as she put on the chain-lock, muttering to herself as she did so. He glimpsed her as she passed by the doorway, holding her high heels in one hand, her suitcase in the other. His heart skipped a beat at seeing her again and realizing how beautiful she was. He listened intently as she padded up the stairs. Then he heard nothing more. Quietly, he followed after her.

Liza was sitting bent forward on the couch, looking very tired and haggard. Her hair was a little untidy, and Peter could sense she had been drinking.

'Liza?' he whispered.

She turned towards him, a broad grin breaking on her face. He stood across the room from her, wildly excited at seeing her again, but still angry that she had done nothing to keep in touch. From where she sat on the couch, Liza motioned him over, giving him a coy, little-girl smile and looking up at him out of her big blue eyes, which were slightly bloodshot even so.

'Where did you get to then?' Peter asked coldly.

'Oh, Peter, nothing about that now. Come here and kiss me. I am so very tired.'

He ached to go straight over to her, to caress her, but instead heard himself saying in a wooden voice: 'In five days I didn't get a word from you! I tried ringing you night and day from Wisconsin. Then I come back and the place looks as though a goddamned cyclone hit it. Jesus Christ, Liza, what is going on here?'

Liza stared at him, then broke into a teasing laugh. 'Peter, don't be so mad. Oh, I am glad to see you. I missed you every minute. How could you think –'

'So where was the hardship in calling?' he snapped back.

'I've really been very busy. I did try calling you. You weren't exactly easy to get hold of up there.' She pouted as she spoke the words.

However hard he tried, Peter could not persuade himself into believing that she had actually attempted to ring him. 'So where did you get to?' he asked angrily.

'I've been up in New York, for the flower convention. It's their great annual event.'

'And what was this party? It looked like some damned army had been through here.'

Liza giggled and brushed back a stray lock. 'Oh, that . . . A mob of the flower people came over for drinks. They'd flown in from New York.'

'But when I tried to call you last night – very late – there wasn't any answer!'

She glared, then shouted: 'Peter Watkins, don't you dare to use that tone with me. I'm no child. I don't have to account to you for everything I do . . .'

'Look, this *is* my house. You had some big blast in here, then just took off. You left behind you a big mess. You never even called me. If you don't have that much regard for me –'

'So that's where we've got to. *Your* house, your rules, your everything! Maybe I don't have a place here?'

For a moment, Peter said nothing. He walked forward to stand over her and demanded: 'I want to know where you were last night.'

She looked back at him, clearly amazed and giddy with drink. 'Why, you're jealous. I don't believe it!' She laughed and reached out a hand, but he turned, left the room and went upstairs, slamming his way in at the bedroom door. He lay down in the darkness, feeling bitterly angry. A dozen confused emotions were running through him. Yes, he *was* jealous, terribly jealous. He could hardly bear the thought that somewhere there could have been flirtations with other men – with another man. Here he had been longing for Liza for days, missing her terribly, and then had returned to an empty messy house, only to have Liza walk in, happy as a lark, after maybe being out all night with some guy. He tossed and turned in a fury, too tense to sleep.

The door opened softly. Liza was whispering beside the bed, 'Peter, I'm sorry – please.'

He lay with his back to her, unmoving.

'I had to fly to Boston last night, after the party,' she said. 'I had an early meeting there this morning. I wanted to be here ready for you

103

when you got back from Wisconsin. Truly I did. I felt so happy for you, so glad you'd won.' She had begun to cry quietly.

Peter felt overcome with melancholy and exhaustion as he turned towards her and held the covers open. She slid into bed, her chilly body completely naked. He drew her to him and began stroking her tear-stained cheeks. She started to kiss him hungrily, teasing her tongue against his. Their naked bodies lay together for the first time in days, and all the frustrations, struggles and worries of the past week melted away in the force of an overpowering passion. After their eager love-making, they drifted off to sleep in one another's arms.

18

They did not stir before noon, but felt relaxed and rested and decided just to spend the rest of the day quietly together. For a time, they simply lay there talking, Liza smiling at him sweetly as she said, 'You looked so sad and defeated last night when you stormed off up the stairs. I expected you'd be on cloud nine after the win in Wisconsin.'

'Oh, it was a long day yesterday . . . I felt tired. I'd been lonely for you.'

'I'm sure you had a lot to do with the Senator doing so well in the debate. All that work. I only hope he knows how valuable you are.'

'I think so. Well, he did say it was as much my victory as his.'

'So isn't this the right time for you to move up in his organization?'

Peter looked a little puzzled. 'Move up? How do you mean?'

She sighed as she smiled. 'You've been in Washington six years, yet you act like you just got off the bus from Snowflake, Arizona. Come on, he *likes* you. You're *in* with him. You should be reaching out to get more authority, aiming for a defined title with clear responsibilities.'

Peter turned on his side and, looking into her blue eyes, laughed a little. 'You know, I can't get over you.'

'How's that?'

'You're always thinking things out so carefully. I can see why America has such fabulous flowers with you organizing the flower growers.'

She ran her hand over his bare chest. 'I just want to see you get all you deserve. I want Senator O'Donnell to appreciate you as much as I do.'

He began to fondle her under the sheets, saying, 'Well, I hope he won't appreciate me *quite* as much as you do . . . not in certain ways at least.'

She laughed as she removed his hand from her warm body. 'It's serious, Peter. Don't you see how important it is for you to make a move at once?'

'How should I do that?'

'Well, what's your present position called exactly?'

'A foreign-policy aide to the Senator.'

'Fine – but how many others are there? Who's over you? Who's your boss? What are your responsibilities? How often will you be getting direct contact with the Senator? All these things make *big* differences.'

'The fact is, I've got pretty close to the Senator and in quite a short space of time. He seems to trust my judgement. I guess he'll be relying on me more and more.'

'Not if you don't push . . .'

'But that's not my style, Liza. I've done pretty well in my own way so far, haven't I?'

'Sure, and I'm proud of you. But you've got to be realistic. As the campaign picks up, Timothy O'Donnell will have more and more people hustling to get close to him. You could be squeezed out.'

'I doubt that. He and I have an understanding.'

'You should prepare to move in to becoming his chief adviser on foreign policy, head up the National Security Agency, just like Kissinger under Nixon. You could be not just *an* adviser but *the* adviser.'

She was looking at him with her eyes flashing with an excitement that could have been erotic. Peter stared at her, at her uncovered breasts as she lay half-tangled in the sheets. Her drive and ambition left him breathless, even overawed.

'Liza,' he said, 'he hasn't even been elected, and already you're planning his White House staff!'

She gazed back, seriously. 'He will be elected – so long as he makes the right moves. A candidate has to take a hundred difficult decisions. One simple wrong decision can trip him. That's where you should come in. You've got to be looking at the implications of every decision, each trip he makes, each word he utters. He's got a whole staff of people thinking about this stuff for him, but he'll come to rely more and more on only two or three men. Every candidate does that. So does every President. You could be one of those men for Tim O'Donnell.'

Peter smiled. 'It sounds like you should be working for the Senator, not me.'

'Maybe it's your innocence that I find attractive, Peter. I'm not even sure that you really care how high a position you get to.'

He ran his fingers through her long, silky hair as he looked at her earnestly. 'No, really I don't. I want to serve the Senator as best as I can. He and I share the same values . . . ideals.'

'Ideals are empty unless they can be made real. That means power . . . politics. Your ideals rest on *your* power. I'm only telling you the facts of life in Washington – or anywhere else.'

'Well, I do have a certain secret influence,' Peter replied sombrely.

She glanced at him with alert surprise. 'Oh, and what does that consist of?'

'This . . .'

Peter snatched all the sheets off Liza in one swift movement as she tried to grab them back.

She laughed as she lay there, naked with the afternoon sunlight streaming in on her. He admired the tint of her flesh, warm and golden in the shaft of light. Then she became silent, and stared at him strangely, her eyes lit up like those of a watchful cat.

'Time to get up!' he suggested cheerfully.

Instead, she gave a slight lick to her lips and began to caress her own breasts and nipples, round and round. As Peter watched, he felt his desire begin to stir again. She ran a hand down between her legs, which rustled against the sheet as, slowly, she spread them apart. He watched her hand's rhythmic movements as she softly murmured, 'Oh,

Peter . . .'

Later, as he lay sprawled in the fading sunlight, his thoughts drifting and swirling, he wondered at his luck in having found this enchantress, who could possess his body so magically and completely.

It was dusk before they managed to get downstairs for breakfast. Both were as hungry as hunters. Peter had writing and reading to do, and Liza a number of letters to type. They agreed to stop work at seven for dinner – if they could hold themselves apart that long . . .

As Peter sat down in front of his stack of books on the Middle East, the old feelings of confusion and futility returned. How could anyone ever figure it all out? If only there were people at hand he could ask, people who'd lived there and could help to fill in the gaps. The face of the Palestinian girl at the hearing came into his mind, and he remembered how he had slipped away from the first hearing, not wishing to hear her speak for fear her story's sadness might mar her beauty.

Peter was startled to find Liza standing behind him as he finished scribbling his last few notes. He'd been too deeply engrossed even to think where he was.

'I thought you must be asleep over your papers. There hasn't been a sound in four hours,' she said.

Peter shut the books and gathered up his notes. 'Oh, just some snippets of research.'

'Research? My God, you look more like a graduate student on an all-nighter,' she said with a laugh. She surveyed the scattered books on the Middle East. 'What are all these?'

'I'm trying to get some more depth on the Middle East. I never feel I really understand what happens there.'

'What is there to understand?' Liza frowned. 'You've got a stagnant Arab civilization that lives in the Middle Ages, a few oil-rich sheikhs and one country of smart dedicated Jews who are trying to build a decent life for themselves. Is that so very complicated?'

'Well, no doubt you're right – but I have to see it for myself.' Peter began to replace some of the books on the shelves.

'How do long-winded books help? Most of them are nothing but academic garbage . . . if you really want to know what's going on there, I can put you in touch with people. Nearly all of my friends have been to Israel.'

'Well, Israel isn't exactly the *whole* Middle East.'

'From the American viewpoint it is. What has America in common with the Arabs? But Israel is democratic, highly advanced. You'd really better talk to some of my friends, Peter.'

'At this stage, I'll stick to books. How could I judge how objective your friends were being?'

'So you don't think Israelis trustworthy? Is that it? Then who do you think trustworthy? The Arabs? Don't make me laugh, Peter.'

Peter sighed, shut the folder of notes away in the safe and stretched himself. 'It's not a question of trust – the point is objectivity. I don't want to talk to some American Jew who's just back from a two-week trip to Israel. And talking to an Israeli would be as confusing as talking to a Palestinian. They are all too emotionally involved. I need to work this thing out by myself.'

He crossed the room and embraced Liza, who was sulking a little, and began to kiss her ears, her neck. At first she resisted, but then she began to kiss him back.

Peter whispered, 'Let's not fight over this stuff. It's not important. I want you, Liza.'

Liza looked firmly and steadily into his eyes a moment before they linked hands and turned to climb the stairs together.

19

Three weeks later, Tim O'Donnell beat Willie Lamb in the Maryland primary, receiving about 54 per cent of the vote. Despite this second victory, Tim remained cautious. He knew Lamb retained a firm grip on his home state of Texas and would thus as a matter of course be carrying a very large bloc of votes to the Democratic convention in August. The Maryland primary had been important, being the first real test of O'Donnell's new national campaign apparatus, and he had begun to receive some important endorsements, the governor of Maryland being an influential help here. Vic Kovacs's strong hints that the United Federation of Labor would probably endorse Tim O'Donnell had also born fruit. Vic had kept his word.

Two weeks after Maryland, O'Donnell ran against Lamb in the Indiana primary. By now, the campaign was picking up speed. Tim needed to fly all over the United States, preparing for other primaries, making contacts, delivering speeches, attending endless fund-raising dinners. He spent far less time on personal appearances in Indiana than he had in Wisconsin or Maryland.

Lamb, on the other hand, campaigned hard in Indiana. He was well-known and liked there. His record in support of the steel industry gave him a strong base to work from, whereas the people of Indiana were a little wary of O'Donnell. Conservative by nature, they were suspicious of a candidate who was young and divorced – and from crazy California. The strongest asset of O'Donnell's was that he had the *look* of a winner. The national press had begun its love affair with the dynamic young Senator, and hardly a day passed when his picture did not appear on the cover of some magazine. He had even become a bit of a sex symbol. Young girls and housewives, not to mention grand-mothers, had begun to crowd the parade routes to catch a glimpse of him, just as they had done for JFK in 1960.

There was a higher voter turnout than expected on election day in the Indiana primary. As returns came pouring in after the polls closed, it looked like a close thing. The three national networks weren't making any firm projections. For about an hour, Lamb seemed to be outstripping O'Donnell. Tim and his staff sat quietly in their hotel suite in Indianapolis to watch the returns and take phone messages from their operatives around the state. Barney Shaw sat and ate his way through large bags of pretzels, and with no shoes or socks on. By midnight, with 80 per cent of the returns counted, Lamb was leading with 51 per cent and O'Donnell trailing at 49 per cent. The networks still had no projected winner, but several commentators were predicting the end of Tim O'Donnell's meteoric progress.

Tim O'Donnell went to bed ahead of the rest of his staff. His mind was already preoccupied by the other primaries he would be running in during the next few months: Oregon, Arkansas, Texas, California, New York. It was again to be constant motion, jet flights and a brutally intense schedule. He'd made eighteen appearances in one day in Indiana, followed by a meeting with his staff at midnight.

He was awakened at 6 a.m. by the booming voice of Barney Shaw, who leaned over his bed and yelled, 'You've done it again, boy! They're not exactly calling it a landslide, but you've done it.'

He tossed the morning papers down on the pillow as Tim felt his heart begin to beat wildly. He looked at the headlines: 'O'Donnell Squeaks By – Lamb Loses on Home Ground'. Also: 'The Front-runner Stumbles . . . And Runs On'. He had beaten Lamb. It had been the closest yet. The message was mixed. Tim felt a glow at winning but a despondency at doing no better. It was bad news for the other primary campaigns – especially for Oregon coming up in ten days. He would need to double his efforts to rebuild his momentum as front-runner. He complained bitterly to his staff that more time should have been spent in Indiana. There should have been more appearances and speeches. Barney responded by chewing him out in front of everyone, saying he was damned lucky to have beaten Lamb at all in a place like Indiana. And besides, Barney added, if there was a landslide in every primary, people were going to be pretty mindless by election day.

The Oregon primary came round very fast, and Tim was popular there. They took to his sense of motivation, his independent spirit. Lamb was also pressing, but his poor record on environmental issues was a drawback in Oregon. Then, half-way into the campaign, the press uncovered some irregularities in Lamb's fund-raising organization, forcing him to spend half his time issuing denials and explanations.

The real dark horse of the primary, however, turned out to be Senator Lerner. Michael Lerner's announcement that he would run for President had been anticipated for weeks. But, it was said, he would save his main push for a few of the big-ticket primaries where he could be certain of doing well: California, Illinois, New York, New Jersey. Then came the abrupt announcement that he would run in Oregon only a week short of the primary. The move caught everyone by surprise. There were a lot of people in Oregon who did not even know who Michael Lerner was.

Barney Shaw expressed delight at the impulsive challenge. In his view, Tim could beat Lerner easily, which would look good later on –

when he ran against him in New York. But then came signs that Lerner's campaign might catch fire. His staff had a plane-load of a book by Lerner sent out in paperback. It was called *Energy – the American Challenge*, and had been published several years before to the admiration of specialists, but not attracting much attention from the public. One chapter had been devoted to the environmental policies of Oregon, proclaiming the state as America's energy showcase.

The people of Oregon glowed as copies of the book were distributed, liberated from their two-year incarceration in a Yonkers warehouse. Oregon newspapers reprinted the chapter relevant to their state and Lerner began an intensive campaign, working through environmental groups which already had energetic political networks. He quickly made an asset of his chief drawback – his campaign's total lack of advanced planning. He turned up unexpectedly wherever there was any sort of gathering, stressing that his was an informal campaign but still gaining intensive media coverage. He kept close to the environ-mental issue, and it worked like a charm.

Rumour had it that the New York money had begun to pour in for Lerner. A stunning TV campaign was prepared for him in a matter of days, and was networked against Tim O'Donnell's own spots. The polls showed Lerner pulling up quite rapidly on O'Donnell, with Lamb dropping to third place.

Close to the finish, Lerner, desperate to pull out in front, called for a debate with O'Donnell, or even a series of debates. Tim welcomed the idea, but Barney was appalled. Lerner, he said, was now something of a golden boy in Oregon. Tim was in the race for the long haul: the Presidency itself. He shouldn't blow it, just because his ego wanted another airing. It was all too sudden. The people of Oregon had had no time really to examine Michael Lerner, who was riding the crest of a transient wave of support, mostly founded on one issue. Nevertheless, Tim questioned, how would it look if, after all the guff he gave Lamb in Wisconsin, he backed away from debating now? Barney said he would just damned well have to take the heat for a few days.

Tim made the most of rejecting Lerner's request for a debate, asking why, if he was really so serious about the people of Oregon, he hadn't been there a month before, campaigning from end to end of the state as Tim had done. He inquired where Lerner stood on the other major issues: on the economy, on disarmament and defence spending, on civil rights and jobs, on American leadership around the world.

Tim closed his speeches by saying: 'I am not here today to lead an environmental crusade. As much as any man, I recognize the importance of the environment. But it is only one issue among a great many others – *all* of which are vital. Mine has been a campaign of months – not of days. The question which the voters of Oregon face is a question of leadership, of the broad vision which that leadership requires, of the quality of leadership required for the Presidency. I ask for your support with confidence.'

These final speeches made a strong impact during the closing hours of the campaign. Most people in Oregon realized that Michael Lerner, for all his appeal, fell short in making a convincing shot at the Presidency. They also saw that Tim O'Donnell was a determined battler who meant business. They liked his style; they sensed a winner.

By election day, the polls showed Lerner beginning to slip back. Political wiseacres began to say he had 'peaked' too soon, that if he had only kept to his momentum of ten days earlier, he could have trounced O'Donnell. An hour after the polls closed, all three networks were projecting O'Donnell as the big winner, correctly as it turned out.

It was a sweet victory, but the time for celebration was short. With hardly a moment to catch his breath, Tim was aboard a plane for Little Rock, Arkansas.

20

Three days later, Tim O'Donnell sat in the campaign headquarters in Washington, brooding silently and looking down on the traffic in New York Avenue. He had been beaten, and beaten badly. Lamb had won by a good 17 per cent. The press were making a lot of Arkansas having broken Tim's winning streak, although the more astute columnists agreed with Barney's view: that, for a California boy, Tim had not done at all badly in Willie's back yard.

The following week was that of the Florida primary, which Tim had kept out of. He intended to spend every minute of the next three weeks planning the campaign for Willie's home state of Texas. That would be a very big primary which no one imagined he could win. He certainly intended, though, to give Willie a run for his money.

The Florida primary turned out, as it happened, to be an exciting occasion. The state had a large Jewish population and a high proportion of liberal Democrats of Michael Lerner's stripe. The dramatic race had both the Lerner and Lamb forces pouring millions of dollars into their campaigns. From the O'Donnell viewpoint, a strong win by Lerner this time would help him greatly by slowing down Willie in Texas. He had even phoned Michael Lerner and suggested in jest that he come down and campaign on his behalf.

In the event, Willie Lamb chalked up a big win. It was his third straight victory, and it put him in a position where he was poised to overtake Tim as front-runner.

Tim was hardly alone in being concerned at the direction the campaign was taking. One afternoon, a group of visitors filed into his campaign office. Nathan Pflug of the Israeli Political Action League had five 'concerned Jewish citizens' in tow, and after the formal pleasantries, came straight to the point. Both he and the Jewish community he represented were perturbed by the defeat of Senator Lerner in Florida. On the contrary, Tim interrupted, he thought Lerner had run a very strong race.

Nathan shrugged. 'But he might have won! Nevertheless, you're right – Senator Lerner has demonstrated that he is a capable campaigner . . . as you discovered in Oregon, I believe. What concerns us, and I speak for everyone here, is Willie Lamb.'

Tim gazed back innocently. 'So what do you want from me? I'm working day and night to defeat Willie Lamb, and I'll beat the guy, one way or another.'

'Maybe. Lamb's very powerful. He has plenty of oil money behind him. He's popular in the South. He'll be no walkover.'

Tim laughed lightly. 'Well, to be honest, I never thought any of this would be easy.'

'We could help . . . help quite significantly.' Nathan gave Tim one of his coldly appraising looks.

'I've always been a loyal supporter of the Jews, Nathan. You know that. I'd be happy to accept whatever support you can offer.'

One of Nathan's five companions spoke up. 'Yes, we much appreciate your work, Senator. My wife's family, in Los Angeles, have voted for you ever since you first ran for Congress.'

'Well, you must give them my warm regards.'

The man smiled back, flattered. 'I think,' he said, 'that what Nathan is getting at is your views on Michael Lerner – as a possible running-mate . . .'

Tim leaned back and sighed. 'I've made no secret of my respect for Michael. I'll certainly give him my closest consideration as running-mate – provided I get the nomination.'

One of the others said, 'But if we could just know for sure, know you would take Michael Lerner, we could help you now in your race against Lamb. The present is the time you need our help. Later may be too late.'

'Let me reply in all sincerity,' said Tim. 'Nothing would please me more than to be able to give you a "yes". Believe me, Michael is right at the top of my list. But you must see I can't do that. I have to keep my options open. We're four months from the convention. Anything could happen in that time.'

Nathan sat up rigidly, gold-rimmed bifocals propped on his high, balding brow. 'Let me put the case a little more abrasively, Senator,' he said, 'because there is very little time left for you or for us. We want from you a pledge regarding Senator Lerner, and we want it *now*. We believe that your chances of winning the nomination are reasonably good – if you have our backing. If you don't, then Willie Lamb will wipe the floor with you. Do I make the options clear?'

Tim had only just been able to contain himself as Nathan spoke. Now he glared at him as he let fly: 'You already pulled this number on me last January. Maybe there were a few more threats then, but I don't like what you're trying to do, and I cannot accept that a majority of American Jews support your tactic. Marty Rifkin already tried to strong-arm me up in Wisconsin, and now I've had it with both of you. I'm sick to death of your threats. If you want to support me – fine. You know where I stand on Israel, and on every issue of importance to American Jews. I'm running for President and I'll be elected – *with* or *without* you.'

Pflug began to shake an admonishing finger at Tim, who interrupted him in mid-motion.

'Now I have another appointment.'

He shook hands with each man, and showed them to the door. The moment they were out of it, he strode swiftly to the wall cabinet and poured himself a stiff Scotch. The door reopened just as he raised the glass to his lips. Nathan Pflug looked paler and more angry than he had ever seen him.

'You think this is all a big game, don't you?' said Nathan, his voice shaking. 'Do you have any idea of what the stakes truly are? I tell you – and it will be the last time I do so – if you don't give us a commitment, and shortly, the going will get rough, rougher than you could imagine.'

After Pflug's disappearance, Tim sat down and tiredly began to study his staff's briefing books on Texas. His schedule for the Texan campaign had him booked from dawn till midnight every day for two weeks. Later that evening, when Peter Watkins stopped by the office to leave some papers for the Senator, he was surprised to find him so late at his desk.

'Come in, Peter,' Tim waved to him.

115

'Senator? Still here at this hour?'

'I'm looking at the impossible state of Texas.'

'You'll beat Lamb all right. I really think so. He's overrated.'

'Maybe the way God's a little overrated in Heaven . . .'

'I can't say I've ever taken to him.'

'God? Or Willie Lamb?'

They paused to chuckle, and then Peter asked, 'So are you thinking Lamb will win, get the nomination, be elected?'

'I aim to see he doesn't,' the Senator replied. 'Who knows?'

'If you hold your own in Texas, the rest of the campaign will be cake. You'll do all right in California. Lamb won't stand a chance there.'

The Senator stared out into the night. 'Maybe you're right. I hope so. But I'm not sure we should be in such a hurry to see Willie go down.'

'Why not?' Peter asked, beginning to feel impatient with Tim's despondency.

'Because it becomes clear to me that he'd be the best man for my running-mate . . . with him on the ticket with me, there's no way President Randall could beat the combination.'

Peter gazed at the Senator in astonished dismay. 'What about Lerner? Aren't you still giving him some thought?'

'Lerner would be good, sure, but Lamb can deliver more votes – practically the whole South. Michael and I are too closely identified as liberals – Lamb would give the ticket a better balance. I need Lamb. It's the simple truth.'

'Is this your final decision?'

'Well, I'll be talking it over with Barney and some of the others during the next few days.'

'Would Lamb accept the Vice-Presidency under you?'

'At the moment, it looks like I may end up accepting the Vice-Presidency under him, if I don't get moving.'

Peter relaxed and laughed, then set down the papers on the Senator's desk.

'Oh, and Peter, this work you've been sending in the last few weeks . . . it's really first-rate. I've been campaigning so hard, there's been no time to talk much.' The Senator laid a hand on his shoulder. 'Let's spend some time together when I get back from Texas, OK?'

The Senator had, as Peter left, reverted to being a solitary figure, hunched over a desk covered with precinct maps of Texas.

21

With Tim O'Donnell launched into his Texan campaign, Peter Watkins found himself tied up day and night, preparing various foreign-policy papers for the Senator. Once every day or two he dropped by at the O'Donnell headquarters to check on progress, and every night he watched the TV news and caught up on the newspapers. One item surprised him: a story in the *Washington Post* which claimed that Willie Lamb had had meetings with Michael Lerner. Rumours were rife that Lamb had offered him the role of running-mate. When questioned, Willie Lamb had only said, 'Well, I guess anything's possible. One of the founders of the Texas Rangers was Jewish, as perhaps you already knew.' Senator Lerner made no comment beyond saying he had paid a courtesy call on the Governor.

The implications for O'Donnell seemed instantly clear. The Jews had decided to back Lamb – had no doubt made a deal with him. With Lerner in line for the Vice-Presidency, Lamb would receive powerful Jewish support and O'Donnell would find himself squeezed out in the middle.

A week later, a poll on the evening newscast had Tim running a good twenty points behind Lamb in Texas. Several nice clips showed Tim speaking to enthusiastic audiences, but they seemed nowhere near as enthusiastic as the rowdy rallies being held for Willie Lamb, the favourite son of the Lone Star State. Lamb was, in his confidence, even arrogance, treating Tim's campaign as a good-natured joke. A subsidiary news item concerned the Israelis insulting President Randall's negotiator at the peace talks and threatening a walk-out. There were speculations that Israel had deliberately stalled the talks, hoping to gain a stronger negotiating position after the elections.

Then, next morning, the papers contained a bombshell, one headline reading: 'Lamb Blasts President – Cites Zionist Influences'. In a late-evening news conference in Austin, Texas, it seemed, Lamb had flown off the handle, charging President Randall with being reduced to impotence, even as Israel had shown a wilful and appalling contempt for the American people. As he rounded off his remarks, a reporter asked why the President was having so little success in dealing with Israel. Lamb replied without hesitation, 'Well, I don't think it's exactly a big secret that there's an awful lot of Zionist influence at the White House. It's a stranglehold I intend to break if elected.'

Lamb's remarks about 'Zionist influence' and a White House 'stranglehold' rocked the country. Within twenty-four hours a thousand editorials were crying out against the crudity of Lamb's anti-Semitism and the dangers of his attitude to Israel. His judgement, maturity and sense of public responsibility began to be called into question throughout the media, and every Jewish organization in the country was up in arms. President Randall responded with uncharacteristic sternness, blasting the 'shrill and ignorant forces of reaction which try to turn the clock back on religious equality and which attempt to sabotage delicate peace negotiations with loud words and ugly rumours'.

Peter felt dazed by this sudden development, and was just sitting down to write a long memo to the Senator, analysing the consequences of Lamb's outburst, when the phone rang. It was Tim O'Donnell calling from Dallas.

'Have you been watching the papers?'

'Like a hawk.'

'I'd never have believed it. He's got the whole country in an uproar.'

'It should make quite a few inroads on his chances.'

'Are you kidding? The guy could be washed up. Everyone knows the Jews have had the last eight Presidents by the balls. Only Willie Lamb has come out and said it.'

'So is Lamb right?'

'Well, he is, in a sense.'

'What do we do next, then?' Peter asked calmly.

'That's exactly why I called you. The press is screaming for a statement.'

'You could say it was an unfortunate choice of words and showed very poor taste. Alternatively, you could come down hard on Lamb's lack of experience in dealing with the complexities of foreign affairs. Maybe you should demand some kind of retraction from him. That could look smart.'

'At the same time, we mustn't lose sight of the Jews.'

'The Jews?' Peter asked.

'It seems to me it could be a golden opportunity. If I lead the attack on Lamb, I'll have every Jew in the country behind me, and the Pflugs and Rifkins can screw themselves. If we throw Lamb out now, they'll have no choice but to back me.'

'Time enough – but what about Texas? The primary's in a few days. How will a tough attack on Lamb play in his home state? They're going to be mighty defensive, I think.'

The Senator paused. 'You could just be right. The Jews aren't exactly popular in most places in Texas. The people here agree with Willie Lamb. They probably think he hasn't gone far enough.'

'I suggest some kind of statement, chiding Lamb for showing very poor judgement and being insensitive, and leave it there – no more than a general statement. Then you can wait and watch what happens over the next few days before turning up the heat. You'll have to judge the timing yourself. That's very important.'

As it happened, Willie Lamb held a press conference next day, amid the rapidly gathering momentum of the campaign. He apologized for his statement and said that no insult to the Jews had been intended. He admitted his remarks had been intemperate, and regretted offending many fine Americans. Then, in an amazing tack, he swung about to begin blasting the President and Israel. While never using the term 'Zionist', he reaffirmed his conviction that Israel had held a disproportionate degree of influence over the President, and that this was playing havoc with the peace negotiations. If his beliefs came under fire, he said, so be it – as a loyal American and a *proud* Texan, he stood by his principles. Peter had to admit, before turning off the television, that as a performance it had been a political *tour de force*. Lamb had, on the one hand, defused some of the charges of anti-Semitism while, on the other, refusing to back down from the substance of his original remarks.

The attacks on Lamb continued unabated in the national press, but in Texas it was a different story. The people of the state rallied behind Willie, the polls showing that most of them agreed with his views. Tim therefore avoided all references to Willie's remarks in the speeches he made.

Two days before the Texas primary election, the O'Donnell camp held an early-morning staff meeting. A current of intense frustration ran through the room. It seemed crazy to believe anyone could beat Willie Lamb in Texas, like thinking you could beat a Kennedy in Massachusetts. But, Tim O'Donnell stressed, he would be satisfied with nothing short of a win. Barney's advice to him was to stay cool, even a little aloof. He figured that people could be burning out on Willie Lamb, having heard him too much, seen him too much. They were beginning to weary of him, as of a favourite uncle who'd overstayed his welcome. By contrast, Tim O'Donnell's dignity, freshness and seriousness could just tip the balance in the end, Barney felt. In any case, the really important thing was that practically every newspaper and network reporter in the country was in Texas to cover this, the biggest primary to date.

None of them could have foreseen that all their assumptions were about to be turned on their heads once again. That afternoon the news came through, just off the UPI wire, that Willie Lamb's son, Keenan, had been arrested on drug charges in Los Angeles at about eleven o'clock in the morning. The news hit the campaign like a warhead. Keenan, twenty-four, had always been the apple of his father's eye, and it had long been rumoured that Willie was preparing to set up his son in a congressional district. For about an hour, until the news became clearer, all campaigning came to a dead halt. Barney Shaw got on the phone to a mate at the *Los Angeles Times*. He sat firing off highly strung questions as the team in the room listened in absolute silence. After hanging up, he turned and slowly addressed the Senator and his staff. 'Keenan Lamb was arrested this morning by an undercover officer of the Beverly Hills police department. He had attempted to sell the officer twenty-five grams of cocaine, which were in his possession at the time of the arrest.'

The Senator could hardly conceal his astonishment. 'It's unbelievable – happening right on the eve of the election.'

'Unbelievable?' Barney shrugged. 'I reckon he's paying the price now.' He rubbed his red nose. 'Let's just put it this way – I don't think it entirely escaped their attention who the boy's father was.'

120

Half an hour later, the news was heard that Willie Lamb, deeply shocked, had flown with his wife to Los Angeles to be with their son. He had said he'd be making no further campaign appearances in Texas before the primary. The announcement caught everybody by surprise, including Barney Shaw, and the O'Donnell team immediately reassembled for a strategy session. What ought Tim to do next? The situation was highly volatile, full of hidden dangers. The conservatism of the people of Texas had received a nasty jolt. It took a lot of argument for the O'Donnell staff to agree on a general approach for the time remaining. Tim, it was decided, should not comment on the Keenan scandal. He should also avoid any personal attack on Willie Lamb, even on political grounds. Instead, he would emphasize his own record, his success as a primary candidate in every part of America, and his excellent chances for winning against President Randall in November. If there was going to be a backlash against Willie in Texas, then the O'Donnell campaign would let it develop of its own accord.

That night the news featured the Lamb drug arrest as its number-one national story. A brief clip showed Willie Lamb and his wife accompanying Keenan from jail after bail had been posted at $500,000. Willie, looking sombre and grey, brushed aside the reporters thrusting microphones into his face. He could be heard to make only one comment in a very low voice: 'We have come here to be with our son.' No further statements materialized, either from Lamb or his campaign headquarters.

Tim O'Donnell did not relish his last day of campaigning. He was feeling sorry for Willie Lamb, the story having been spread all over every newspaper in Texas. The reports contained a note of censure, although no one could guess how this might translate into votes. Tim's declining to use the issue for his own gain meanwhile attracted a widespread admiration.

The turnout of voters for the primary was in fact much lighter than had been expected. It was said that many Lamb supporters, confused and uncertain, had chosen to stay home. As the returns began to come in that evening, the networks remained reticent about making any early projections. Not till around midnight did the Lamb headquarters issue a statement from Willie Lamb conceding the victory to Senator O'Donnell and congratulating him on a strong, clean campaign. The win had been a fair one, O'Donnell leading Lamb by 55 per cent to 45 per cent. But, as everyone knew, it had been the drug case and Willie's withdrawal from the race which were the real turning points.

In the circumstances, Tim O'Donnell was unable to feel any real joy in his victory deep inside himself as he went downstairs to the ballroom of his Dallas hotel campaign headquarters. There his supporters broke into waves of cheers and applause for which he had to wait for twenty minutes before they subsided. He spoke only briefly, thanking everyone for their many weeks of labour. Then, in a more subdued tone, he spoke of Willie Lamb for the first time: 'This campaign was, in its closing hours, marked by tragedy, a tragedy which removed my opponent Willie Lamb from active participation in the race. I think, as you all know, Willie Lamb is one hell of a campaigner. He's surely no quitter.' A brief burst of applause cut in on his words, and he raised a hand firmly for silence. 'It was therefore with great regret and sorrow that the unfortunate news was received by me and by my staff. In closing, I'd like simply to express our concern for the Lamb family during this most difficult time, and to say I look forward to running against Willie in a dozen more primaries between now and the convention. Thank you all. God bless you all.'

The Senator's eloquence and graciousness evoked a powerful and dignified response. The applause lingered long after he left the ballroom.

As soon as he was clear of well-wishers, O'Donnell hurried back towards his room. The figure of Nathan Pflug standing in the corridor outside his door seemed like an inevitable manifestation. Pflug looked at Tim with a smile that almost had warmth in it.

'Congratulations, Senator,' said Pflug, shaking his hand. 'You ran a most impressive race. I wanted to say that. Nothing more . . .'

'It's good of you, Nathan,' said Tim O'Donnell, skirting his way round him. 'Thank you. I have to get ready to leave for Washington directly.'

Pflug, looking down at the carpet, was jingling change in his pocket. 'A terrible pity, what happened to Lamb . . . really a big shame.'

He gazed directly at Tim O'Donnell for a few silent moments before turning and walking away. The glaring reflection of the corridor hall lights had been caught in Nathan's glasses, so Tim had not been able to catch the expression in his eyes. Really, he thought to himself, Nathan was quite preposterous, so how was it that every time he met him he feared him a little more?

122

22

Peter was working at home next day, so Liza asked him whether he minded some of her friends stopping by in the afternoon. They'd stay up in the living room and wouldn't disturb him. He agreed and gave Liza a long, warm kiss before shutting himself away in his library. He had to write an up-to-the-minute briefing on NATO for the Senator.

At around three, he slipped upstairs for some coffee. As he came to the top of the stairs, he was surprised at what he saw in the living room. Various large maps and documents lay about unfolded on tables and over the rug. Two typists were busy at the dining-room table, while a group of four were busily making notes as they watched video tapes of Willie Lamb's major campaign appearances in North Carolina. Stacks of envelopes had been dumped on the floor.

Liza greeted him with a cry of welcome and a kiss and introduced him. They congratulated him on the nice work he was doing for Senator O'Donnell. Peter recognized a few of the names – colleagues Liza worked with. Almost all seemed to be Jewish.

He went to the kitchen to get a cup of coffee and some cookies, then, hearing Liza's voice speaking, decided to look in on the living room again for a few moments. Liza had just stood up to address the meeting. She looked very commanding, dressed impeccably as she was, in a long white dress, her blonde hair swept back neatly. She glanced down at some notes before saying: 'I think we're all agreed that we concentrate attention on Rhode Island. The Rhode Island primary comes on the 19th. The vital thing is to stop Lamb. Michael Lerner will be running. He's quite well known there, and well liked, so we have to do two things – fast. The first is to broaden Michael's appeal as much as possible, secure as many votes as we can, and I mean from people who will get out and *vote*. The second – and it's the more important – is make very, very clear to the people of Rhode Island all the negative things Willie Lamb stands for. I don't care how it's done, but by the 19th I want the people of Rhode Island to hate the guy. Oh, and something else – Rhode Island has the highest percentage of Catholics in any state. We need to develop some literature and have some pickets carrying the message: "Willie Lamb hates the Jews . . . will the Catholics be next?" . . . Something along those lines.'

Liza checked through a list and confirmed the task of each person in the room for the Rhode Island primary: fund-raising, media coverage, direct mailings, committees organizing public speakers, contacts at universities, voter registration drives, telephone canvassing, compiling computer data based on precinct demographics. The list left out nothing. Peter felt amazed at the thoroughness of the operation and the evident competence of every person in the room.

Then one of Liza's friends spoke up, a tall, older woman. 'What about New York, Liza? I mean, suppose Lamb doesn't lose in Rhode Island? Shouldn't we be doing a little advance planning on New York?'

Liza sighed and frowned. 'Shirley, we've been over it twice. Lamb isn't going anywhere once we're done with him in Rhode Island. Don't concern yourself about New York. Worry about Rhode Island.'

It was about an hour later that Liza came into the library, walked over to his desk and began to massage his back and temples. He sighed in relaxation, swivelled his chair about and pulled her on to his lap. As he looked into her blue eyes, he asked, 'So what was that all in aid of?'

'What?' asked Liza, mockingly innocent.

'The Jewish mafia,' said Peter drily, pointing upwards.

'Oh, just people I work with, and some friends.'

'My God, you looked to me more highly organized than the O'Donnell campaign!'

'We're concerned about Willie Lamb. About this thing he has against the Jews. He's got to be stopped before it's too late. We're just trying to do our bit in Rhode Island.'

Liza walked across to a mirror and began to fiddle with her hair as Peter watched in fascination.

'You gave me the creeps for a moment,' he said, 'you looked so damned organized.'

'So what's wrong with that?'

'Nothing, I guess. Only it did sound rather like you were setting up the vigilante patrols or some kind of smear campaign . . .'

'I don't care for your implications, Peter,' Liza suddenly flared at him. 'I think you owe me an apology.'

He sighed helplessly. 'Liza, I only –'

'That man's *got* to be stopped!'

There was an unexpected edge of steel in her voice. It took Peter completely by surprise. He began to put his papers and books away.

'Willie Lamb is personally repellant to me,' he said. 'But, to be perfectly honest, I agree with him when he says Israel exercises too much influence on the White House – and over Congress. I think it's doing plenty of harm to America's foreign policy at this moment.'

Liza stood blank and icy in her disbelief. 'My God, I never thought I'd hear such a thing coming from you, who's supposed to be the big expert on the Middle East. Don't you realize how little power Israel really has? It has *nothing*! Nothing except enemies. The US government controls its very existence, while the Jews here in America, too, have nothing but enemies.'

'But Lamb is doing no more than making a criticism of American foreign policy, a criticism that has some truth behind it. Anyway, I'm not at all sure how helpful it is to have Jews all over the United States ringing alarm bells and organizing paranoid committees.'

Liza was red and shaking in a fury he had never seen in her before. She stalked about the room as she started shouting: 'We are Americans! We are exercising our democratic rights! Willie Lamb is allowed to speak out. So am I! So are my friends!' Her voice had grown shrill and unattractive with aggressiveness. 'And no one stands in our way – not you or anyone.'

Peter was aware of keeping his own massive upsurge of anger coolly under control as he looked Liza in the eye. 'I'm not asking that you remain silent. I think it's great you're active in the campaign, you and your friends. All I question is your objectivity – and your methods. I begin to doubt if you can tell the differences between American and Israeli foreign policy . . . There's a difference, you know . . .'

In her rage, Liza grabbed his notes and hurled them across the floor.

'Screw you! Screw your goddamned notes!'

She turned and ran out of the room, and only minutes later he heard her slamming the front door behind her with a bang.

Nursing his anger, Peter took a shower before getting dressed to go down to the Federalist Tavern. There he had two quick Scotches, and sat gazing into his third, a double. He felt as limp as a wet rag. With the campaign becoming increasingly demanding, he was starting to feel the pressure. He took a sip and all at once was overtaken by nostalgia for his work on the Subcommittee. It had been a great job, he thought. It had been orderly. There he studied things, analysed them, made sense of them, tried to render them clear to the Senators. It was all a little slow, but it was steady. Then he thought of the last hearing – Shavinsky making jackasses of the whole bunch. So much for nostalgia!

The memory of his quarrel with Liza had begun to sicken him. Perhaps he had been over-critical. He understood that he had touched on a sensitive area, but the fact that Liza could be so violent-tempered was a revelation to him. When he finally reached home, Liza was already sound asleep – in the other bedroom. It was the first night since she moved in that they had slept apart.

The next couple of days passed grimly. Liza left for work early each morning, before he was up. She arrived home late and barely spoke to him. He felt miserable inside, and held himself constantly ready to apologize, but Liza was behaving in such an utterly withdrawn and coldly distant way that he felt almost afraid to speak to her. By the second afternoon, a real depression began to sink in. It was affecting his work, since he was making a new start on that damned Middle Eastern stuff. He sat daydreaming, hardly able to get down a word. Everything spun about in his head – Shavinsky, that crazy Jewish guy Rifkin at the debate in Wisconsin, Liza and her group of hot-heads. It was all growing hellishly complicated, and came right on top of his current reading about the grim history of Palestine from the time the British took over after the First World War up to the establishment of the Jewish state in 1948.

He began to think again of the refugee hearings, and of the black-haired young woman who had been testifying when he peeped in on the proceedings. He wondered who she was, what she was doing in the United States, what she might have to say concerning the events he'd been reading about.

In the end, he looked up Senator Daniels's number in his confidential congressional phone directory, introduced himself, explaining that he was trying to put together some papers on the Middle East for Tim O'Donnell. He said that he'd been particularly struck by the young woman, Miss Azoury, and Daniels agreed she had been their best witness. She was a Christian from Haifa.

Peter paused. 'Do you think she'd be open to any further interviews? I'd like to get in touch with her, perhaps have her meet Senator O'Donnell.'

Daniels was enthusiastic. 'By all means. Hold on a second. I'll get my notebook with the information about witnesses.'

By the time Peter hung up, he knew her telephone number, the fact that she was a student at Georgetown University, living up near Dupont Circle, and that her full name was Aida Azoury. It took him about an hour to get his nerve up and give her a call. He explained who he was, how he had briefly seen her testify and was now working on Middle Eastern policy for Senator O'Donnell. Would she be willing to talk with him? She sounded soft-spoken, friendly and polite, and suggested they met at four in front of her building. Then they could go out for coffee and she'd be glad to answer any questions and suggest other sources for him to read. As Peter hung up the phone, he felt a slight lifting of his depression, even a slight elation. A line of inquiry to get him temporarily out of his library and away from his books seemed the right move in the present state of things.

He arrived at the address he had been given at four exactly, and found himself standing outside a five-storey building which dated back to the 1900s, situated on Swann Street, a few blocks from the Washington Hilton. Aida Azoury came down the steps a minute or two later, wearing jeans. She was really tiny, much smaller than she had seemed at the hearing. They walked down to Dupont Circle to talk in the open air for a while as the weather was warm and spring-like.

'Is living over here difficult for you?' he asked. 'I mean, especially being a Palestinian?'

She looked at him shrewdly. 'It's nice to hear someone being frank about things for a change. Whenever I'm introduced here, I get these suspicious little sideways looks, as though they expect me suddenly to produce a bomb.' She smiled a little sadly and exclaimed, 'Most Americans know nothing at all about us. Neither do they wish to know.'

Peter looked out at the Circle and saw the beginnings of the heavy evening traffic rushing past. He touched Aida lightly on the shoulder. 'Can I buy you a Chinese dinner at the Mandarin Garden, or will that

127

wreck your study schedule?'

Aida looked pleased. 'Sounds a great idea. You've no idea how much biochemistry goes into cooking a Chinese meal . . .'

They talked as they walked to the restaurant, which was only a few blocks away. The Mandarin Garden was one of Peter's favourite secluded spots, and this being a Tuesday, it was not especially crowded. The lack of bustle added a special intimacy to its charm. They ordered an elaborate array of dishes and sat back. Peter felt that Aida was beginning to relax a little, but was aware that she was still trying to make him out. He knew himself that he didn't fit the pattern of the usual Washington political type. For one thing, he lacked the cynicism.

'How do you come to end up at Georgetown, in biochemistry?' he asked.

'When I was at secondary school in Beirut I got interested in biology. A cousin of mine lived in New York, and so I came to stay with her for about a year. I worked as a waitress in a restaurant so I could register for night classes at NYU. Later I applied to Georgetown, and luckily got a partial scholarship. Now I'm about half-way to my Master's Degree. It's taking a long time because I can only attend part-time. I have a job working as a lab technician.'

As she spoke, Peter could sense her total determination to succeed. There really was something remarkably impressive about this girl.

'Did you say you'd been reading up the history of Palestine?' she asked.

'I must admit I'm coming a bit late to the subject of the Middle East. I wanted to try and see how all that complexity arose in the first place. It's really not easy to sort it all out – or not for someone who's never been there and seen it close to.'

Aida leaned forward with interest. 'So tell me what you've discovered.'

'Well, maybe it will seem pretty basic in your view, but I've found it all rather disquieting. I started with the Arab Revolt – how the British encouraged that for military reasons, holding out hopes of independence to the Arabs. Then I moved on to the Zionists and the Balfour Declaration.'

Aida simply commented, 'It makes a grim chronology which gets worse as the years pass. More promises, more betrayals. In 1937, a British Royal Commission recommended Palestine be partitioned to create a Jewish state. The report advocated the forcible transfer of the Arab population to achieve such an end!'

128

'After all that happened, the Palestinians must have had little trust in the British.'

'They were deeply suspicious. At this time, also, the Zionists themselves turned against Britain. They organized more and more underground groups to back illegal immigration. By 1942, there were increasing Zionist terrorist attacks on the British.'

'So, I guess, after the war ended, the British felt in no mood to try and hold things together in Palestine.'

She nodded. 'That's right. They asked the Americans to join in another commission of inquiry in 1946, which called for the immediate immigration of 100,000 Jews and an abolition of all limits on land sale. By now, the Zionists had made major propaganda efforts in the United States. They had realized more quickly than most the decisive influence America would have in the post-war world.'

'But didn't the UN get involved after the war?'

'Yes. In 1946 a UN commission advocated the partition of Palestine into Arab and Jewish states. The United States exerted pressure on many countries to vote for this measure. It was thus approved by the General Assembly . . .' She paused for a moment, before continuing, 'At this time, there were 678,000 Jews in Palestine compared to 1,269,000 Palestinians – a ratio of two-to-one.'

'But the Zionists were still chalked up to receive half the country.'

'Yes. At that point, the British announced they were terminating the Mandate in May 1948. In April that year, the Zionists began their major terror offensive which led to the flight of thousands of Palestinians – who became refugees, as they remain to this day.'

She suddenly had the appearance of a tired child as she brushed her hair back under the restaurant lights. Softly, she thanked Peter for dinner, then looked at him a moment before asking, 'Do you understand a little more now?'

'Yes, yes, I think so,' he replied, sensing in Aida the full weight of the sadness of history.

23

It was a glorious spring morning in New York City. The sky was a translucent blue, and, for once, the smell of trees and flowers got the better of the exhaust fumes. The amiable mood of the weather affected the crowds of passers-by, who cheerfully walked their dogs, pushed push-chairs or window-shopped. In Central Park, dozens of joggers criss-crossed the well-worn paths. Lovers lay on the grass. A few blocks distant, at the new Hillel School, butterflies shortly out of hibernation flickered above the school area as teachers supervised Jewish pupils in setting up folding chairs on the lawn. Decorations were also being hung. The atmosphere was festive, the kids overjoyed to be missing class for a few hours.

A blue Lincoln limousine was making its way from the UN Building to Central Park, threading through the late-morning traffic. Alone in the back seat rode Jason Cardozo, America's Ambassador to the United Nations, a brilliant and astute politician who had had an influence on the Vietnam peace negotiations some years before. He had also served as a valuable intermediary during the Iranian crisis and had played a prominent role in organizing relief efforts for Cambodian refugees. His work in the field of human rights was widely acknowledged.

He sat and mused, watching the familiar streets of New York, which he had known since boyhood. His parents had been Russian Jews who immigrated from Minsk in 1897. His father had been a tailor. Jason thought of the fact with wonder as he gazed down at his impeccably tailored Savile Row suit. While he had come a very long way, he had in reality travelled no great distance – only from the Bronx to the UN Building. He loved to contemplate such ironies.

Throughout the whole of his career, he had always maintained a home in New York. He would often ask his mystified driver to pass through a certain street in a very rundown part of the Bronx. There he would gaze out at the battered stoop of an ageing brownstone tenement, and all the memories would come rushing back. It had been a big Jewish family – five brothers, three sisters. Father and Mother had encouraged his studies right from the time he was six. He remembered when he graduated from Harvard Law School, his mother threw a party for every family in the neighbourhood – to show off the diploma! He was the only one of them left in New York now. For him, it would always be home. He had been born here and raised here, and here he wished to die.

His task today was to dedicate a new school, founded by his friend, Rabbi Herman Rubinstein. The Rabbi was a high-spirited, energetic old soul, a mainstay of every social and cultural activity in New York. He had been working to get the school established for twenty-five years. Part of the funds had been donated by Israel, as an expression of thanks for American aid, and Herman had hoped the Israeli Ambassador might be there today, but he had been out of the country.

The Lincoln swung off Fifth Avenue on to the street where the school was located. It was 11.30 a.m. Jason was beginning to feel hungry. He wondered whether they'd serve a lunch, even a skimpy school one. As the car pulled up, he saw Archie Tompkins coming out. Tompkins, an old friend, was currently Under Secretary of State for Middle Eastern Affairs. Archie opened the car door for him and greeted him warmly. 'Jason, welcome to Hillel School. Hey, but you're looking great. What do you do to stay so youthful?'

Jason smiled. 'I avoid all forms of pleasure.'

Archie grinned. He knew Jason's wit was only one sign of a formidable intellect.

'Come on,' he said. 'The kids are out on the playground, waiting for you. I think you'll find all this a little more exciting and rewarding than a Security Council session.'

131

They met Rabbi Rubinstein in the entrance hall, who greeted Jason with a bear hug. 'Thank you for coming, Jason,' he said. 'It is so good that you can be with us today.'

'My pleasure, Rabbi. I needed a little fresh air today. And I know what a helluva school this will be with you masterminding it.'

The Rabbi took Jason's arm and looked him seriously in the eye. 'Jason, if I could have had you go to *this* school instead of that place up in the Bronx, you might have amounted to something!' The three men laughed heartily as the Rabbi guided them out to meet the principal, a lively red-haired woman in her forties, and to begin the dedication ceremony. As they walked across the lawn, a small choir of boys and girls started a chorus of Jewish songs.

Jason and Archie were seated behind the Rabbi as he led a prayer before making a brief speech expressing the joy he felt on this day, the most fulfilling of his life. Then he introduced Archie, who spoke on the importance of education and the special friendship existing between the United States and Israel. After that, as the Rabbi's old friend Jason was introduced, the children were clearly in awe. Jason was perhaps the most widely respected Jew in the country, and certainly among the best-known in the world.

As Jason rose to take the podium, he noticed two reporters moving forward from the back with notepads. A photographer had also begun to snap photos. Finally, a technician from Channel 5 in New York walked forward and crouched on the lawn, pointing upwards with a portable colour camera. Jason was so used to media paraphernalia that he hardly noticed it any more, though he would always wait courteously until the cameramen were ready. He began by greeting the children warmly, touched by the sight of their fresh, young faces. He spoke of his own boyhood and schooling, the importance education had played in his life, not as something that led to material reward, but as a source of constant spiritual enrichment. He commended their new school to them and advised them to make the most of the many opportunities it offered. Finally he praised the dedication of Rabbi Rubinstein.

Behind him stood two young oaks, freshly planted and linked by a blue ribbon. He took up a pair of scissors from the podium.

'I'll get along with this now. Most of you must be about as hungry as I am.'

As a giggle ran through the children, Jason held up the scissors and turned towards the ribbon. No one paid any attention to three men who had quietly emerged from a utility shed and begun to cross the lawn. Jason was smiling broadly, poised to cut the ribbon as he said, 'Children, it gives me inexpressible honour to dedicate this –'

His words were cut short as a violent burst of automatic weapons fire sprayed the podium. Children shrieked, ducked and scattered in terror. The Rabbi and Archie Tompkins were slumped over in their seats. Jason Cardozo lay face down on the lawn, the scissors still gripped in his hand. Among the front row of tumbled chairs were several children, bleeding heavily as teachers ran about in hysterics. The three killers paused only to glance at the slaughter, and one threw down something on the ground as he gave an abrupt order. They ran out the back gate and jumped into a car waiting in the alley.

In only minutes a stream of ambulances and police cars was descending on the school. Jason had been killed instantly. The Rabbi died on his way to hospital, and Archie Tompkins died that night from multiple wounds. Four schoolchildren were wounded, one critically. In the middle of the area the police found a red kerchief which carried a small white emblem on it. This was soon identified as the symbol of the PFL – the Palestinian Freedom League – a little-known, left-wing terrorist organization.

By noon, a deeply shocked nation was viewing the horrifying videotapes of what came to be known as 'the Manhattan massacre'. The Channel 5 cameraman, a veteran of news coverage in Vietnam, had coolly kept his camera rolling throughout the gunfire. The picture was jerky, the camera having been buffeted by fleeing children, but the gunmen could be quite clearly picked out, firing their weapons and then dropping the kerchief. They had been wearing bandanas across the lower halves of their faces. In the blow-ups of the photos, their dark, menacing eyes were to gaze out from the front covers of hundreds of magazines around the world during the following weeks.

President Randall at once called a day of national mourning. Following an emergency meeting with the National Security Council and the CIA, he flew to New York to accompany the body of Ambassador Cardozo back to Washington, where it was to lie in state in the US Capitol. The President was scheduled to give a brief address from the floor of the United Nations before he returned to Washington.

As the initial shock began to subside, a single emotion swept the nation: outrage. Outrage at the death of the beloved Cardozo, the death of a State Department official, the death of an elderly Rabbi, the wounding of four young schoolchildren. Americans had long distrusted the Arabs, but now a deep and vengeful spirit gripped the country as a thousand editorials cried out at such horror, and as network reporters stood with their microphones before the scattered chairs of the fateful playground.

Peter had been home writing in the afternoon when he first heard the news item. At once he felt sickened and profoundly depressed. Watching that TV film of the gunmen, the dead bodies, the helpless, panicked children, was almost beyond bearing. He felt, moreover, a sense of personal sorrow: he had always admired Cardozo, and had met him on several occasions in the Senate.

The irony of it all struck him as immense. Only a week before he had spent an evening with a delightful girl, bright, sensible and brave, and a Palestinian, just like these gunmen. He had listened to her story, and had now read every book on the subject he could find. He had been aware of a deep change within himself, a very gradual but new realization that the history of Israel was one that had been flawed from its beginnings. America's alliance with Israel had, from the day it was founded, been marked by illusion and ignorance of the Middle East. He intended to make all this very clear to Senator O'Donnell as a man who could become the next President of the United States.

A lot of things had gone towards changing his thinking recently. There had been the wretched events of the Intelligence Subcommittee hearings, the blackmail he'd seen being practised in the O'Donnell campaign, the Palestinian hearings and all that he'd been reading. More than anything else, there had been the few hours he had spent listening to Aida, whose own life was living history, more persuasive than any book. He felt at least he could understand a little of what had driven those three men to commit such an act of slaughter. At the same time, he loathed what they had done with all his heart, and recognized the futility of violence. In a few seconds on a sunlit playground in Manhattan, those three men had defeated their own chance, destroyed any hope that their people's grievance might be understood in America.

Senator O'Donnell rang, his voice sounding very subdued. 'Peter? It's hard to take in. This cold-blooded murder in broad daylight! Schoolchildren! What do these bastards think they're doing?'

Peter felt thoroughly distracted. 'Is there any inside news? What are they saying at the Capitol?'

'Only that it looks like it was a very professional job. No one got a look at the car. The FBI and the CIA are going over the TV footage

134

with a fine-tooth comb. They might be able to identify them, but they're probably out of the country already.'

'So what will your statement be? They'll be wanting a comment.'

'That's what I want to discuss. Naturally, I'll express condolences to all the families, condemn such a barbaric act.'

'A personal tribute to Cardozo would be appropriate,' Peter added.

'Sure. Then I was thinking about Lamb . . .'

'Lamb?'

'Yes. Maybe I should come down on the climate of fear he's been creating among the Jews – "anti-Semitic passions" and all that. I wouldn't need to mention his name – the message would be clear. Sympathy for the Jews is running at a peak now, and it'll make Lamb look like a heavy after all he's been saying.'

Peter paused a few seconds. He knew the Senator was right – some telling points could be scored against Lamb now, but they seemed inappropriate in the circumstances, even in poor taste.

'You're right,' he said, 'it would work against Lamb. Only I couldn't recommend this as the time for it. Should we drag the campaign into a human tragedy?'

The Senator let a few seconds' pause go by before he finally said, 'I expect you're right, Peter. Leave it alone for now. We'll talk again tomorrow. Thanks a lot.'

Later that evening, Peter watched President Randall's address from the UN. The President spoke with superb eloquence, insisting that no single act of wreckless violence should be allowed to stand in the way of the quest for peace in the Middle East. O'Donnell came later in the news, making a statement deploring the senseless murders and expressing his sympathy to the bereaved. Then he hit out at the mood of intolerance which had recently become a feature of the political scene, directed at these same people who were victims of the Manhattan tragedy – the Jews. So the Senator had ignored Peter's advice after all. He had not been able to resist exploiting the incident for his own ends by making a thinly veiled reference to Willie Lamb. A fresh fit of despondency overcame Peter as he switched off the set and headed for bed. Maybe he didn't really understand politics at all, he thought to himself, and maybe he'd much prefer not to anyway.

24

Slowly the initial shock-waves subsided. The three slain men had received honoured burial amid a great outpouring of grief from right across the United States. The one bright piece of news was that the child who was most severely wounded was off the critical list and rapidly improving. The other children were no longer in hospital. Yet the incident was not to be allowed to lie. It was, if anything, beginning to loom even larger in the political landscape because of the efforts of one man – Jesse Lusk.

Lusk, a Congressman from Florida for twenty-eight years, had risen to that most august of positions, the Speaker of the House. He had been Speaker for six years, and ran the House as though it were his own baronial manor. When he cracked the whip, Congressmen sprang to attention. The control he exercised over committee appointments, campaign funds and agendas had made him something of a legend. Some commentators said he was the most powerful Speaker the House had witnessed since the nineteenth century. He had squashed the movement towards greater independence in Congress, and vigorously reinstituted the seniority system. He was a short man with straggling white, unruly hair, who made up for his small stature with a caustic combativeness.

The Manhattan Massacre had struck an especially sharp nerve-end in Jesse Lusk, he being half-Jewish and always 101 per cent loyal to Israel. He had expressed outrage and bitter resentment at the time of the killings. As the days passed, he sensed a vaster rage in the country than was grasped by the press or the men in Congress. It was a great reservoir of antagonism which he aimed to tap. For years, he had made no secret of despising the Arabs. He was disappointed that America had not done even more for Israel than it had. And now, in the wake of these horrific murders, Jesse Lusk saw his chance to air his viewpoints.

On the first day when the murders were no longer receiving front-page coverage, Lusk addressed a major press conference in the House. He pledged that America was not ready to forget this heinous crime. The American people were, he claimed, crying out for action by their elected officials. He tipped up two huge mailbags on a table and let the letters cascade to the floor. This, he said, was only a small part of the response condemning 'the Arabs' his office had received. Taking up a letter from a nine-year-old girl in Oklahoma, who had been terrified by the news and asked him to make every school in America safer for children, he read it out in a speech, making the most of its highly emotive content.

Then he demanded immediate Congressional action, asking that all Palestinian students in the United States be expelled within sixty days. The Bureau of Immigration and Naturalization should, moreover, carry out an immediate security check on every Palestinian who had been in the country less than ten years. He blasted the President for his inaction, and said he ought to summon home all American ambassadors serving in countries which recognized the rights of the Palestinians. He called for the United States to put forward a UN resolution, condemning 'all acts of Arab terrorism for whatever cause'. He also launched a bitter attack on Willie Lamb, whom he described as 'a hater of Jews and a leader of the forces of darkness'. Finally, he made clear his intention of taking major initiatives in the House to achieve the actions he had outlined.

Lusk's statements made headline material again. The fact that he was able to get away with launching such an overtly rabid assault against a particular people was a measure of the climate of hatred which the incident had engendered. His fulminations had immediate results, as did a half-dozen other Lusk outbursts in the days which followed. Four Arab students were beaten by a mob of twenty citizens

137

in Los Angeles. A Palestinian doctor's car was blown up in Ohio. Vandals sprayed graffiti over the home of a Palestinian family in a New Jersey suburb. An Islamic school in Washington, DC, was burned to the ground. A Palestinian student at the University of Georgia was wounded by a gunshot from an unknown assailant. A vast demonstration outside the Hillel School in New York was accompanied by repeated chants of 'Arabs out! Arabs out!' And each night Jesse Lusk won his niche on the news as he threw a little more gasoline into the blaze. It all seemed disturbingly reminiscent of the McCarthy era in Peter Watkins's mind.

Meanwhile, the news also contained increasing reports of a major military build-up in Israel. The Israelis had put in an emergency request for the immediate purchase of thirty new American Warrior missiles and as many as forty F-9 fighter jets. The request was being debated, and, in the current situation, support for Israel was running high. President Randall's popularity had meanwhile reached its nadir. The Middle East peace talks which he had pressed for so forcefully now lay in shambles. His chief negotiator had stepped down over policy differences, and there were rumours that the Secretary of State was also about to resign. Israel chose this point to deliver a blistering attack on Randall, claiming that he had been playing into the Arabs' hands for a year now, that it was his own indecision that had invited the boldness of the recent massacre in New York. They attacked him for opposing their most recent weapons request, claiming that he was responsible for 'further endangering the security of Israel'.

The Presidential campaign itself was almost lost to sight beneath the turbulence and upheaval. Willie Lamb, under fire from all directions, including Liza's tight-knit group, had been forced to withdraw from the Rhode Island primary. Michael Lerner, now running unopposed in Rhode Island, had nevertheless campaigned hard and honourably, refusing to profit from the effects of Jesse Lusk's attacks. He publicly deplored the violence and vandalism that were being directed against Arabs living in America. At the poll he won a very large vote. The heavy turnout was attributed in part to Lerner's campaign, but it was also widely seen as a public vote of support for Jews in the wake of the massacre.

Peter Watkins often thought of Aida during these difficult days. He had wanted to call her, but what was there for him to say? America was showing a very ugly side of itself just now, and Peter felt a sense of shame. He was also rather disappointed in Tim. As the mood of the

138

country had shifted under the baneful influence of Jesse Lusk, so Tim had changed as well. He had missed no opportunity to remind the populace of his long-standing support of Israel. Whenever he was questioned over Lusk's proposals, the Senator would say that they were excessive measures, but he avoided making any direct attack on Lusk.

Peter found it hard to accept that, for the time being at any rate, the Senator would not be able to advance any new positions on the Middle East. He had suggested to him that, since the Manhattan Massacre was having such a profound impact on the Middle East situation, he might undertake a little research on the various Palestinian movements. A lot of the sources which he had developed during the years on the Intelligence Subcommittee could come in here, while Ronnie Montgomery might be able to produce some background. With powerful emotions prevailing everywhere, including in the media, Peter kept firmly to the line of advice that they should maintain objectivity, keep trying to view the whole thing as rationally as possible.

Tim O'Donnell was favourably impressed with the idea. He had not the slightest notion who these Palestinian Freedom League people were, therefore the more they could find out about them the better. Perhaps Peter might even be able to locate a PFL sympathizer or spokesman among Arab students in Washington. They must be around there somewhere. It was not unknown for needles to be found in haystacks.

25

Peter was taking a bus home from the O'Donnell headquarters, but got out half-way, deciding to walk the rest of the distance in the spring twilight. The cherry blossoms around the Tidal Basin were still in bloom. Yes, he thought, he loved this city. He began to think how life might be for him if Tim were actually elected. What kind of office might be his in the White House? What did the Oval Office really look like? He felt sure they could accomplish much together. In a flight of fancy, he saw himself in the position of revolutionizing foreign policy, becoming the architect of a new American role in world affairs.

The New York primary was coming closer – the week after next, to be exact. Tim O'Donnell had already spent a lot of time up there. The time seemed to have been rushing past ever since that day when he and O'Donnell had met over lunch at the Senator's house. The primaries were going by in a flash. Meeting the Senator had certainly changed his life, he thought. So had meeting Liza. But, at the thought of Liza, his spirits drooped again. He hardly knew what to make of that relationship any more. He didn't even want to think about how it had been going lately.

Peter had trouble putting his finger on the moment when things had begun to slip. He had been totally preoccupied with the campaign whenever he wasn't immersed in the Middle East research. Liza had herself been increasingly busy. There had been many late hours with her work for the flower growers. Someone was always coming to town who had to be taken out. There was always some party or gala to be attended in order to corner some Congressman or other official. The result had been that, over the past six weeks, they had spent less and less time together.

Sometimes, Peter sensed, Liza seemed to resent his growing involvement with the Senator these days. She had begun to make a point of belittling his Middle Eastern research. And then, as he watched her with her friends, Peter had begun to see an especially hard side to her which disturbed him. Sex between them was still very good, but there was less and less of it. He knew he still felt deeply for her and very much wanted the relationship to work. Once the election was over, he thought, things would calm down and they would find more time for each other. He didn't want this to be just another dead-end affair between two Washington career people.

He stopped off for a quick drink at the Federalist Tavern, and as he sat drinking began to turn over in his mind how much it really meant to him that Liza was sharing his home with him. Some nights, when they were both at home, they made love before dinner on the living-room rug. Then they'd eat late, watch an old movie or sit up in bed and read. Tomorrow they had a lunch date at Rive Gauche to celebrate their six months as lovers. It was something to look forward to. They seldom spent any time together during the afternoons now.

As he approached the townhouse, he could see, through the kitchen window, people moving about. Reaching the entryway, he heard a lot of noise from upstairs. He recognized the tone of the voices – Liza's campaign group again. There were at least thirty people crowding the living room, talking and eating. He made his way to the kitchen, where Liza was busily supervising. She greeted him distractedly, let him kiss her on the cheek and asked him to put some dishes on the table. Dutifully he obeyed before grabbing a piece of chicken and a drink and retreating down to the library.

The door remained open as he began looking through a bunch of foreign-policy journals which contained discussions of Palestinian nationalism. Before long, he heard Liza telling them all to be quiet. There was a burst of clapping for their victory over Willie Lamb – for his withdrawal from the Rhode Island primary. Now, Liza said, it was surely essential that they should respond to the post-massacre situation. It was a time for action by all concerned Jews. She outlined a proposal for tightening the pressure on President Randall to support Israel's request for military aid at the same time as criticizing the support he had shown for the Arabs during the peace talks.

Liza suggested that they set up a series of demonstrations against the President, timed with his primary appearances in New York. Once they were through with him, he'd be afraid to appear anywhere, even as Lyndon Johnson had been during the Vietnam War. A major letter-writing campaign should be initiated among American Jewish organizations. Her list of proposals seemed never-ending: media contacts, fund-raising, the placing of editorials. It began to grate on Peter as he heard Liza repeat over and over that they must never let America forget what happened in Manhattan, that it must be *used* to the hilt. It was the kind of exploitation that stuck in his gullet. The last thing he overheard Liza saying before he shut the door was that while Jesse Lusk's methods may have been crude, you could hardly overlook their effectiveness.

It was getting close to 11.30 before he heard signs of the party breaking up – these enthusiasts really worked late! Peter sat on, unable to write, feeling hungry and tired and with a sense of emptiness. Liza came in at the door, a drink in hand, a facetious grin on her face. He hated her in this particular mood.

'Hi, stranger! What've you been burying yourself in down here?'

'Just trying to get through a little work.'

'Why didn't you eat with us, help out at the meeting? You could help a lot . . . they all like you.'

'I'm not so sure I like what you and they are doing, Liza.'

'Oh, not all that again! Don't you see that it's in your interest, too? We all want to see Randall defeated and we don't want to have an asshole like Lamb nominated. Who does that leave us with? Who is our support to go to?'

'To Lerner, no doubt.'

'Come off it, Peter. Michael Lerner isn't going to make President. We're not dreamers, you know. The next President of the United States will be Tim O'Donnell. You know it, and I know it, and everyone who was at that meeting tonight knows it.'

Peter frowned and opened an academic magazine.

'Look, Peter, we're getting behind Tim's campaign. You *need* us.'

'Maybe . . .' said Peter tonelessly.

She put her supple arms around his neck. 'Come along upstairs,' she whispered.

Peter shrugged her off. 'No, I've got too much to do here. Things to get drafted.'

Liza looked down at the books. 'Still on the Middle East stuff? Enough's enough!'

'I'm putting together a report on the Palestinian Freedom League for a briefing for the Senator. I've still got a way to go on it. You carry on up . . . I'll follow later,' he said distantly.

Liza went out of the room. Peter felt angry and irritated. He'd been looking forward to a productive evening, but his concentration had been undermined and little had been accomplished. Now he was determined to sit and write notes until he had the beginnings of a report. He wanted to get it to the Senator before he left for New York tomorrow afternoon.

Within a few minutes, when he heard Liza come back into the room, he decided to ignore her, no matter what. He'd done with her games. As she stood behind him, he became aware of her gardenia-scented perfume in the air about his head.

Liza spoke softly. 'Peter . . .'

He continued to write notes. She said nothing more, but as he glanced backwards over his shoulder, he saw she was standing there naked, leaning on the chair back, smiling. When he raised his hand, it had been to push her away, but instead he used it to cup one of her gorgeous breasts. At once she pressed herself up against him, and as he kissed the smooth flesh of her belly both note-taking and report were forgotten.

They made love in the bedroom, lights on, the windows open, as the spring air caressed them and Liza reached one powerful climax after another, moaning in his arms. Once it was over, Peter felt a return of sadness and emptiness. He also felt regret at having come upstairs at all, at having let his anger towards Liza slip away, at having thrown away the chance of the report being done in time.

As they showered afterwards, he gently soaped and massaged her body, admiring its perfect curves and proportions. It was then that he saw the marks – livid scratch marks across her back. But not *his* marks. There was a sudden feeling like lead in his guts and a jealous rage so intense that he thought of choking Liza right there, under the shower spray.

As he dried himself, he found he was rigid and shaking with jealousy and despair. All those late nights, all those trips to New York, became,

143

in an instant, a terrible revelation.

Liza, still under the shower, called out, 'Oh, I forgot to mention that I'll have to break our lunch appointment for tomorrow. It's our special day, I know, but there's a group of Japanese flower growers coming in from California. Can we make it Thursday? OK with you?'

He pretended to be already asleep as she quietly slipped into bed. He did not turn and hold her as usual, and couldn't sleep a wink the whole night for brooding. The thought of her other lover, of her unfaithfulness, had been sprung on him as a torment.

26

For the whole of the next morning, Peter tried to work on the report. He made a few calls, seeking information, but drew a complete blank from everyone – including Ronnie Montgomery. He felt a complete wreck, and every time he picked up a pen the vision of those goddamned scratch marks came back. What a bitch! He had trusted her, trusted that their relationship meant as much to her as it did to him. The thought of the eager love-making last night had become sickening.

Towards lunchtime he took a cab down Maryland Avenue, towards Liza's office. He got out about six blocks short and looked at his watch: five to twelve. Liza was usually punctual. She'd be coming out at noon, and then he could catch a glimpse of these 'Japanese flower growers from California'. If necessary, he'd follow her on foot or by cab. He had to know the truth, before he went crazy from rage and anguish. He hurried along the crowded sidewalk, stopping about half a block from the entrance and waiting, feeling exposed and foolish.

There was some highly important work he should have been getting on with, and here he was, hovering in the street like a seedy private eye. Perhaps it all existed in his imagination? Maybe Liza was innocent. He realized that he felt very possessive towards her, but what man wouldn't? The marks could mean nothing. There was probably a very simple explanation.

Then there was Liza stepping briskly out from the glass doors, wearing her navy-blue suit. As her head half-turned in his direction, he saw there was a radiant smile on her face as she gave a little wave to someone. A tall, blond man stepped promptly forward from the crowded sidewalk and embraced her. As they walked away, he kept his arm around her shoulder. Peter leant against a tree. His veins were running with ice water; he could hardly breathe. The lead weights were back in his stomach.

He walked aimlessly for a while and eventually realized he was in Georgetown. He wandered along a path, through the gardens at Dumbarton Oaks, and sat down on a shaded bench. He had hardly settled before a voice called his name. 'Dr Watkins?' He looked up, hesitant and confused. Aida was looking down at him in some surprise, even with concern.

'Are you all right, Dr Watkins?'

She set down the books she was carrying on the bench beside him.

'Oh, me. I'm fine,' he said. 'How are you? It's nice to run into you.'

He felt his smile was strained as she continued to look at him closely.

'Are you sure you're all right?' she persisted. 'You're not looking at all well to me.'

Peter tried to gather his resources. He sat up straighter and ran a hand back over his hair.

'No, I'll be OK. I had a touch of influenza this week, and I think I've been working too hard. I'm tired and a bit hungry, I guess.'

Aida reached inside her bag. 'Here, eat it. I made it myself. It's only a roast beef sandwich.'

Peter shook his head, declining politely. 'No, I mustn't eat your snack.'

Aida was insistent and made him take it. 'Go ahead, eat. You need

145

it more than I do.'

As Peter took a bite he realized the extent of his hunger and wolfed the sandwich down. Then Aida took out an orange and an apple. Peter accepted the orange and began to peel it as Aida bit into the apple.

'Feel a little better now?' she asked kindly.

Eating so fast had left him slightly breathless, so he only nodded. Aida was gazing off between the handsome trees.

'Do you know this park well?' she asked.

'I used to come here a lot of the time, to read and write and, well, you know, daydream, I guess,' he said. 'These days I don't get over this way as much as I'd like.'

'Same here,' said Aida with a lightly musical laugh. 'I think this must be one of the few places in Washington where there's no one after something.'

Peter smiled. There was something about her spontaneity and freshness that gave him a lift, made him feel a bit alive again. Aida herself seemed to embody spring as she sat in a simple yellow dress, her hair tied back by a ribbon. As they talked inconsequentially, Peter found himself beginning to relax for the first time in days.

Then the ugliness of recent events came into his mind, and he remembered his concern for Aida after the Manhattan Massacre and Jesse Lusk's rabble-rousing crusade.

'It had me wondering how you were getting on,' he said. 'I almost got in touch . . .'

She frowned, and a look of pain came into her face.

He looked at her earnestly as he asked, 'Has something happened, anyone said anything . . . You could tell me.'

Aida kept her eyes down as she answered, 'This would have been a bad time for us anyway – after the killings. But as soon as this Lusk man began . . .' Her voice trailed off and she lifted her head and looked sorrowfully across the park. 'Yes, people here said things to me at the university, crude things. Then, at the lab, there's been pressure to let me go. All of that's not easy, but last week I began to get obscene phone calls. Some man said he'd kill me if I didn't have sex with him. Every night he called. I thought of going to the police, but I knew I'd get no help from them as soon as they knew I was Palestinian.'

She stopped abruptly, as if the act of remembering the fear had crushed the spirit out of her. Peter watched carefully, waiting for her to continue in her own time, and eventually she went on: 'On my way

146

home from work a few nights back – I walk from the lab to my apartment, you see – I felt as if someone was following me. It was only a feeling at first. I couldn't see anyone. The next day walking home I caught a glimpse of a man from several blocks away. I began to be afraid to go out, but was determined I would not live in fear. The day after that, I saw him behind me again. If I hurried, he hurried. If I slowed down, he did the same. Going out to work that night, I took a taxi to the lab and back again afterwards. But as I went up the steps, from round the side of the building a voice called out hoarsely, "Aida!" It was the voice of the obscene caller. Oh, dear God, I was so terrified! After that, I haven't been out again . . . until today, when I couldn't stand being shut in any longer. So . . . so . . . you see me here in the park . . .'

Her emotions cracked as her voice broke and she buried her face in the handkerchief which Peter promptly handed her. He felt overwhelmed by his pity for her, and by his own sense of helplessness. He kept an arm firmly round her as she clutched the handkerchief to her eyes. For a while they sat motionless in mutual sympathy, as a pair of robins argued energetically in the tree overhead.

The sun was getting low amid the trees by now. Aida suddenly took Peter's hand firmly in hers and held it as she looked him full in the face. Her smile was radiant again. It was as if the night terrors had departed for the moment. She jumped up, snatched up her bag and darted off along the path.

'Aida! Aida!' Peter called after her, 'I'd like you to feel you could always . . .'

But she was gone, as if, in the end, his voice had never reached her.

27

The powerful rhythms of the primary campaign had begun to reassert themselves. In only three days, the Democrats of New York would make their choice between Senator O'Donnell and their own Senator, Michael Lerner. It was expected to be another very close race. Lerner was popular on his home ground, and the Jews there were counting on big wins for Lerner in both the New York and California primaries. With that style of success, Michael Lerner could reach the convention as a most attractive running-mate. Thus, while a number of Jews were working for O'Donnell in New York, the Jewish community was for the most part solidly behind Lerner – which meant heavy campaign contributions coming in his direction.

As for the killings in Manhattan, no trace of the three gunmen had been found, even though police artists' sketches of their faces had been widely circulated. Jesse Lusk's inflammatory attacks on the Arabs had begun to fizzle out as public opinion reacted against his tendency to provoke violence. The idea of deporting all Palestinian students was still being debated, but attacks on Palestinians and Arabs in general were becoming steadily fewer.

The main surprise was that Willie Lamb's popularity had started an upward climb. He naturally avoided any reference to 'Zionist influences' now, and had even ceased attacking the President. As he continued to make appearances around the country, he had chalked up a good primary victory in Missouri, running against a former US Senator from that state. He was proving to be as highly popular in the West as in the South. In only a few weeks' time, he'd be taking on Tim again in California – in the last and biggest of the primaries.

As O'Donnell and his staff surveyed the national scene, they saw plenty of obstacles – more than they could have anticipated a few weeks before. President Randall and Willie Lamb were both doing better, while O'Donnell faced a major battle for New York against Lerner. A win seemed unlikely, with the Jews going solidly for Lerner. Losing to Lerner in New York would be no help to Tim's campaign in California, where he'd be running against Lamb *and* Lerner. Lamb's many primary victories in the South and West were starting to look threatening. If Lamb could do well in California, then there was every chance he could go on to a nomination in the first ballot at the Democratic convention.

For his breakneck campaign in New York, Tim O'Donnell was appearing day and night at rallies and factories, at gatherings of university students and ethnic associations. He was trying to catch up on the twenty years of goodwill that Michael Lerner had built up in New York. It wasn't an easy challenge. Barney Shaw had laid down one golden rule for the New York campaign: speak only good of Lerner. It had been good advice, too. The joke went about that O'Donnell had become Lerner's strongest supporter.

Peter arrived at the new headquarters at about noon. At the Senator's request, he was spending most of the last week of the primary in New York, and they had been devoting an increasing amount of time to discussion on foreign policy, especially on the Middle East. As he entered the Senator's office, he had the impression that Tim was positively overflowing with good spirits, despite the strain. He was due at a major rally at NYU in ninety minutes. Even as he motioned Peter to a chair, the intercom buzzed.

'Senator, Mr Shaw wants you in his office for that meeting now.'

Tim switched off the intercom. 'Come on, Peter, let's enjoy a real ballbuster next. Rifkin's called by to go through his friendly vampire routine.'

In Barney's office, Marty Rifkin was all smiles. 'Nice to meet with you again, Senator . . . and with you, Dr Watkins.'

He wasn't a man to forget a name, even after a brief meeting. As they sat down, Barney ordered in some coffee.

It was Tim who spoke first. 'I'm truly glad you stopped by, Marty. It's great to see you. Unfortunately, though, I have to be at the big rally in NYU less than an hour from now.'

Marty smiled ingratiatingly. 'Listen, if this is a bad time to talk, I can call round later or –'

'Not at all, Marty. Let's hear what's on your mind,' suggested Tim cordially.

'All right, then. Well, let me say straight off that you guys have been running some campaign. A-1 all the way! Arkansas and Texas – both fantastic! I'm sure you'd have had Lamb beat even without that drugs mess . . .'

Marty seemed to be pausing for effect, so Barney gulped down the last of his coffee and said, 'What else did you expect from us? We're geniuses, Marty. You know that. And what's more, we'll beat Michael's ass in New York on Tuesday and again in California in two weeks' time. After that, it'll be our ball game at the convention.'

Marty reacted boyishly to Barney's brash bluntness. 'Well, Barney, my friend, I wish you all the luck in the world, because I happen to consider you have a very fine candidate on your hands – the best.' He sipped his coffee. 'That's precisely why I'm here: I think Senator O'Donnell should be the next President.'

'It's nice to hear that, Marty,' said Tim ironically, 'because I value your opinion. I'm sure Barney could find a comfy niche for you on the campaign staff.'

Marty laughed, took out a Winston and lit it up. 'A handsome offer, but not this time . . . In fact, I came here to make you an offer, one which I think looks pretty attractive . . .'

As Peter observed Marty, he felt repelled by the insinuating manner, by the smooth intermingling of obsequiousness with coercion. He had to admit it was quite a performance, but he could hardly bear to sit and watch its progress.

Barney was rubbing his big nose impatiently. 'I only hope it's something we haven't heard before.'

Marty blew out a stream of smoke, then stubbed out his cigarette nervously. 'Let me put it to you straight. You're in trouble here in New York. Sure, you're running strong, and you just conceivably might beat Lerner by a hair. I kind of doubt it. A loss here isn't going to look good in California. And once you get out there, you're going to be fighting off Willie Lamb, who's going to lay more money into that

150

primary than anyone ever spent anywhere before in history. You're going to be battling Michael for your own Californian constituency – the Jews and liberals, the academics and professionals and so on and so forth. And you know what that means? It means that you and Lerner will split the liberal vote and rip the party down the middle. So who will it help? Willie Lamb, of course. He'll be nominated on the first ballot at the convention.'

They stared in silence at Marty as he lit another cigarette. What he said was perfectly true and in line with their own analysis. O'Donnell was finding himself caught in an incredible bind with Lamb still presenting a formidable problem, especially if they needed to fight off Lerner in California.

'Then what do you see as the solution, Marty?' said the Senator neutrally.

Marty flicked ashes into his empty coffee cup. 'If you will give me confirmation, here and now, that you'll take Michael Lerner as running-mate – I am prepared to ensure you get the nomination on the first ballot.'

Marty looked straight at Tim, never batting an eyelid.

Barney shrugged, uncharacteristically fumbling for his words. 'Are we to assume that you are personally representing Michael Lerner . . . that *he* sent you?'

Marty smiled modestly. 'Let's put it this way. I merely represent interests that can play a decisive role in any action taken by Michael Lerner.'

Tim O'Donnell looked jumpily at his watch. 'So just what can you deliver, Marty? We've been over this ground before.'

'I can make sure the vote here in New York is *very* close. And I can make sure a lot of Jewish money and support comes your way in California. The Lerner campaign out there could be just a formality, for the sake of appearances. Maybe he'd even withdraw . . . Either way, I can assure you of a massive win against Lamb and of mighty support at the convention.'

'And if I say no?' asked Tim, his voice unusually flat.

Marty paused, picked a piece of lint off his suit. 'You'll probably lose in New York, and in California – and at the convention. If Lamb wins the nomination, that's bad for you and bad for the Jews. But let's assume you somehow pull through in New York, and in California – maybe this is even your line of thinking right now. If you go to that convention and win that nomination, and then take Willie Lamb as

151

your running-mate, you'll have every Jew and every Jewish organization in the country against you. And don't imagine they'll let the American people forget the Manhattan Massacre, or Willie Lamb's loose talk. You'll be torn to shreds by November.'

Tim looked away from Marty's cold eyes and across at Barney as he asked, 'What do you think?'

Barney sighed, slouching in his chair like a bedraggled bear. 'I don't like what he says one bit. But he's right. Lamb could chew us to pieces if we're not careful. Besides, Michael Lerner *would* make a good running-mate. You've said so yourself. And if giving him the OK now would line up the Jews – especially in California – I'd have to give the notion mighty close consideration.'

Now Tim looked at Peter, who had been watching the charade with a grim look. 'So how does it all strike you, Peter?' he asked.

Peter gripped the arms of the chair angrily, feeling unprepared to say anything. 'I think you're going to win in New York on Tuesday. I think you'll beat Lamb and Lerner in California. I think you'll go into that convention as unquestionably the strongest candidate, the best proven vote-getter in every region of the country. And I think you'll be nominated on the first ballot, no matter what Willie Lamb thinks, or Michael Lerner or Marty Rifkin . . .' Peter glared at Rifkin before looking back at Tim as he pleaded, 'My view is you'd be crazy to màke any kind of guarantees, especially when these goddamned threats are being held at your head. In Wisconsin, they had a Lamb–Lerner ticket all worked out. Now all they want is a body to attach Lerner to as the next Vice-President. I would trust, if you have any confidence at all in your candidacy and what it represents, that you'll show the right contempt for this kind of bargaining.'

Tim rose and walked over to the window to look down on the busy streets of New York. There was no sound in the room, and Marty Rifkin sat rigid and white-faced. As Tim turned about to face them, he looked Marty in the eye and said coolly, 'Thanks for looking in, Marty.'

Marty jumped to his feet, nodded his head deliberately two or three times and, without a word, stalked out, letting the door bang behind him as he went.

Barney sighed, then frowned as he stared at the Senator. 'Could be you'll regret this for the rest of your life.'

Tim had got his jacket on and straightened his tie by now. As he looked back at Barney he said, 'One thing I do know that I'd have regretted for the rest of my life would have been if I'd said we had a deal . . .' He gave Peter a smile. 'Well, over to NYU now to convince a few thousand more people I'm just as wonderful as Michael Lerner.'

He left them with a cheerful wave, and Barney sat silently for some moments before he spoke. 'Peter,' he said, 'you and I haven't seen eye to eye on a lot of things during this campaign. But I've learned to listen to you . . . I've learned from you. All I want to say is that I truly admire you.'

Peter felt he was almost mesmerized by the other man's big bloodshot eyes as Barney continued, 'But I'm not sure you really grasped what just happened in here. It's going to mean trouble like you haven't dreamed of in your life before. Just never tell me I didn't say so.'

28

To Barney, it was a hollow satisfaction to have the Senator sitting on the other side of his desk, looking shattered and bewildered with all the stuffing gone out of him.

Barney poured him a drink. 'You got yourself into it.'

'I did? How?' demanded Tim angrily.

'You thought Marty Rifkin was just fishing around in here yesterday? Just feeling you out, or something? Brother, were you mistaken. When he walked out and slammed that door yesterday, your balls were caught in it, believe me . . .'

'Marty . . .?' The Senator was afraid that he might add to his humiliation by being physically sick.

He had campaigned hard all day, making one appearance after another, until, late in the afternoon, someone handed him a copy of the same tabloid which had printed the article about Tim and the starlet. Now it was on the streets with a second lurid scoop. Its front cover once again featured the same bleached blonde, wearing a skimpy halter top and cuddling a cute, two-year-old girl in her arms. The headline ran in huge red letters: 'Why Won't Tim Visit His Baby Daughter?', the byline under the picture reading: ' "He refuses to see us," Bambi Winkler charges.' Then followed a long, two-page story complete with black and white photos – one showing Tim O'Donnell and Bambi in front of the Twenty-One Club in New York City, which they'd already used once, and a 'new' picture of Bambi and her little girl standing outside a Malibu beachhouse, where the Senator had supposedly been a 'frequent visitor'.

When Tim was handed the copy of the tabloid, he had just delivered a real beauty of a speech on a sidewalk on Wall Street to a crowd of office workers on coffee break. An aide passed it to him as he got back into his limousine. The moment he looked at it, he felt his head go giddy. He'd probably expended no more than three hours on this Winkler dame, had dinner with her and that was it. He hadn't even *liked* her – she was unusually stupid and an unbelievable chatterbox. And now here she was in the limelight of this scathing and viciously motivated piece of rubbish. There were thousands of fervent readers of tabloids in New York, and the circulation figures were huge! The public reaction to it could be unimaginable with only two clear days to go before the election day itself.

That evening, Tim spoke at the University of Syracuse. Students constituted his favourite audience, and in New York they represented an important group of voters. He made a brief speech, and then, as was his practice, threw the floor open to questions. At the back of the hall, an overweight girl stood up, holding the tabloid in her hand. 'Senator, I'm not a regular reader of this kind of publication, but there's a lot of talk concerning this current article. I was just wondering what your response might be?'

A tense silence came over the packed auditorium. Tim had felt his stomach churning as he saw her produce the tabloid. Just the same, he

154

smiled, aware that his audience was as uncomfortable about it as he felt himself.

'Well,' he offered, 'let me first say that I'm glad to hear you are no regular reader of this kind of publication . . .' A low laugh ran through the crowd. 'As for Miss Winkler, I *am* acquainted with her. She and I had dinner together on one occasion at the Twenty-One Club in New York. If that baby girl is related to me in any way, she can only have been conceived during the course of the meal.' The crowd burst into uproarious laughter as Tim amiably grinned and added, 'Perhaps the waiters should be interviewed . . .'

There was another burst of steady applause. He had won the students over wholesale and the exchange got a wide showing on the evening news right across New York State, even being picked up on the national news.

The next day, the day before the election, it became clear that the sniping tactics had grown even more ruthless. A story appeared on the front page of the *New York Daily Reporter* with the headline: 'O'Donnell Ten-Year-Old Under Treatment – Family Problems Cited As Cause'. The article, written by Aaron Mandel, reported that Senator Timothy O'Donnell's son Jeffrey, who was in fact eleven, had been receiving psychiatric treatment for more than a year. The article stated that Jeffrey, who lived with his mother in Charlottesville, Virginia, had been making weekly visits to a psychiatrist, Dr William Alexander, in that city. An unnamed source, close to the family, was quoted as saying that Jeffrey had been deeply disturbed by his parents' divorce, to the extent where, for the past year, his school work and sports activities deteriorated dramatically. At the heart of the problem, it was implied, lay Jeffrey's feeling that he was being neglected and ignored by his busy father, Senator O'Donnell.

As Tim O'Donnell set the paper down on his desk, his eyes were stinging with tears of anger. He felt an impotent outrage at this gross invasion of his privacy, but, more importantly, of that of his son. There was a framework of truth behind the story. Jeffrey *had* been in therapy, following an incident two summers ago when, in a boating accident at camp, he saw his best friend drown. As a consequence, he had suffered recurring anxieties, nightmares and problems at school. What sort of set-back in the boy's treatment might result if someone showed him the article? Already he was striving to come to terms with the gnawing guilt he felt about failing to save his friend's life. Now he could find himself being used to harm his father's race for the Presidency. The more Tim

O'Donnell brooded on the front-page item, the more his anger boiled. On a sudden impulse, he stood up, swept out of the office and hailed a cab.

At the *New York Daily Reporter* he asked a receptionist where he could find Aaron Mandel's office. She stared in surprise when she recognized him, but said nervously that Mandel worked on the fourth floor. Tim waited a few seconds for the elevator before springing impatiently up the staircase. In the city room, amid a clutter of reporters' desks, he asked which man was Aaron Mandel. At the sound of his voice, heads turned and someone pointed hesitantly towards the back. At one of the desks sat a short young man with glasses, who stood up, an embarrassed smile on his face. He was clearly bemused to find the Senator coming towards him and pulling a creased-up copy of that morning's paper out of his coat pocket.

'Did you write this?' Tim O'Donnell demanded, throwing the paper down on the desk top.

Mandel raised a hand and stroked his sideburn. 'Why, yes . . . yes.'

Tim was red in the face and trembling. 'You could have called me to check it. I'm always accessible to the press. You people know that.'

Mandel shrugged and smiled nervously round at his colleagues, who had gathered in an interested group. 'Look, I –'

'Because this consists of fabrications, distortions, lies and half-truths with which I am not concerned, except for the harm they'll do my son. Yes, my son *is* undergoing therapy, but not for any of your reasons. Besides, that's a matter for his privacy, or has the muck-raking of the press reached a point where it no longer regards the relationship between a doctor and patient as private? What makes you think you have the right to exploit an eleven-year-old boy in a squalid political move? How would you like it if it was your son?'

Mandel had taken off his glasses and was blinking at O'Donnell smugly. 'Now then, Senator, all's fair in love, war and newsgathering –'

Before he could finish, a blow in the face had felled him to the ground, three flashbulbs popping simultaneously. This was, after all, the city room of a leading newspaper. The Senator rubbed his knuckles as he looked down at Mandel, who crouched resignedly, his lip bleeding. As he turned to leave, Tim found himself looking into the faces of at least twenty reporters. He straightened his tie and walked out calmly.

The story was an instant nationwide sensation, the photograph of Tim slugging a reporter appearing in all the evening editions. O'Donnell

156

looked chastened himself as he sat later on with Barney and Peter in Barney's office. Barney gripped a glass of neat whisky in his fist as he paced the floor and exploded with exasperation. 'What are you gonna do tomorrow,' he asked, 'beat up some nuns? Jesus Christ, I've never seen the likes! Where the hell do we take it from here? Tomorrow's election eve . . . Will you hide, or campaign, or explain, or what?'

'I'll campaign my ass off. You know that, Barney. And I'll not breathe a word about any of this.'

Barney poured himself a few more shots of whisky. 'Maybe another time you won't get on your high horse and send Marty Rifkin packing quite so fast . . .'

A sudden knock on the door startled them, but before anyone could make a move to open it, Michael Lerner came in, walked straight across to Tim and shook hands.

'Tim, my friend,' he said, 'I don't know how to say how sorry I am about that story appearing. I know, as well as anyone, how those people can hurt those you love. I wanted you to know that I've put out a statement deploring the piece, and I haven't minced any words.'

'Michael Lerner,' said Tim O'Donnell, 'I think I sense a lightening of the atmosphere in this room at this moment. What can I say in return? . . . What can I do?'

'Say and do nothing,' said Lerner.

'There goes another theory out of the window,' said Barney. 'The moment you think that gentlemen are extinct in the world, one walks in at the door.'

29

To his surprise, everywhere he went next day, Tim O'Donnell found himself being cheered and applauded. As soon as the full story of his encounter with the reporter became known, he was caught up in an accelerating wave of sympathy and support. The people of New York took delight in Tim's haymaker. It had seemed well aimed and well deserved, especially in the light of articles correcting the Mandel story which included denials by the psychiatrist and Allison O'Donnell.

The voting on election day was heavy. Predictions during the day had it running neck and neck till near midnight, at which point O'Donnell began to pull slightly ahead. When all the results were finally in, he had won, in Lerner's home state, by 3 per cent.

In the hour when dawn was breaking, Peter Watkins got home to Washington, straight off the plane and tired beyond imagining. He would, he thought, never be able to adjust to the crazy hours of a campaign schedule. It had been an important victory, but the ugliness of parts of the campaign, the tabloid story and the piece on Jeffrey O'Donnell had been disillusioning and gave the victory itself a sour flavour.

As usual, Peter had got back to an empty house. He had seen very little of Liza during the past couple of weeks. She and her group had been very active in New York in the Lerner campaign, and he had made no attempt to confront her with having witnessed her meeting with another man outside her office building. She did not seem to have noticed how cool he was that evening, how tired and worried he looked. It had been an excellent working lunch, she told him. The Japanese flower growers had been courteous and charming. At least, Peter had to admit, she lied with the same stylish elegance she brought to every other facet of her life.

The days after that had sped by as he put all his time and energy into the primary campaign. Perhaps he had been trying to lose himself in the skirmish, to avoid having to face his feelings. It had perturbed him to discover the power which Liza held over him, the extent to which she could hurt him.

It was next day before Liza finally turned up. He was busy writing in the library as she walked in.

'Hello,' she said, her voice husky with fatigue as she put down her travelling bag.

'Hi,' said Peter with little emotion.

'Congratulations.'

'Thanks. Lerner ran a good campaign. I saw him briefly up there. He's a good man. Tim thinks so too.'

'Then why the hell doesn't your damned Senator take him as running-mate? It'd make life a lot simpler all round.'

'Liza, that's a line we've heard over and over. Tim will make his decision when he's ready. There's nothing more to be said.'

'Well, the going's going to get rougher for him. That I can promise.'

Peter stared in amazement, then went back to his writing, hoping she'd take herself off upstairs. Instead, she stayed hovering about in the room so that Peter could scarcely bring his mind to bear on his work. He stood up and gathered his papers together before walking out of the room without so much as looking at her. When he reached the front door, he found she had followed him.

'And where are you off to now, Peter dear?' she asked sardonically.

'To get some air,' he said. 'I need some clean, fresh air.'

As soon as the door was shut behind him, he felt freer than he had in many weeks. All through the mêlée of the New York primary, the thought of Aida had kept coming back to his mind. He had tried reaching her on the phone several times, and once more this morning. There had been no reply, but that could be because she had stopped answering her phone after the series of threatening calls. He decided to

159

go to where she lived. Only seeing her would relieve his anxieties about her, and in any case, he wanted to show her the draft of the paper on Palestine that he was preparing for Tim O'Donnell.

When he reached her building, he tried her buzzer several times, but there was no response. It was a bit late in the day for class times, and he knew she did not start work till much later. He could not suppress a sick feeling of apprehension. Suppose something had happened to her? As he stood there, a middle-aged woman with a friendly face and holding a pass key came up the steps, looking at him inquiringly.

'Can you help me?' he said. 'I'm trying to contact Miss Azoury. We're old friends. She's not been answering her phone and I'm afraid she might be ill.'

The woman replied that she was acquainted with Miss Azoury, but hadn't seen her about lately. Noticing the look of concern on Peter's face, she let him in with her key.

Peter knocked gently on Aida's door, but could hear no sound. There was a light showing under the door. He knocked more loudly, and again, but still could hear nothing. As a last resort, he began to call Aida's name. The third time he called there was a faint rustling and Aida's voice asking, 'Yes? Who is it?' but sounding very faint and far away.

'It's Peter Watkins. Can I come in?'

The chain came off and the catch turned. Slowly Aida opened the door. She looked out at him with large, dark and solemn eyes before ushering him into the apartment, which was quite dark since all the curtains were fully drawn. Aida was wearing a blue house robe that came down to her ankles, and looked frightened and exhausted. Her course books and papers lay scattered over a desk and couch. Shyly she asked Peter to sit down, then curled up on the sofa in a nest of papers. The room was hot and stuffy and seemed to be saturated with Aida's fear and depression. It occurred to Peter that she had probably been shut in like this for days.

'You must excuse all the mess,' she said, indicating the scattered notes and books. 'I'm trying to catch up on some homework. I've missed many classes.' There was a look of fatalism in her eyes, disturbing to Peter since it contrasted so sharply with the spontaneous high spirits of which he knew she was capable.

'You mean you've not been back to college, not since I last saw you?'

She looked down at her hands. When she spoke her voice was barely audible. 'I've been feeling unwell.'

160

Peter saw it clearly. 'It's because of your fear – your fear of the man who was pestering you. You've been too scared even to go out, isn't that it?'

He went to stand over her, put a finger under her chin and gently raised her head until their eyes were meeting. At that point, she began to tremble, then broke into tears. He knelt down and put his arms round her, rocking her back and forth, reassuring her, sensing her tension beginning to relax a little. She clung to him for a minute or two before she stopped crying. He brushed back her hair and suggested: 'Let me read you something. It could make you feel better.'

Aida nodded, her face still puffy from weeping.

'Right,' he said, 'but first let's get some light in here – and a breath of air.'

He swept back the curtains and opened a couple of windows while Aida stayed curled up on the sofa, blinking her eyes at the unaccustomed daylight.

He sat beside her and, slowly and clearly, began to read over his manuscript pages on Palestine. When he got to the end and looked up, he saw her looking at him intently, the colour slowly coming back into her face. But she said nothing, only smiled. After a few minutes, she suggested they go to the kitchen, where she began to heat up some home-made lentil soup.

'I think your piece calls for a celebration,' she said, as she took down a bottle of wine from a shelf. 'I've been saving this for a while. Now seems to be the right occasion.'

Peter decorked the bottle and poured them a glass each. He could tell that she hadn't sat down to a decent meal in days, and insistently helped her to a second bowl of soup when she'd finished the first. After that, they went back into the sitting room to continue drinking the wine and watch the sun begin to set behind the neighbourhood roofs.

There was a long but very relaxed silence between them until a point came where, still unspeaking, they both stood up simultaneously. He realized, as he looked at her, that she had a rare and delicate beauty that moved him deeply, and which he wanted to gather up and protect. As he took her in his arms, they kissed.

'Peter . . . I . . .' she began, but he blocked her words with another kiss, and felt her begin to return his kissing with a matching passion. He ran his hands down her sides as she embraced him tightly in return. He kissed her cheeks, her eyes and ears, felt her warm silky hair against his cheek. Aida sighed as he touched her, quivered to the movements of his hands.

'I want us to make love, Aida,' he whispered in her ear.

She sighed and drew him closer, pressed her body against his. Then, all at once, she broke away again as she said, 'I'm not sure . . . I don't even know . . . I mean, I've never made love before.'

Peter felt almost shocked, and drew back a moment, but then, as he looked into her shining eyes, he felt a powerful emotion rising inside him: a deep yearning that seemed a new sensation and not something he had ever felt before – not for Liza, and not for any woman. He despaired of giving the words the fresh meaning they warranted, but they escaped from him nevertheless: 'Aida, I love you!'

It must have been the expression of surprise on his face that drew from her a sudden light laugh like a tiny burst of music. Then her own face became serious again as she took a deep breath and stepped back a little way, never taking her eyes away from his. As she unzipped her blue robe she let it slip from her shoulders, then reached to take Peter's hand and place it on her naked breasts.

'I will be yours,' she simply said.

30

The next couple of weeks were, Peter felt, among the most satisfying of his life. The last and biggest of the primaries in Tim's home state of California was rapidly approaching. A big win there, after all his other victories, should just about clinch the Democratic nomination. And then, along with the work and excitement, there went Aida. The suddenness of their relationship still left him amazed. He had initially been so fascinated by her life as a Palestinian exile that he had hardly been aware of the growing love that must have been there. The day in the park, when he had put a comforting arm round her, had been a very confusing day altogether. The night before he had not been able to sleep for jealousy, and then he had seen Liza throw herself into the arms of another man.

A new routine was asserting itself in his life. After writing for a few hours each morning, he would snatch a quick lunch and dash off to meet Aida in Dupont Circle on her way back home from college in the afternoon. Then they would walk back to her place hand in hand. The radiance of her beauty and personality seemed to shine through more each day as her fears and tension relaxed. The afternoons were long ones, filled with fresh pleasure and the brightness of summer.

Peter was meanwhile seeing less and less of Liza. They appeared to be almost completely estranged. She would leave the house early, work all day, then go on for meetings with her campaign group. He found it very strange that she had never even commented on the change that had obviously come over both him and their life together. Perhaps, if she did notice, she didn't care at all.

One day, an early-morning call came through from Tim O'Donnell. He had, he said, just flown in to Washington from Los Angeles the night before. He'd appreciate Peter joining him as soon as he could manage it. They met in the campaign office on New York Avenue, and the place was in chaos. Tim had been going pretty well flat out for six months now, and there was certainly no time to stop and do some tidying up.

'I have a half-hour scheduled for this talk,' said Tim, greeting him with a brisk warmth.

'Here's that report on the Soviet economy you asked for,' said Peter, handing him some papers.

The Senator glanced at them before locking them in his briefcase. 'Peter, your efficiency is almost frightening! I don't know where I'd be without you. But that can wait. The reason I asked you to come by today is that I've made an important decision. I wanted you to be the first to hear it, and I want your reaction. Tuesday's primary vote will determine who's to be the Democratic nominee at the convention – in other words, Willie Lamb or myself.'

'How are the polls looking in California?'

'I'm out ahead, but not by much. I'm only about ten points ahead. I'm at 40 per cent with Lamb at 30 per cent. Lerner's running at 20 per cent with 10 per cent undecided. So as you see, Lerner has really cut into my lead. If he weren't in on this one, I'd have the nomination in the bag.'

'You really think Lamb could beat you? You're *from* California.'

'Yeah, and Willie Lamb's from Texas. That didn't help him there in the end. You never know what'll happen. With all the publicity of Keenan Lamb's trial, Willie could win by a landslide, just by picking up the vote of every drug addict in California. There must be ten million of them.'

Peter laughed, then quickly grew serious again. 'And if Lamb wins, you think he has the nomination for a certainty?'

Tim sighed. 'Can't say. Barney still reckons we'd have a fighting chance, with Lamb being a bit too much of a redneck by the Democratic standards. You could say that by putting all the primaries he's won in the South and West together with a win in California, he'd be up in the driver's seat.'

'So, are you saying you'll take Lerner as running-mate? That's the obvious answer, isn't it? Send Marty Rifkin the high sign and California's yours for the asking. I mean, if it comes down to you losing the nomination if you don't go for Lerner now, what choice does that amount to?'

'That's it exactly, the same damn dilemma we've been kicking about for months.' Tim paused, sighed, stood up and looked out the window. 'Anyway, I've made my mind up . . .'

'Have you called Lerner yet?'

Tim turned and smiled. 'I'm surprised at you, Peter. Don't you think I've learned a little something by now from your approach?'

Peter caught his breath. 'You mean you'll take Lamb?'

'It may cost me my ass, but, the way I see it, there's no way I'll win a national election against an incumbent President without Willie Lamb on the ticket. I don't exactly adore the guy, but he's a better sort than most people think. Look at Kennedy. He had to take Johnson – and it worked. He squeaked past Nixon by a hair.'

'It means a real ding-dong in California – I mean, from the Lerner supporters.'

'For sure. And they'll get wind of my decision soon. I've got to meet with Lamb and some of his people to make it clear that, if I win on Tuesday, I shall be strongly considering Lamb as running-mate. He's got to know, so that he doesn't make too harsh a personal attack on me during the next few days. Of course, he'll act like he's going to win in California, but he knows as well as anyone that the odds are running my way.'

Peter's smile was ironic. 'Strange how it's all turning out. We all admire Michael Lerner very much, think he'd make a great running-mate. Then Rifkin's obnoxious tactics make Lamb seem the only solution.'

Tim looked at Peter. 'Well, don't imagine we've heard the last of Rifkin and the other cohorts. They'll be trying to get the knife in right up to the convention.'

'You're making the right decision,' Peter said. 'I know you'll win on Tuesday. I can feel it.'

Tim shook his hand. 'Listen, I want you to start on a foreign-policy briefing for Lamb and have it ready in case we win in California. I want him fully informed of our policy directions. I don't think he realizes

165

there's a big wide world outside of Texas!'

With Tim O'Donnell back into his hectic round of campaigning before some of the largest and most enthusiastic crowds of his career, Peter was taking the chance to pick up again on his research into the Manhattan killings. He had still turned up next to nothing on the PFL – the Palestinian Freedom League. Nothing but a few old clippings and some declassified documents. He felt the time had come to give Ronnie Montgomery a ring. They had not spoken together for some time, and after a chat catching up on the Washington and election gossip, Peter came to the point: 'Look, Ronnie. I've been doing a lot of work on this Middle East thing. The Senator and I have been trying to uncover a bit more about the PFL – you know, the Manhattan killers?'

Ronnie groaned. 'One thing I can tell you: we've a million miles of filing cabinets buried out there in Virginia, but everything the agency knows about the PFL would go on the backs of a few postage stamps.'

'Nothing at all you could call a lead?'

'Well, it's plain to see the three killers were complete professionals and we're sure they were transported out of the country immediately. The PFL's reputed to be an extremist leftist splinter group, but no one knows how many members it's got or who its leaders are. It seems they've refused all association with other Palestinian nationalist groups. Our people in the Middle East are working on it day and night. We ought to have some information fairly soon.'

'Hey,' Peter changed the subject. 'What do you think? I just got to know a Palestinian girl.'

'Palestinian?' Ronnie chuckled. 'Watch it. She may be loaded.'

'I don't think so, not this one. She's a real honey.'

'Sounds a piece of all right,' said Ronnie lecherously. 'Hey, what happened to that Liza you were going around with last winter?'

'Going around with? Are you kidding? Liza moved in months ago.'

Ronnie paused before asking, 'So how are things there?'

Peter sighed. 'Well, you know, you always hope these things will work out, but I reckon that as soon as the campaign finishes we'll be splitting up.'

'That's tough.'

'Well, don't be too sorry. I'm in love, after all.'

'How can we keep up with you? Don't tell me – that Palestinian honey . . .'

'Well, as a matter of fact, yes. Her name's Aida. I first saw her at a Senate hearing, of all places.'

Ronnie whistled. 'From a Jew to a Palestinian . . . you're really becoming expert in shuttle diplomacy.'

'I don't remember ever mentioning that Liza was Jewish,' said Peter.

'Liza Samuels? Why, I . . .' Ronnie trailed off, awkwardly for him.

'Do you mean to say you know her, Ronnie? You never said a word.'

Ronnie's voice suddenly dropped its pitch. 'Oh, heck, Peter, I must be losing my discreet touch. I never wanted to move on to this.'

'You know something, Ronnie? Something I don't?'

Ronnie paused, even longer this time. 'I don't know what she's told you about herself. I can tell you that Liza Samuels is heavily involved with a group of Israeli radicals who've been floating around Washington for years. They are *very* political. Legitimate, mind you, but very strong-arm. They run quite an impressive operation. Liza's their American representative. We get a regular lot of complaints about them from people in Congress, people who feel they're being pressured by them. But then, it has to be said, they stay on the right side of the law. The Israelis are on legitimate visas and use Liza as their go-between. She's the one who really runs things, though. That's my impression.'

Peter was trying hard to cover up his dismay as he said, 'I knew Liza was very involved politically. She's held meetings of her friends here. Do these people have some kind of headquarters office?'

'You must be joking. They operate from one of the handsomest offices in Washington. It's at 3200 N Street.'

'Well, I'm sure Liza does a great job for them. Look, Ronnie, thanks for your help on the PFL. I'll come back to you if more emerges.'

'Sure thing. Let's crack a bottle together after the campaign. Be seeing you.'

Peter hung up in a daze. In an odd sort of way, what Ronnie had said about Liza had not been a surprise. It all fitted in somehow. He had to laugh at himself as he remembered how unpolitical he thought Liza was when they first met. A few weeks back, this conversation with Ronnie could have wrecked his life. Now it barely mattered. About two hours from now he had a date with Aida.

167

31

When election day arrived at last in California, it was the culmination to intense campaigning beyond anything the state had ever witnessed. Tim, Lamb and Lerner had appeared in every corner of the state. The television channels had been saturated with campaign ads for all three candidates. As the early returns began to come in, Tim seemed in the lead, but the networks were reserving their predictions. A good showing by Lamb could still inflict damage. Peter was nervously glued to his set, constantly referring back to his notes on California and its various election precincts.

He had seen nothing of Liza for two whole days. She had been getting in late each night and leaving at the crack of dawn, and he only knew she had been there because the bed in the other room had been slept in. Peter could not get Ronnie's revelations about her out of his mind. He was desperately anxious to find out more, but the thought of prying was repellent. Suppose that she did work for some powerful Israeli lobby, but didn't want him to know about it. That was *her* business. Even so, he felt wounded and deeply disturbed. They had lived together half a year, after all, and he had trusted her, and been open with her about his life as well as about a lot of the sensitive work he did. Maybe Ronnie had her confused with someone else. Maybe he exaggerated. Certainly she was politically active, but she and her friends did not seem to represent more than a small pressure group, and he had never met any actual Israelis among them. If he was so curious, he kept telling himself, why not come right out and ask her? Why should he be afraid?

As the election evening wore on, a trend emerged from the returns. Senator Michael Lerner was not doing as well as expected, not even in the heavily Jewish-populated areas of Los Angeles. Exit polls indicated that many Jewish voters liked Lerner, but felt he didn't really stand a chance. They had gone for O'Donnell because they thought he could win – and because they were nervous of Lamb. A high proportion of the Lerner vote from the opinion polls had begun to swing towards O'Donnell. By 8.30, the networks were all projecting an O'Donnell win by a substantial margin. A great sense of elation began to fill Peter. This was it. They'd done it. The long struggle was over. Now, with that in the bag, he decided, he'd slip out and settle another matter.

When he got out of the cab outside 3200 N Street, he found himself looking up at a large office building. It looked recently built: an eye-catching design by some smart young architect. Even if Liza wasn't here, he thought, it would get back to her that he'd dropped by. The glass doors were locked, but a security guard got up off a seat inside, and opened one door slightly to ask him his business. Peter said he'd an appointment with Liza Samuels. The guard motioned overhead. 'Miss Samuels's office is on the third floor. On your right.'

As Peter walked to the elevator, the building seemed to be bustling with action. People rushed past, carrying papers, folders, sheafs of computer printout. On the third floor, the atmosphere was even more hectic. Dozens of phones were ringing and typewriters clicking, while multiple televisions blared out the campaign coverage. A vast and brilliantly lit room opened out before him. He assumed it must be the nerve centre of this massive election-monitoring operation. At least thirty or forty people were working in it, and the desk tops were covered with printout charts and precinct diagrams as a set of eight telex machines clattered unceasingly.

Amid the activity sat Liza. She was talking on two phones at once, scribbling notes, giving instructions, calling out people's names. Peter felt astonished by the degree of her control. She seemed to be transformed into a machine as she coolly and efficiently command-ed this overwhelming operation. The American Flower Growers

169

Association had suddenly dwindled into an absurd charade.

As Peter walked across to Liza's work area, her alert eyes spotted him coming between the cluster of assistants who were leaning over her. 'Peter! What brings you here, tonight of all nights?'

Peter smiled sourly. 'I was on the verge of asking you a similar question.'

Liza looked at him indifferently. 'Surprised at this?'

'Let's just say disappointed.' He stared angrily.

More and more papers were being heaped before Liza. Every detail of the latest in the California returns seemed to be there the moment it was known. They had clearly been paying very close attention to Lerner's progress and Tim's victory.

Peter turned and walked away, but Liza hurried after him, leaving her bevy of assistants standing immobilized round her desk. In the corridor outside the elevator she grabbed his arm.

'Look, we're working for the same thing. We want the best man elected to national office. That's all there is to it.'

Peter's voice was grating with contempt as he replied, 'No, that's *not* what you want. You really don't even care who the men are. Michael Lerner means nothing to you. Neither does Tim O'Donnell. All you're after is gaining a degree of control, so you can manipulate your interests. It's a good thing for this country that there are still a few people like Tim O'Donnell in it – people whose integrity you can't touch.'

'That's what you think, Peter,' she said, breaking into a remarkably hard-edged laugh as he stepped into the lift and the doors shut behind him.

As he left the building, Peter felt an intense relief to be out of it and back in the clean air of a late-summer evening, though he could not imagine what it was that had triggered off Liza's sarcasm.

He was back in the living room, sitting in the dark to watch the last of the primary coverage, when he heard Liza arriving home. Tim had delivered his victory speech about half an hour earlier, having beaten Lamb by a good 15 per cent. It was a brilliant triumph.

Liza came up the stairs, let her heavy briefcase drop to the floor, threw off her coat and sighed. Without a word, she went to pour herself a stiff Scotch.

'It's been a long day and a long night,' she said tiredly.

Peter made no reply as Liza sat across from him and kicked off her shoes. She glanced up.

170

'You still sulking? Why aren't you on top of the world? Your man won.'

For a few more moments, Peter stayed silent and clutched his own glass. When he spoke, his voice was quite low. 'There's more to life than elections, Liza.' He tipped back the last of the neat Scotch in his glass. 'I cared about you. I trusted you. I thought that had some meaning.'

When the phone began to ring, Peter rose wearily and went to the kitchen to answer.

'That you, Peter?' The Senator sounded very tired himself.

'Senator! Congratulations! What a fantastic race. I knew you'd do it . . .'

'I'm tied up here right now. I've only a few moments,' said Tim O'Donnell, his voice sounding unnatural in some way – almost as if he were half-strangled.

'Is something wrong?'

'It's just this. There's been a change of tactic. I've . . . ah . . . altered my plan. I'm asking Michael Lerner to be my running-mate. I wanted you to know before . . .'

Peter could hardly speak. 'But we'd agreed . . . What's changed the picture . . .?'

'I can't go into it now. Just wanted you should know. I'll get back to you some time tomorrow. Sleep tight, now.'

Peter hung up and walked slowly back into the nearly dark living room. His mind was dazed as he looked across at Liza.

'I guess that was your Senator,' she commented in a flat voice. 'He's taking Lerner, right? Just like I said.'

Peter turned his back on her and went upstairs to bed. His heart was pounding like a dull lead weight. He had almost dozed off when the door opened. Liza crossed the room without putting on the light and got into the bed in which she had not slept for weeks. As Peter pretended to be asleep, he felt her nakedness curling up against him as she started to kiss the back of his neck and whispered breathlessly, 'I want you now, Peter, I want to feel you inside me, filling me, like you used to . . .'

He stayed completely still, but she pressed herself up even closer as she slipped a hand inside his pyjamas and began to caress him subtly, intimately. All at once, his desire for her was as strong as ever and he rolled over into her arms, feverishly returning kiss for kiss. As he slipped his sex between her thighs once more, he was perfectly aware

171

that his love-making was fired more by anger and helplessness than it was by any impulse of love.

32

At the bottom of a deep pit, far away and half-buried in rubble, a phone was ringing, on and on insistently. It cost Peter a tremendous effort to drag himself free from a sleep which seemed reluctant to let him loose from its grip. He sat up and looked at the time. The morning was half-gone. At his side, Liza slept on unstirring, and as he looked at her his memories of the night returned and he felt a faint churning of shame and revulsion. He went out to the landing, shutting the door quietly behind him. The phone showed no sign of stopping. He got to it in the library and lifted the receiver.

'That you, Peter?' said the Senator's voice. 'You're sleeping late today. Would we were all so lucky.' There was an unusual note of nervous irritation in his voice, as if he resented the fact that Peter had not been sitting on top of the phone ready for it to go. 'Listen,' he continued, 'I've an important – a more than important – meeting coming up at four this afternoon. I want you to be there. I'll send a driver round at 3.30.'

'Where do we go?' asked Peter.

'It's terribly confidential this – not a word to a soul. We go to the

White House. President Randall's asked me to pay him a call.'

'Three-thirty's OK, but could he pick me up at the Library of Congress? There's one or two things I want to look up there.'

'Good man. I'll be seeing you.'

Even as he hung up, Peter was trying to figure it out. It was astonishing, almost unprecedented. Why should the President be summoning the leading Presidential candidate to the White House at this stage of the campaign? Even so, whatever the reason, it would be getting him his first glimpse of the inside of the White House. He made himself some coffee and toast, then took a shower. As he stepped out of the shower, he heard Liza calling. He hesitated before slowly walking into the bedroom, with a towel wrapped around him.

She looked up at him languorously, her eyes shining like those of a cat as it marks its prey. 'Good morning, Dr Peter Watkins.'

'Liza.' He stood by the doorway.

'Don't I come in for a good-morning kiss?'

He stepped across and gave her a routine peck on the cheek. Nevertheless she smiled, as if all was now again as it had been in the early days.

'Last night . . .' she said, 'you were wonderful, really. I realized how much I've missed our love-making.' She ran a hand over his bare chest and went on talking. 'These last few weeks have been such hell. We've both been so busy. We kept having those arguments. Now that's all over. We mustn't let it happen again.'

She began to try to untease the towel from round his waist, but he stood up suddenly and pulled it tighter about himself.

'I've got to leave now, Liza,' he said blankly.

'Oh, no, please. *Please* sit down here, only for a minute,' she said, letting the sheet fall clear from her breasts.

'I've got to get to the Library of Congress today,' he said, and turned away, grabbing up his clothes to go and dress downstairs and write a few quick notes. He heard Liza calling his name as he went out of the front door, but paid no attention.

At 3.30 sharp, as Peter stood outside the Library of Congress, Tim O'Donnell's driver drew up and picked him up before driving on to headquarters to pick up the Senator. Tim was looking tired and burnt out, and he kept staring distractedly out of the window.

Peter felt himself grow tense almost with a kind of stage fright as the car passed through the west gate to the White House. They stopped in front of the West Portico, and were quickly escorted in, following the

173

official who led them down a long hallway and into a richly designed reception area, where they were greeted by Nick Flynn, the President's appointments secretary. 'Good afternoon, Senator, Dr Watkins. Congratulations on the California win. The President's in the Oval Office, expecting you.' Flynn escorted them up to some white double doors. 'Go right in, please.'

As they entered the famous room, the President rose from the vast desk of dark oak and came forward. 'Senator. It's good of you to come at such short notice.'

'This is my assistant, Peter Watkins.'

The President shook Peter's hand. 'Dr Watkins. I've heard good things of you and your work for the Senator. Come and sit down now.'

The President, a tall, lean, silver-haired man in his late fifties, was known as a reticent person who liked to hear the opinions of others. The moment they were sitting down, he seemed to be going out of his way to make them feel at ease. Then, after a few minutes of pleasant conversation, he stood up and went over to the window, staring out on to the Rose Garden, his hands behind his back.

'If you ever come to occupy this strange office, Senator, and one way or another it looks a probability, you'll find it a job that's filled with sorrow – with sorrow, conflict and intolerable demands. I can't imagine that any President has ever really been happy while he lived in this house.' He looked up at the face of a deeply melancholic and brooding Abraham Lincoln in the picture frame on the wall, and said: 'That man's face says it all.' Then he turned and smiled thoughtfully. 'The reason I wanted to speak to you was to ask a favour. Mind you, I'm not accustomed to asking Democratic opponents for favours, so don't think it comes easily.'

Tim looked back earnestly as he said, 'Mr President, if I can be of any help on any issue so important as to prompt you to ask for this meeting, then you have my word that my full co-operation is yours to ask.'

The President stayed silent for a moment, then said, 'These have been very difficult times with the Middle East problem. There have been many charges made about me and the peace talks, charges that I have been pressuring Israel and so on. There have been reports, for months, of a so-called Arab military build-up. And then there were the terrible murders in New York, followed by Jesse Lusk blustering in most unhelpfully.'

The President sighed wearily as the Senator interjected, 'It has indeed been an ugly series of events. We've been trying to get to grips with the Middle East picture, and Dr Watkins has done some really excellent work for me on this.'

The President looked at them a shade wistfully as he said, 'Well, I hope you're making better sense of it than I am!' He walked over to his desk and picked up a thick folder, which he opened. 'I have had in a number of reports over the past few weeks, as well as a detailed study by the CIA, which confirm an on-going, full-scale military build-up in Israel at the present time. This build-up is being conducted with the utmost secrecy, but it represents a movement of massive proportions. Their entire army and air force are on the alert. There's been heavy movement of weaponry and supplies, shifting of planes from one airbase to another, diversion of troops, imports of a variety of armaments purchased on the black market, and an intensification of intelligence activity. We have been monitoring all this for some time, and the evidence for it is overwhelming.' He tossed the folder back down on the desk.

'Has the Israeli government made any attempt to keep you informed?' asked the Senator.

'Not a solitary goddamned word!' the President replied bitterly. 'And I've been bending over backwards for them for four years. Whenever there was a problem with Israel – peace talks, aid packages, state visits or whatever – I always walked that extra mile. And small thanks I got for it!'

'They must realize you'd find out,' Peter queried.

'You might think so, but let's put it this way. Their self-confidence has seemingly reached a point where they look on the US government as a conglomeration of naïve buffoons.'

'So is the Israeli action a defensive move against the Arab build-up?' asked Tim intently.

The President frowned as he shrugged. 'Senator, there never was any Arab build-up. The Syrians have been considering a few very minor manoeuvres close to their border. The Jordanians have built a couple of new airbases. No big deal. The rest that you've heard is moonshine.'

Tim was looking perplexed, even apprehensive. 'So what set the story going in the first place?'

The President smiled grimly. 'Well, there's one giant Israeli rumour mill in this country, and it's called the New York media. The moment Israel's about to ask for aid, the talk begins about an Arab military build-up, or Arab war threats or Palestinian terrorism. And you

175

always hear the same things when an election's brewing. I hardly think I'm telling you anything you don't know already.'

As Peter had listened, so had thoughts of the Subcommittee hearings, of Shavinsky's testimony and the hijacked plutonium begun to run swiftly through his mind. Should he raise that now? It could be of vital importance. On the other hand, it ought to be coming from Ronnie Montgomery. He was the expert on national security, after all, and it was not for Peter to pre-empt any of his moves or inquiries.

Again Tim spoke up. 'Might I ask what you plan to do next, Mr President?'

The President smiled ruefully. 'Senator, you soon discover you can't plan a damn thing here. You just wait for whatever hot potato drops into your lap next. I have requested Israel's Foreign Minister to meet with me, at which time I will confront him with all the information we've gathered. I'll make it clear that nothing less than an immediate de-escalation of all military operations in Israel is acceptable, and that I'm prepared to sacrifice my re-election to whatever steps I need to take in that regard.'

'So how can I help? You said you were asking a favour.'

The President looked directly at Tim O'Donnell. 'The situation is extremely fluid at the moment – and hazardous to a degree. This country's been in an uproar over the Middle East for weeks, and it's only just begun to settle. What I would ask from you is that you refrain from any intense public debates concerning the Israelis or Arabs for the present. I want to see this Middle East issue played down as much as possible during the remainder of the campaign. I know I've been taking all the flack from these negotiations for quite a while, but, for the good of the country, I'm willing to go on doing so as long –'

'Mr President,' Tim interrupted. 'You have my word on it that I'll handle this as discreetly as possible. Naturally, I have to take certain stands on foreign policy, but I'll soft-play the Middle East in any way that's feasible.'

The three men stood and the President shook the Senator's hand, then Peter's. 'I'm obliged, Senator, Dr Watkins. I'll keep you informed of new developments. In the meantime, take this copy of the report for reference. It's top secret so please handle the file accordingly.' The President passed over to Tim the thick folder. 'Thank you for coming here today, gentlemen.'

Tim O'Donnell remained unusually silent until they were driving out through the White House gates, when he handed over the folder and said, 'Here, I'll need your analysis of this pronto. You know the procedure. Keep it under lock and key.' Then he paused, picking nervously at an ear lobe before continuing, 'Peter, you're wanting to know why I'm taking Lerner instead of Lamb?'

Peter replied reproachfully, 'You said yourself that Lamb would be a better running-mate. Then, the next thing I know is . . . well, you ring and tell me otherwise.'

The Senator lowered his head and seemed lost in thought. 'These people can be ruthless,' he said.

'So it's pressure that made you take Lerner?'

The Senator turned towards him, a strained look on his face. He drew something out of his coat pocket. 'This is just to round off your education . . . Take a look.' He handed over an envelope full of photographs and Peter found himself shuffling through pictures of Tim naked in bed with a woman, in various positions and various bedrooms. The pictures were clear and in colour. Peter stared at them stonily as the Senator spoke with great difficulty out of his shame and humiliation: 'I know the press once made me out to be quite a playboy, but it was never really true. I've seen very few women during the last few years. Sure, I've been lonely – and the campaign's involved a lot of pressure. I met her by chance, at a restaurant I used to eat in a lot. We hit it off – became friends and then lovers. I had no idea how they were . . .' The Senator's voice trailed away.

Peter stared out of the car window at the Washington Monument, his eyes blank, his face grey. There had been no mistaking Liza in the photographs. He said nothing, had nothing to say.

33

When the driver dropped Peter off in front of his townhouse, he felt exhausted, consumed by rage and a deep sense of betrayal. Looking up at the townhouse windows, he could tell Liza was home. The very thought of seeing her made his stomach heave. The bitch had been screwing Tim O'Donnell these many months – God knew who else! He remembered the blond man she met that day, remembered their love-making of last night, the false, seductive words she had spoken that morning. He felt himself ready to crack – wrenched between a helpless despair and a violent fury.

He found Liza curled up on the couch, calmly watching the late news. Peter avoided her glance and, briefcase in hand, headed for the stairs.

'So where has the clever Dr Watkins been all day?' she asked.

Peter froze, his hand on the banister rail.

'Still pouting about your visit to my office? I thought we'd got over all that.'

He went on up the stairs without replying. In the bedroom he took off his jacket, tie and shirt, flung down his briefcase on the bed. There was a sound of Liza's steps running on the stairs, and she came smiling into the room and walked up to him as he stared vacantly into the mirror. From behind, she wrapped her arms around his chest. He saw her face next to his own, a beautiful face become repellent. He pushed her hands away from his chest as he turned to face her. As she pursed her downturned lips and leaned forward to kiss, he struck her as hard as he could across the face. She reeled, but reached out once more as he struck her again with the back of his hand – a sharp, brutal slap. She fell on to the bed, her eyes brimming – and burst out laughing.

The mockery behind her laugh seemed to explode in his head as he flung himself down on her and began to strangle her. She choked and struggled, but he only squeezed the harder until she went white, her blue eyes widening with terror. He loosened his grip slightly, but kept on shaking her head, battering it again and again against the bed. At last he jumped back, horrified at this spring of violence within himself. He strode out of the bedroom and went into the bathroom; where he filled a basin to the brim with cold water and sluiced the water on to his face. Drying himself, he sat on a bathroom stool for a few minutes, waiting for the shaking in his arms and knees to quieten down. When he got back to the bedroom, Liza was sitting up weakly, holding her throat and coughing. As she raised her head, she gave Peter a fearful, sickly smile.

'He must have shown you . . . the pictures,' she said. 'I wasn't sure he'd do that.'

Peter glared, the tide of his anger returning, but she only looked at him with contempt. Then she thrust her face towards him as she screamed and spat: 'You're nobody! Nothing! I made you. I can make a dozen more just the same. I can crush you and always find another.'

'Yes, and it seems your ambitions extend to making Presidents. To you, men are just there to be manipulated, used up and then –'

'Oh God, Peter, you sound *pathetic*!'

'But not everything's worked out as you planned, has it? You can't completely control everyone and everything, can you? When it came to it, with me –'

'I controlled you from the start. I found you, sitting on that goddamned rinky-dink Subcommittee. You were just the person I wanted – frustrated, bright and talented, but not *too* talented. And lonely – like a dog that doesn't get enough pats on the head. *I* made you go up to the O'Donnell headquarters. When Barney Shaw wasn't interested, and you were so fucking depressed, I made sure he *got* interested. And when Howard Mattingly cut you off because of your foreign-policy views, who do you think got you out of that? Lady

Luck? God, you're blind and stupid!'

Peter stared, dumbfounded, incredulous. Everything she said made a horrible, twisted sense out of the past six months. He could hardly utter a word, but managed to whisper, 'You make me really sick, Liza. I don't believe one word –'

'I don't need you to believe me. How about that day you got the call from Senator O'Donnell? You think he would ever have called a nobody like you if I hadn't been pulling a lot of strings? It hasn't been easy getting you to where you are, I can tell you. Then, the whole time I had to put up with the old love-sick routine, and you say I make *you* feel sick!'

Peter looked at her grimly, aware he had never felt such an intense hatred before. 'What in hell drives you, Liza? It's so –'

'We like to keep a close eye on all the candidates, especially those who look likely to win. If you hadn't gone so crazy on the Middle East, you could've been really helpful to us. And while I think of it, on the subject of your little girlfriend, that Palestinian bitch, you can tell her she can come out of hiding now. I've instructed the guy tailing her to let her alone.'

'Liza . . . you're that vicious? That was your doing too . . .?'

'I'm leaving now, Peter.'

She turned, picked up her purse and sweater. Only a minute later he heard the door slam downstairs. He sunk into a chair, a tight constriction about his chest and the events of the last few hours blurring together in his mind. As he looked towards the bed, he noticed that the catches on his briefcase were undone. Looking inside, he found the President's report on the Israeli build-up still there, but its pages had obviously been rapidly turned over and muddled up. He began to rummage through all the drawers in the bedroom, although he had no idea exactly what it was he hoped to find.

34

Some months later, the driver assigned to Dr Peter Watkins, special counsellor to Timothy O'Donnell, the President of the United States, dropped off Dr Watkins at his home address. Peter had become something of a neighbourhood celebrity as soon as his photograph began to appear in various papers and magazines. The public attention still made him feel odd and nervous. It took a good bit of getting used to. The moment he opened the door and went in, Aida, who had been hiding directly behind it, stepped out and tickled him on the back, above the hips. He turned, grabbing her hands and kissed her happily. It was still a novel delight to arrive home and find her here each night. All the cares and frustrations of his new duties at the White House vanished the moment he came in and found her there. As they went up the stairs together, he could smell the delicious scent of lamb roasting. It never ceased to amaze him how wonderfully his wife cooked.

As he went to wash, she was singing to herself in the kitchen. He smiled happily as he remembered the day of their wedding, with the new President for best man. The ceremony and reception had all taken place in the Blue Room of the White House, and he had only been allowed the afternoon off to be with Aida. What with the new Administration just getting settled, there had been no time yet for any honeymoon.

The thought of the piles of work waiting on his desk, however, suddenly dragged his spirits down again a little. He had spent the whole of that day reviewing a comprehensive array of the import-export problems between the United States and Japan. Next week there was to be the visit of the President of France, for which he would have to brief Tim. It was a relief to hear Aida calling that dinner was on the table. Tonight they would have an early night, he promised himself. Tomorrow was another day.

The next morning, as he sat at his desk looking over various reports on the French economy, his appointments secretary buzzed him and announced that Ronnie Montgomery was here to see him. Peter told her to send him in straight away.

Ronnie, carrying his battered old briefcase, was looking preoccupied. He managed no more than a faint smile as he shook hands, then sat grimly across from Peter as he took out two bulging file cases.

'They tell me the President's gone for the day,' he said. 'Where to? When'll he be back?'

Peter could sense something unusually serious. 'He's in New York, dedicating a housing project in the Bronx. Then he's meeting the Mayor. Should be back around noon tomorrow. What's in the air?'

'One of our Damascus agents was approached last month by a member of the Palestinian Freedom League.'

'Something from them at last. Did he give a reason for the killings?'

Ronnie rubbed his brow. 'He was very reluctant to say anything about them at first, but after a while he confirmed the PFL had certainly sent some men to New York . . .'

'Then they're admitting –'

'No, that was after the killings . . . they only sent their men in after the killings, at great personal risk, he emphasized.'

'How does he mean, *after* the killings?'

'He denied the PFL had anything to do with the actual killings in Manhattan. He claimed they played no part in them, had no prior knowledge of them, and that none of their members was involved in any way. He stated that he, personally, could account for the whereabouts of virtually every member on the day of the killings. Not one had been in the United States. He deplored the murders, said how much they had harmed the Palestinian cause. He felt it had been the work of madmen or . . .'

'Or what . . . who?'

'The moment the PFL was linked to the crime, a decision was taken by their higher command. They would send one of their own teams to New York to investigate. They had no faith in the American police or the FBI.'

'But it seems incredible . . . I mean, that they could somehow sneak in their agents at the height of the anti-Palestinian demonstrations and with all the tight security at immigration. How weren't they caught?'

Ronnie looked at Peter seriously. 'Don't make the mistake of thinking that these guys are in any sense amateurs,' he said.

'So how could they have got anywhere, after the New York police, the FBI and your lot at the CIA drew a blank?'

'Maybe we didn't know what we were looking for . . .'

Peter stared back at Ronnie, disturbed by the implications. 'Are you meaning to tell me they did?'

'They knew they weren't the killers, and they knew that whoever it was had to be someone out to get them. That was a point we'd never even considered. The case against them looked so air-tight.' Ronnie sighed as he continued, 'I know it all sounds crazy, but sometimes you have to take whatever lead is offered, however bizarre. Their men did a lot of checking around New York. They even went over the scene of the killings – the schoolyard itself – late one night. Can you imagine if they'd been caught? There'd have been a lynch mob nobody could have stopped.'

'Did they turn up anything?'

'Not at the school.'

'But they found something somewhere else.'

'Not exactly found . . . more found out . . . found out that one of the individuals they suspected had been sighted in New York around the time of the killings, at the Port Authority Bus Terminal.'

'Who was it?' asked Peter, leaning forward eagerly.

'A man known as Amram Yariv.'

'Amram Yariv? That sounds more . . .'

'Precisely. An Israeli.'

A long and wordless stare passed between the two men, Peter becoming acutely aware of the tick of the clock on his desk.

'You've heard of Deir Yassin,' Ronnie continued.

'Yes, one of the atrocities in the 1948 war.'

'Before the war began,' Ronnie corrected him. 'It happened in April, when the extremist Zionists were doing their best to strike terror into the Palestinians before the Mandate ended. Deir Yassin was a little village near Jerusalem, which the Zionist terrorists entered one night. They slaughtered virtually all its inhabitants: 254 people, mostly women, children and old men – including 35 *pregnant* women. They threw the bodies down a well. They tried to cover the whole thing up, but the International Red Cross went in and made a full report.'

'Yes,' said Peter, 'I've seen some of the documents.'

'And it worked. It scared the shit out of the Palestinians. That's why so many fled Palestine *before* the war broke out.'

'So what does all this have to do with Amram Yariv?'

'According to our source in Damascus, Amram Yariv works with an extreme Zionist organization called Deir Yassin, after the massacre. Their viewpoint is that this is just the kind of action which is needed against Palestinians today . . .'

'But, so far, it's all no more than rumour, from some member of a hole-in-the-corner splinter-group of Palestinian radicals. How can their version be allowed any credibility?'

Ronnie stood up and went across to the window, looked out at the bare trees of the Rose Garden, gazed at the heavy black wrought-iron fence that surrounded the White House grounds in the distance. 'I wish to God their version had no credibility. Our line, at first, was that it had none.'

'Didn't the CIA hold some information on their Zionist group?'

'We knew a little about the Deir Yassin, knew of various bombings and killings attributed to them. But we had very few names to go on.'

'So how could your PFL source know so much?'

'He said the PFL had been working to counteract terrorist attacks by the Deir Yassin in the Gaza Strip area. There had been a series of clashes between them over the last couple of years. It had taken time, but the PFL had identified a number of their key figures.'

'And that was all?'

Ronnie wrinkled his brow. 'All that our source had to say for the time being. It gave very little to go on, but we were interested enough to begin a search, without much hope.'

'What about contacting Israeli intelligence?'

'That didn't seem advisable. We had no idea of the status of the Deir Yassin group. Then our source made contact again two weeks ago. He told our agent in Damascus that Yariv and the other two – Shemesh and Yaacov – were now in Haifa. He gave us a description of where they were and what they looked like.'

Peter could hardly bear the suspense. 'So did you then find them, or

184

was this another wild-goose chase?'

'We found them, all right. Turned out that all three were living in this very expensive condominium-style village – a luxury complex of some kind – with heavy security, guards and all the rest of it. There was no way for us to penetrate their villa or establish a tap on the line. After a few days of constant surveillance, however, we got some excellent telephoto footage of all three men.'

'But what good would photographs be when you didn't even know who they were?'

Ronnie, walking to the desk, opened one of the folders and took out a number of large glossy colour prints. 'These are blow-ups of some of the shots of the three men. That's Yariv . . . here's Shemesh. There's Amos Yaacov.'

Peter studied the faces carefully. All were young, unshaven and dark. Then Ronnie opened the other folder, took out more photos.

'These are special enlargements,' he said, 'of stills taken from the Channel 5 footage of the Manhattan killings,' and handed them across.

Once again, as he looked, Peter saw those faces concealed by bandanas which had glared out from the front pages of newspapers and magazines during a whole terrible week, again saw those menacing eyes.

'It's the eyes you have to compare,' Ronnie said.

Peter laid down the Channel 5 pictures, then arranged the blow-ups of Yariv, Shemesh and Yaacov under them. It took him no time at all to match up the photos. He looked up at Ronnie in shock. 'My God, Ronnie, it is the same men. It's definitely them!'

Ronnie smiled. 'Yes. Our people in Virginia have done a very high-magnification blow-up of just the eyes from both the Channel 5 footage and our shots from Haifa.'

He tossed down more photos, huge blow-ups of eyes this time. Peter whistled as he held up the pictures.

'The resemblance is . . . is exact!' he said. 'But, dear God, Ronnie! This is saying that Jews killed Cardozo, Tompkins, Rabbi Rubinstein – and wounded those kids! No one will ever believe it. It will be like when the Nazis burned the Reichstag and pinned it on the communists. The Deir Yassin gang is willing to sacrifice their own people just to intensify anti-Palestinian propaganda. It's beyond the credibility –'

'There's more to come. The match-up of the eyes is 95 per cent certain, especially since all three sets of eyes match so perfectly. But we've also made a positive identification of Amram Yariv.'

'Identified him?'

'We got a thumbprint off the broken back lock at the Hillel School, which was never revealed publicly. When we matched it up with one of Yariv's thumbprints, lifted off the handle of his car door in Haifa, it was the same.'

'So there's no question –'

'Right. We've been watching all three now for two weeks. They're spending money like water. They live in this fancy place, drive expensive cars, do a lot of shopping. Getting through their pay-off from the killings, most probably. Once we can get their place wired or get a bug on their phone, we hope to find out who did the paying. Then we'll make our move. There's a full report on everything I've just told you in here.' He handed over the folders. 'I think the President should see the material and report immediately,' said Ronnie gravely.

Peter looked at his watch. 'He'll be through with the Mayor of New York in a few minutes. I'll call him, tell him to fly back immediately. It can't wait till tomorrow.'

'What about Lerner?' asked Ronnie.

Peter looked at him. 'You think we should tell him now? He's the one who's been closest to the Israeli government. Prime Minister Peritzsky and he are old friends.'

Ronnie rubbed his jaw. 'That's just what I'm wondering about. Maybe he's too close . . .'

Peter stared at Ronnie wide-eyed. 'My God, Ronnie, you wouldn't suspect Michael Lerner! We've worked with the man for years. You know him through and through. You CIA guys really go off the deep end at times.'

'I don't suspect anything. What I'm concerned about is, if it's made known to him, he might overreact and even call Peritzsky. He trusts them, and it could blow the whole thing. We've got to nail those three in Haifa and find out who they're connected with, whether it's terrorists or the Israeli government.' Ronnie looked at his watch. 'You call the President. I'll get back downstairs to see if we've any more information coming in.'

'How many people know about this report, Ronnie?' asked Peter.

'You, me, and about three guys out in Virginia. The surveillance team in Haifa has no idea who it's watching.'

'Fine. I'll see you in a little while.'

Peter began rapidly to dial a secret service code number in New York. President O'Donnell had just finished his meeting with the

Mayor and was about to shower for dinner. Something very urgent had come up, Peter told him. The CIA had identified and located the killers from the Manhattan Massacre. Certain highly sensitive issues were involved, and Peter suggested an emergency night meeting of cabinet officials, National Security Council and CIA people. The President gave him the OK to convene the meeting. He would fly back within about ninety minutes.

Peter sat in a daze, shaken by all that Ronnie had just said. He gazed out of the window at the ice-covered branches. It still seemed impossible to believe. He flipped through the folders, looked at the pictures again, and sat back in his chair as he wondered what Tim would make of it all. At that point, the phone went on his desk. It seemed rather late in the day for anyone to be calling. He picked it up, but there was only a silence on the other end until a familiar voice asked, 'Peter?' His heart nearly stopped dead.

'Liza,' he said drily.

'Peter, we have to meet.'

He couldn't believe it. He hadn't seen or spoken to Liza since the night she walked out. He'd done his best to erase every trace of her from his life. But now, here she was, calling him at the White House and sounding like a nervous rabbit.

'What is this, Liza?' he asked. 'Another one of your games?'

'I've got to see you, Peter. Now. Straight away.'

'On what business?' asked Peter coldly.

'I'll come round to your office. We can talk . . . I can be there in fifteen minutes.'

Peter paused, then replied frankly, 'No.'

But before he could hang up, he heard Liza call out, 'Don't put that phone down, Peter!'

He listened in silence.

'You see, I know you've got the report from the CIA . . .'

Peter's heart skipped a beat. She knew! She already knew about the sodding report, and Ronnie had only brought it to him an hour before.

'What report would that be, Liza?'

'The Deir Yassin group, the pictures . . . everything. I know you've got it.'

'I don't know what in hell you're talking about, Liza.'

'That report's a lie, Peter – believe me. Because if you don't –'

Peter contained his righteous anger. 'Do you realize, Liza, that I could have you investigated from pillar to post for even mentioning

187

this report's existence? You've violated top security, and I could get your ass in jail.'

'Listen again. I know about your work on the new peace plan, your briefings, the Palestinians you've brought to the White House. You've got O'Donnell wrapped around your finger. Not at all bad. But what disturbs me most is Michael Lerner . . . You've poisoned his mind, too. He's no use to us now, he's –'

'He's brilliant, courageous and independent-minded. He'll do more for American Jews than anyone ever –'

Liza cut in sharply. 'I want the terms of the peace plan changed. And I want you to use your influence on O'Donnell – he must not betray Israel.'

'Liza, he is not betraying Israel! He only wants the best solution for the Middle East.'

'And the report, Peter – it must never be made public. It would only destroy the faith of people in Israel. You don't realize the facts behind what it –'

'I'll not discuss any report with *you*.' Peter was shaking with anger by now. 'And if you ever try to threaten –'

'Shut up, you fool!' snapped Liza. 'You don't know what's at stake. I *made* you. Then you got involved with that little Arab tramp.'

'Liza, I'll not listen to –'

'Maybe you'll see things my way when you get home –' She had put down the phone abruptly, almost cutting off her own words.

Peter suddenly had a picture of Aida alone at the house. He remembered how Liza had had her followed previously. A chill of dread ran through him as he held the dead telephone receiver in his hands and muttered impotently into it, 'Liza, if you've done anything to harm her . . .' before slamming it down, jumping to his feet and running from the office.

He urged the White House driver through the city at breakneck speed, and practically leaped from the moving car as it was pulling up outside his townhouse. There were lights in the upstairs window. He rang the bell, knocked on the door, fumbled for his key. Running up the stairs, two at a time, he found the TV was on in the living room, but one of the four high-backed chairs was lying tipped over on the rug. In the kitchen, where Aida would usually be cooking at this time, he saw the shards of a broken tumbler scattered over the tile floor. Three covered pans stood on the oven burners, the heat turned off. Touching each pan, he found them all still warm.

'Aida?' he called out loudly, feeling his panic sweep through him.

Upstairs, in the bedrooms and bathroom, there was nothing. Everything looked as neat as a pin. The sound of a buzzer going off downstairs startled him. It was only the stove timer. He looked frantically at his watch. The President should be landing at any minute. He'd probably helicopter over to the White House from the airport. *What in hell was he to do now?* The very thought of Aida being in danger was more than he could –

As the phone rang, Peter darted downstairs. 'Hello?' he shouted, out of breath.

'Peter?' said Liza's voice.

'Listen, you fucking bitch, lay one finger on her and I'll have the entire US –'

'You've got an hour,' Liza said without emotion.

'An hour for what?' Peter demanded angrily.

'I'll give you one hour to decide. You know more about the terms of the peace plan than anyone. You're its chief architect. You can change it – they'd listen to you. You can swing O'Donnell around. And Lerner. You're the only one who can do it, Peter.'

'Liza, nothing can make me –'

'You do want to see your little Arab wife again, don't you?'

Peter became totally hushed.

'She'll be dead in an hour, and you'll never even find the body, unless we get your absolute co-operation. I don't care how you do it, how long it takes – I want that peace plan changed. We'll discuss details later. And I want the report suppressed. My meaning's quite clear. It's your decision.'

Liza's words cut like a knife. The shattering realization that Liza was, in truth, a cold-blooded killer whom he had loved and lived with and trusted was almost beyond bearing. He could tell that there was not an ounce of bluff in her words.

'OK, OK, I'll do whatever you want,' he said. 'I can shift the peace plan. It'll take time, but then –'

'And the report on Deir Yassin?' asked Liza sharply.

'I . . . think we can keep it under wraps. The President should realize the security risk involved. But what about Aida? Please, Liza . . . please don't –'

'I'll call you back in an hour. Oh, and don't try anything stupid – like contacting the police. You don't want to be a widower so soon, I take it.'

189

As she hung up, Peter sat at the table, dazed and trembling. There was no way he could do a thing that she asked. But now, for Aida, there must be the hope that she could be saved – wherever she was. Hurriedly he dialled Ronnie's number at the White House.

35

The old warehouse stood a couple of blocks off Bladensburg Road, out near Maryland. It was in a rundown area, an area which the office buildings and apartment complexes and Holiday Inns had never quite reached. Deep in the warehouse's entrails, in a small glassed-in shipping office, sat Aida. Her hands and feet were bound, and she was tied to the chair she sat in. She was also gagged, by a rag stuffed into her mouth and masking tape run around her head in tight bands, as well as blindfolded. She had been cooking in the kitchen when someone grabbed her from behind. She had struggled helplessly while a second person gagged and blindfolded her. Then they tied her up and stuffed her into a laundry bag before carrying her out of the house and loading her into a van. Now she sat, unable to move, see or speak, with no idea of where she was or who had seized her. She knew, of course, that crime was bad in Washington, but if this was a kidnapping, it made no sense. She and Peter had no money.

Aida could sense footsteps in the distance. Then she heard the more definite sound of a woman's heels clicking on a cement floor. She strained for the slightest sound, for the slightest clue as to who these people might be. The heel clicks stopped somewhere outside the room and Aida heard what sounded like a woman making a phone call, putting coins in the slot of a pay phone. The sound was too muffled for Aida to catch anything that was said.

Aida must have dozed, because suddenly she was aware of a man and woman speaking in low voices somewhere behind her in the room. The tone of the man's voice sounded worried.

'When will you call him back?' he asked.

'Soon.'

'How do we know he'll keep his word?'

'He will.' The woman sounded sharp and arrogant.

'What about her?' he demanded.

The woman did not respond, only asked, 'Is it ready?'

'Yes. The detonator's finished. It's being transported tomorrow. The crew's standing by.'

'What about Yariv and the others?' she asked in a clipped voice.

'They are ready.'

'Will there be any problem at immigration?'

'Yariv will arrive in New York in three days. He had no problem before.' The man paused. 'Did you get the President's schedule?'

'It'll be with us. Don't worry about that,' the woman answered.

There was a momentary silence, and then Aida felt a cold hand touching her cheek. She shook her head and tried to hunch away and heard the man laugh. Now his hand was on her hair. She was terrified, but sat utterly still.

'Leave her alone,' the woman commanded, evidently standing just behind Aida by this time.

'A very pretty little Arab child,' the man said coarsely.

'Come, let's go,' the woman ordered.

Aida felt a wave of hot breath on her neck as the man whispered a crude sexual remark in Arabic in her ear.

'I really must get a look at her . . . this pretty little one,' he said.

His hands were somewhere round the back of her head as he fumbled with the blindfold.

The woman shouted, 'What are you doing, you fool?'

As the blindfold dropped away, Aida found a man in a dark suit standing in front of her. He smiled a narrow, tormenting smile as he stepped closer, bent towards her and took her chin in his hand as he

191

forced her to look into his face. He was deliberately breathing hard.

'Yes, indeed, very pretty,' he said.

She cringed in fear as he gave an unpleasant laugh, and leaned forward, pouting his lips in a parody of a kiss. He began to toy with her blouse, flicking the buttons undone and fingering her breasts.

'For God's sake!' the woman practically screamed as she suddenly appeared and pulled at his arm with such strength that he almost overbalanced. 'We're not here to play games,' she said.

'Sometimes,' he said, with a sigh of mock disappointment, 'I fear you're such a puritan. Never mind. It can wait.'

Aida felt she was almost fainting with fear as she sunk back against the chair. It was a relief when the couple went out of the room and left her on her own again.

36

The last man had arrived at the Oval Office for the hastily convened meeting. The President had greeted each one pleasantly as he came in, but he was looking worn and tired as he flipped through the sheafs of papers from the two folders on his desk. He looked at this assembly of the key men in his Administration: Secretary of State, Henry Simpson; Assistant CIA Director, Drew Endicott; the head of the National Security Agency, Mason Van Damm; the chief of the Defense

Intelligence Agency, Constantine Chartoff; and last but not least Vice-President Michael Lerner.

'I'm sorry this summons has been so abrupt. We'll send for some sandwiches in a few minutes. I know most of you haven't had time to eat yet.' The President glanced back down at the folders. 'Mr Montgomery submitted a CIA report to Dr Watkins late this afternoon, which I have flown back from New York to read. The CIA has established a contact with a member of the Palestinian Freedom League, the PFL, in Damascus. This member denies his organization's involvement in the Manhattan killings. He states that his group have investigated the case and uncovered an Israeli terrorist group, known as Deir Yassin, behind the murders. He named, in particular, a man named Amram Yariv, and two others – Amos Yaacov and Meir Shemesh – who together formed a terrorist hit squad. Our source was eventually able to locate them for us in Haifa, where we set up an immediate surveillance operation.'

There was an instant sense of shock in the room, and Vice-President Lerner was visibly upset.

'Mr President,' he said, 'I find this too fantastic to warrant any serious thought. You're saying it was Israelis who killed Cardozo, Rubinstein, shot those kids? Dear God! As a Jew, I find the implications –'

'I'm deeply sorry, Michael,' the President interrupted. 'It's shaken me to the core as well. There's plenty more to follow.' The President took out the photos of the Deir Yassin men with the telephoto shots from Haifa. 'Here are some blow-ups of some footage we got in Haifa of the three men.' He handed them around the table.

'And the claim is that these were the men behind the Manhattan killings?' asked Secretary of State Simpson.

'But how can all these really prove a thing?' Michael Lerner protested desperately.

'How many here know about OMI – Optical Magnification Identification?' asked the President quietly and gently.

Drew Endicott of the CIA explained, 'It's a technique where enlarged photographs of people's eyes are used to confirm identification.'

'Exactly. OMI has been used to match up the Deir Yassin group with the media footage of the three killers in New York, shot by the Channel 5 cameraman. These are the two sets of pictures of the eyes.'

The President laid the sequences of photos out on his desk in two rows as the meeting stood to look at them. Constantine Chartoff, the gruff head of the DIA, squinted at the two rows.

'Unquestionably, the same men,' he said. 'No doubt about it. They should be brought in immediately.'

'I agree with Constantine for once,' Mason Van Damm put in eagerly. 'There's no doubt but it's them. I have a group who can make a nice clean job of it. They can be terminated within forty-eight hours.'

'Mason,' said Chartoff in irritation. 'This has nothing to do with the NSA. If they need to be terminated, I have people who can handle it.'

Michael Lerner looked aghast as he asked, 'We're surely not discussing the liquidation of these men in cold blood, are we? Not when we have no proof beyond these photographs? I admit they seem to match up, but suppose we had a thousand other photos of dark-eyed men here for comparison? We're discussing human lives ... Such an act would be no better than the killings in New York.'

'Amram Yariv,' the President intervened, 'has been positively linked to the site of the killings. A thumbprint was found on the back lock of the Hillel school. It matched a thumbprint of Yariv's we obtained in Haifa. It seems a clinching proof.'

A look of despair and defeat spread over Michael Lerner's face as he fell silent. This shocking revelation coming so soon after the Sub-committee hearings and the disillusion they involved was shattering.

The Secretary of State, a quiet, competent official, and a longtime supporter of Israel, posed the next question: 'Is the Israeli government in any way aware of the involvement of these men?'

The Vice-President raised his hands in protest. 'I hardly think,' he said, 'that the Israelis could have had any knowledge of them. Certainly, they would have informed our government if –'

'I take that as a legitimate question, Henry,' the President replied, addressing himself to the Secretary of State. 'A significant question ...'

'From the standpoint of the NSA,' inquired Mason Van Damm, 'I have to ask what would the purpose be of such an attack? What is there to gain from it? There must have been some kind of logic behind it to justify the planning which must have gone into it.'

The President glanced through the papers. 'That remains a central question,' he commented. 'In the light of the gravity of this matter – and its urgency – I have decided to fly to Israel tomorrow morning for an emergency meeting with Prime Minister Peritzsky. There I will divulge to him the contents of this report and demand some kind of response. I'll be prepared to go public with the report the moment after we've met Peritzsky and resolved the situation of the three men.'

Mason Van Damm, looking highly perturbed, protested, 'Mr President, it's not at all advisable for you to travel abroad just now, especially to the Middle East and at such short notice. There's no time to counter the tremendous security risks.'

'I'm aware of that, Mason. But the matter must be resolved if our peace plan's to go forward.' The President, looking across at his old friend, Michael Lerner, and seeing all the anguish, disbelief and sadness in his eyes, continued, 'Michael, I know how terrible this report must seem to you.'

The Vice-President sighed wearily. 'The Jews have always struggled for truth, no matter at what cost. I'd rather the report were known, so that the perpetrators of these crimes – be they Jewish or otherwise – may be apprehended and brought to justice.'

'I'll need your help on this, Michael,' said the President. 'You've known Prime Minister Peritzsky for years. You know how he thinks and how he should be handled.'

'I'll prepare a full background report tonight,' said Lerner. 'You can read it on the plane tomorrow.'

'Thank you, Michael.' The President handed the folders to Drew Endicott. 'The report remains absolutely top secret. Drew, get a copy to each person in this room, please, but on no account are any of your aides to see it.' He rose briskly as he looked across at the Secretary of State. 'Now then, Henry, you'll have to work out some sort of phoney briefing for the press on this sudden trip . . . a visit regarding the peace talks or something. High-level negotiations.'

'Yes, Mr President. I'll prepare it tonight.'

The President shook hands with each man and quickly left the room.

37

Ronnie Montgomery's Buick screeched as it swung off Bladensburg Road. He shut off the headlights and stopped about two blocks short of the warehouse, where he and Peter quietly got out. Ever since his telephone conversation with Peter, Ronnie had decided that Liza was far more dangerous than she appeared. Her close relationship with Peter, the fact she had lived with him, for Christ's sake, and her dubious Israeli connections were all equally alarming. He became convinced she had been using Peter all along.

When Peter became special counsellor to the President, her past relationship with him continued to be a worry to Ronnie. He had briefly had her tailed last month, but uncovered nothing suspicious. Even so, he felt concerned enough to have had a tap put on Peter's phone – for his own protection. If she made any threatening calls, Ronnie wanted to know about them at once. The tap had supplied a trace for the number from where Liza had called Peter, when he reached home and found Aida gone. It came from a warehouse out in the boondocks.

As they went towards the warehouse, Ronnie silently pointed upwards. Peter saw the dim haze of a distant light from a tiny window high up in the building. They must be there – somewhere inside! Peter's

196

heart was pounding rapidly. He looked at his watch – Liza would be calling his townhouse number any minute now. Silently they crept along the side of the building, towards a back alley, Peter feeling startled to see Liza's car parked beside a loading bay. He pointed it out to Ronnie, who nodded and slipped out a gun from a holster under his arm. It quite shocked Peter. He had never thought of Ronnie as someone who carried a firearm.

Ronnie indicated a small screened window – a vent perhaps – over the loading bay, and climbed up to peer inside. The warehouse was practically in darkness, but there was a glimpse of a light from somewhere at the other end. There seemed to be an office area beyond piles of roofing stuff. He climbed down.

'I think they're through at the far end. We'll try to get in here at the back and work our way forward. Maybe we'll hear them.'

It was very dim inside, smelling of bitumen and sheet metal. It was hard to see anything in front of them. Then there was a sound of muffled voices, evidently being raised in argument.

'He's not answering?' asked a man's voice. 'It means he's not home. He didn't get the report. Maybe he's called the police. You've been wrong about him.'

'Shut up, you fool. It's only a delay. He'll get home shortly. I know him. He loves her too much . . . one minute and I'll call again.'

Ronnie had meanwhile edged up to a stack of aluminium pipes leaning against a pillar and begun to nudge them out of position. Several of them suddenly fell with a loud clatter, and the door of the office swung open, a man standing against the light as he loosed off a couple of shots wildly into the shadows. Ronnie's gun also went off with a deafening report in Peter's ear, but the man had leapt back inside and slammed and locked the door.

'Damnation,' said Ronnie through clenched teeth. 'Missed him. Quick, give me a hand with the door.'

'They've found us!' they heard the man shout, as Ronnie's shoulder crashed against the door, which shook but held firm.

'Stand right back,' said Ronnie. 'I'll have to blow the lock off.'

But before he could do so, Peter's blood ran to ice at the sound of two shots being fired somewhere beyond the door.

'Aida,' he whispered.

Then Ronnie blasted the lock and simultaneously sent the door flying inwards with a noise of wood splintering. As Peter rushed in at his heels he saw only, behind a glass partition in the inner office, the

197

small, bound figure of Aida, slumped motionless in a chair, the scorch marks from a gunshot on her white blouse, just below her left breast. Refusing to let his hope die, he knelt and began frantically to tussle with the knots of the bonds, only vaguely aware that Ronnie had turned about again, having realized that Liza and her accomplice had used a route through a connecting office to double back into the warehouse. There was a sound of more shots being fired as Ronnie went in pursuit, of more building materials crashing down, of a big metal door slamming and of a car hysterically revving and spinning as it took off at speed.

As Ronnie got back to the office, baulked of his quarry, Peter had just freed Aida from the rope and tape and discovered, to his intense relief, that she had flung her arms around him and begun to weep hysterically.

'Thank God it was your Liza who fired those shots,' said Ronnie, pointing to the powder burns on the cotton of Aida's blouse, 'and thank God we put blanks in her gun the day our man found it! I figured she just might cause some trouble, walking around with it loaded. I'll go and get the car.'

Peter carried Aida over to a couch, laid her down on it and knelt beside her as she clung to him, unable to stop crying. She was a little calmer by the time they got her into the car, and Peter asked, 'Try to think, Aida, my darling, what was the man like who was there?'

'Tall, blond. In his thirties,' she said. 'Such thin lips. Unkind lips.'

Peter stared out at the passing lights as they approached Washington. 'It must be the man Liza met the day I followed her . . . her lover. Outside her office. The day I met you in the park.'

Aida could hardly follow what Peter was saying, but Ronnie added sympathetically and softly but firmly, 'Aida, these people are very dangerous. We need to find them straight away. Did they say anything . . . anything you overheard?'

Aida's face puckered with the effort of recalling, and she replied in a whisper. 'The man mentioned a crew. The crew was ready. Something was to be transported. I don't know exactly. I'm muddling it up.'

Peter held her tightly. 'You're doing fine. What was this crew transporting?'

'I don't know. I'm not sure he said.'

'Did either of them mention any names?' Ronnie asked.

Aida frowned, rubbed her forehead. 'He mentioned a man. Some man was coming to New York in a few days. His name . . . it was foreign.' She bit her lip. 'I don't remember. I'm sorry.'

'And what did the woman say when he said this?' asked Peter nervously.

Aida thought for a moment, brushed back her tangled hair. Her face was still raw from the tape. 'The man asked if she had the schedule yet. She said not to worry. That's all. I'm sorry . . .'

'The schedule?' Peter asked. 'What schedule? For what? Where? When? This could be so very important, Aida.'

She stared vacantly ahead, tired and shocked. 'I don't know. I just can't recall. Someone's schedule. She said she'd be sure to get it . . .'

Ronnie's hands were gripping the wheel tightly. 'You've done just fine, Aida . . . just fine,' he said as he screeched to a halt in front of the emergency room of Georgetown University Medical Center. It had been a very long evening, and he knew that, where he was concerned, it still had some way to go.

38

Peter slept restlessly, alone in his townhouse. As soon as they had established at the medical centre that Aida was basically unharmed and needed only some treatment for shock, Peter decided it would be safer for her to stay with friends for a few days. There was no telling what Liza might try next. Maybe they would be more likely to go after him another time, but Ronnie had assured him that an immediate alert for Liza and her companion would be put out through the FBI, to bring them in on kidnapping charges and suspected national security violations.

As Peter spent the night tossing and turning, he could not banish thoughts of Liza, which kept flickering through his mind in nightmare images from their past relationship. She had used him, lied to him, betrayed him. Again he thought of the day he saw Liza come out of her office to meet her lover. The picture still filled Peter with rage and disgust: Liza and the tall blond man walking away, arm in arm. And now he had to add the thought of those two tormenting Aida, gagging and binding her before trying to kill her! It filled him with a desire for vengeance, a primitive impulse that he would normally have despised.

He finally dozed off a little before dawn, only to be startled out of sleep by a loud buzzing. Sitting up in a panic, he looked at the clock: 8.30 a.m. The doorbell was ringing, over and over. Maybe it was Liza or one of her henchmen. Peter pulled on his robe and stepped swiftly and silently downstairs. As he carefully slipped open the peephole, he saw an image of Ronnie. Promptly he unbolted the locks and swung the door open.

Ronnie gave him an appraising glance as he hurried in. 'You look like hell's half acre,' he commented. 'Didn't you sleep any?'

Peter brushed back his hair. 'I had a rough night, worried about Aida . . . and then thinking about Liza, that incredible bitch . . .'

'OK, pal. Can you rustle up some coffee?'

Upstairs in the kitchen, as Peter began to make coffee, Ronnie said, 'Look, I called the FBI about Liza last night. We've a lot of information on her. They'll round her up in a day or two, if she hangs around Washington. Aida's going to be just fine. Don't you worry. And I can lay on round-the-clock protection for her, if you want it.'

Peter smiled gratefully. 'Thanks, Ronnie. I think she'll be OK where she is. No one will find her there. But I'll feel a hell of a lot better as soon as Liza and the blond guy are under lock and key.'

'Believe me, it won't be long.'

Peter sipped his scalding-hot coffee in big gulps and rubbed his eyes. 'So what brings you over this way so early, Ronnie?'

'I had to be up to see President O'Donnell before he left from the Andrews Air Force Base, just after dawn. He told me to be sure to thank you for all the work you've done. Said your briefings on the peace plan were sensational.'

Peter smiled modestly. 'I'd like to have gone along, but he said he needed me more over here, to keep an eye on things, the Secretary of State going with him as well.'

Ronnie sighed. 'Actually, the reason I dropped by is that something came up when I stopped back at the office. We've got some coded intelligence reports through on the Deir Yassin killers.'

Peter became suddenly alert. 'What do they say?'

'Ever since we identified those three as the killers and began surveillance in Haifa, we've been trying to penetrate the files of Israeli intelligence, see what they had on them. Well, one of our people there sent in a report early this morning. Turns out Yariv, Yaacov and Shemesh were positively identified as the men who shot up the truck convoy and hijacked the uranium on its way to Beersheba. The Israelis found some prints on the truck abandoned in the desert.'

Peter stood up, stunned. 'Jesus Christ, Ronnie, can we be sure about that?'

'Totally. I've got microfiche copies of the Israeli intelligence files. They've just been flown in.'

Peter rubbed his head, the lack of sleep really starting to get to him. 'You're telling me the Israeli government knew they were the hijackers and then left them running around loose?'

'Let's put it like this. They knew who they were and could always find them. But who says they didn't want the bomb project to go forward? And if they'd come clean on that with us, they'd have lost their heartbreaking story about Arab terrorists building a bomb.'

Peter, in a daze, stared out of the window at the street. 'And Shavinsky knew all of this the whole time – during all the hearings.'

Ronnie nodded grimly. 'Must be. Can you imagine what would've happened if the Subcommittee had found out that *Israeli* terrorists hijacked the uranium? DeAntonio would've blown the lid off it! There'd have been the biggest damned public investigation this country ever saw!'

'The President's got to be informed,' said Peter. 'He'll demand that Peritzsky arrange immediate extradition of all the three. Your CIA people in Haifa can take them within an hour. They've got to be put on trial for the killings and questioned about the uranium hijacking.'

Ronnie lit a cigarette, unusually for him, and blew out a long stream of smoke. 'That's just it – we've lost them . . .'

'Lost them?'

'Our man in Haifa lost them some time last night. His report said there were no lights. They never went out in their cars. So we made an entry. No sign of them in the villa. They must have gone over the roof or out of a basement exit.'

'But,' asked Peter excitedly, 'what tipped them off?'

'We don't know – we just don't. Someone got a whisper to them. The fact is they're gone.'

Peter sat down again, brooding deeply and overcome with a sense of deep discouragement. 'Have you sent word of this to the President? It will affect his meeting with Peritzsky.'

Ronnie nodded tiredly. 'I got a coded message out to the Secretary of State as I left the office just now. He'll have it tomorrow morning. I asked that he call me as soon as possible. I didn't want to go into specifics. The message could have been intercepted.'

'They've got to be found – by our people or the Israelis. Peritzsky must co-operate . . .'

'I wouldn't bet on it. The old bastard will probably stall, deny everything – then put all the obstacles in our path he can think of . . .' Ronnie got up. 'Look, I've got to get back.'

'Please, if there's anything, give me a call.'

Ronnie picked up his cigarette. 'I'm not sure that's such a good idea. Your phone may not be secure . . . you never can tell . . .'

'In that case, I'll drop by later in the afternoon.'

Ronnie smiled. 'That's good. Hey, get a bit more sleep.'

Peter yawned as he heard Ronnie going down the stairs. He felt tired, but there was no going back to bed now. He decided to cook himself a sizeable breakfast and then spend some time in the library. He would work on his papers concerning the Middle East peace plan to take his mind off things.

As he worked, he kept reviewing every detail, changing his notes, thinking of points that needed to be brought to the President's attention. He did not stop for lunch, and it was already well into the afternoon when the phone rang. With a degree of apprehension, he lifted the receiver, but he relaxed the moment he heard Aida's voice.

'I thought you'd never call,' he said.

She giggled. 'I was so sleepy last night. That sedative they gave me at the hospital knocked me right out. I only got up a few minutes ago. I feel I've been asleep for weeks.'

'Is everything OK?' Peter asked with concern.

'Fine. They're treating me so well – I guess that's what friends are for.'

'This house is missing you,' said Peter wistfully.

'Sweetheart, I wish I was there right now. I'd make a wonderful dinner. We could sit by the fire and . . .' But then she paused and went off on another tack, 'Oh, Peter. I remembered something – something Liza and that man said last night. It's probably unimportant . . .' She paused again. 'Well, the name of the man who was coming to New York in a few days. It was foreign, kind of strange. Yakov, something like that.'

'Yakov?' Peter repeated. 'Sounds almost Russian.'

'Maybe not exactly Yakov. It might've been Yarov, Yariv . . . I'm not sure.'

Peter gripped the receiver. 'Yariv! Was it Yariv?'

'Yes, that's it, *Yariv*. Now I remember. She mentioned Yariv and the others – they'd be in New York soon. And then the man said, "Did you get the President's schedule?" '

'The President's schedule? Are you sure of that, Aida?'

'Yes, I'm sure that was it.'

'My God, Aida . . .'

'I didn't understand exactly . . .'

'They were coming to New York to kill the President. That's why they wanted his schedule.'

'Kill the President?' said Aida with a gasp.

'Yes – just like before. Just like the Manhattan killings! Now listen, Aida, I can't talk any more now. Don't mention a thing that you've told me to a soul. I have to go now. But please, please, stay where you are – and please don't go out for any reason.'

'Peter,' she said, a sudden desperate note in her voice. 'Oh, Peter, I do want to see you. Can't you come over –?'

'I'm sorry, my love. This could even take me out of the country for a few days. I'll ring as soon as I can. Listen, Aida, I love you. Never forget that.'

He hung up the receiver in a panic. So many things were starting to converge so rapidly that Peter could barely think. Only a few days before, Yariv, Shemesh and Yaacov had been identified as the Manhattan killers – Israeli terrorists posing as Palestinians. That alone had seemed almost unthinkable. Now, this morning, Ronnie had linked Yariv and his gang with the Beersheba uranium hijackings. And now, from what Aida had overheard, it seemed Liza was mixed up with the Deir Yassin group, with trying to assassinate the President!

What was it that Aida had said last night – about a crew being ready to transport something. Was this the Deir Yassin group again? Maybe it was their guns, the weapons they'd need for another killing. He leapt to his feet, suddenly remembering what Ronnie said about Yariv and the other two escaping. The President would soon be landing in Israel. They would try to kill him there! He must get a warning through. But how? If he called the President, there was no way he could be sure of a safe line. He could take no chances.

Peter looked at his watch. The President would land and be escorted to his quarters to rest. He wouldn't meet with Peritzsky until tomorrow morning. He was safe until then, and meanwhile Ronnie could arrange an Air Force jet to Tel Aviv overnight. There was just time for him to get word to Tim O'Donnell before he went to meet Peritzsky, but only just.

Peter ran upstairs to the bedroom, grabbed up some clothes and stuffed them into a suitcase. Outside, the late-afternoon dusk was already closing in. Back he hurried downstairs to the library to call Ronnie then summon a cab. Plunging back into the nearly dark room, he went to his desk and started frantically putting his papers into folders. He froze as a voice came out of the darkness: 'Peter . . .'

He dropped a sheaf of papers and turned about to find himself staring at Liza standing in the doorway. The gun in her hand was aimed directly at him.

'Hi, Peter.' She brushed back a wave of blonde hair from her eyes, gesturing with her gun at his suitcase. 'Going somewhere?' She stepped closer, gun held out. 'A little trip to Israel, maybe?'

'I see,' said Peter. 'So you did get a bug on my line.'

'You were always so naïve, Peter, never thinking things through. You were always weak until I –'

'Cut the crap, Liza. You're the naïve one now, thinking you can stop me leaving.' He slammed shut his briefcase, locked it, took a forward step.

'No, you're going nowhere, Peter . . .' She held the gun out, aiming it at his chest.

Peter knew perfectly well that she wouldn't hesitate to pull the trigger. He also knew he had to stay alive, get out and warn the President. He remained very controlled. 'You're involved with the Deir Yassin group. You knew about the Manhattan killings. You work with Yariv, the others . . .'

'Your pretty little wife should have kept her mouth shut, Peter. She's made sure you know too much altogether.'

'So it must have been you who warned them we had them under surveillance and told them to escape.'

'They've not finished their work. Not yet.'

'You think they can get away with this one, Liza?'

'With what?'

'Killing the President.'

Liza smiled bitterly. 'We'll do what has to be done, no more, no less.'

'But suppose you succeed, what then? Michael Lerner will be President. Do you think you have him under your thumb? He supports the peace policy as fully as the President. He's aware of the Deir Yassin group. He won't be stopped.'

'We know all about Michael Lerner. He'll be taken care of.'

Peter stared back incredulously. 'You'd kill one of your own people, a lifelong supporter of Israel? You'd do that?'

'That's enough talking,' Liza snapped. 'There's no time for it.'

'One other thing I do want to say,' he said with as much contempt and disgust as he could put into its expression. 'I saw you, one day, walking arm in arm with your lover down Pennsylvania Avenue. A tall blond asshole. A good Aryan type, no doubt –'

Liza arched her fine eyebrows. 'Lover! Lev? My lover?' she said, breaking into a peal of quite genuine laughter.

'But I saw –'

'You fool – Lev's my brother.'

'Your brother?' asked Peter, completely fazed.

'I couldn't believe you hadn't noticed the resemblance between us long ago.'

'But I'd never seen him till that day – I didn't quite catch a look at his face.'

Liza shot at Peter a glance of withering scorn. 'You saw him plenty, you idiot. At your Subcommittee. Lev Shavinsky.'

'Shavinsky!'

Liza stepped towards him. 'The safe, Peter, we'll have it open now.' She motioned towards the wall with her gun.

'There's nothing in it, Liza,' Peter said nervously.

'Open it. I want all your papers.' She held the gun up towards him. 'Simply open it.'

'And then what? You can hardly leave me here to talk, can you? You'll have to kill me, Liza. Can you do that?'

Liza stared fiercely. 'Open it.'

205

Peter carefully turned the combination lock until the safe came open with a soft click.

'Now hand me everything in it,' she ordered.

Peter knelt to reach inside for the papers.

'Here, take them,' he said, standing up with a stack of files in his arms, but, before she could reply, pulling the trigger of the gun which he held, concealed at the bottom of the pile, twice in rapid succession.

Less than twenty minutes later, Peter was in an official car, screeching full pelt for Andrews Air Force Base to catch the special Air Force jet which Ronnie had laid on. As the cab shot through the outskirts of the city, Peter sat in the back seat, his heart still pounding. Thank God that Ronnie insisted he take that gun last night! He had felt so foolish about having a gun that he'd locked it away in the safe. Then he thought of Liza and the look on her face as he fired twice. Then of her long blonde hair spread out as she lay motionless on the carpet.

So Shavinsky was Liza's brother! He had been there in the warehouse that night with Aida. And Shavinsky was involved with Deir Yassin, who had hijacked the uranium. Shavinsky must have run the bomb project from the beginning. Everything fitted.

As the car shot in at the gates of the air base, one of the things that Aida had said came back to him. *The crew was ready . . . ready to transport.* The bomb! Of course! They'd built the bomb. It was ready. They were going to use it! There seemed to be even more at stake than the life of a President.

39

After Air Force One's gruelling fifteen-hour flight to Tel Aviv, the small Presidential entourage had been glad to have the chance to wash and dine and rest itself at the luxury rest-house reserved for diplomats. Now, the next morning, they were on the move again, loaded into four black limousines that were speeding along the highway, up through the hills towards Jerusalem. It was a hot day, with surprisingly strong, dry gusts of wind blowing up from the desert.

President O'Donnell sat in the back seat of the leading car, talking with the Secretary of State and still fuming with anger at the Israeli cover-up of the Arab uranium hijacking and all that Peter Watkins had told him concerning the Subcommittee investigation. He'd been further enraged by Prime Minister Peritzsky's resistance to the peace talks. And now there was this Deir Yassin thing. The problems seemed never-ending. It was time to get everything cleared up – once and for all.

The limousines sped past the Knesset and drew up in front of the Prime Minister's offices. The party alighted, and everyone stretched their legs. The wind blew eddies of sand up along the driveway as the Israeli Foreign Minister, Sol Goldblatt, dashed out of the double doors, followed by a group of aides. Goldblatt, a rotund, jovial man in his late fifties, greeted the President warmly and shook hands with all the members of the entourage. He welcomed everyone to Israel and apologized for the unusually warm day, then led everyone in, taking the President's arm. Secretary of State Henry Simpson was reacting coolly, irked that Peritzsky himself had not come out to greet them. It was a grave breach of diplomatic etiquette, almost a snub, and one hell of a way to begin a high-level meeting.

They were led into a courtyard which had a fountain in the middle, where the members of the group were served iced tea and seafood appetizers. There was an interlude of polite conversation between members of the President's party and some of Peritzsky's staff until, finally, Goldblatt ushered the American President and his party into the Prime Minister's office.

Peritzsky, dressed in an open-necked khaki shirt, rose from his desk in greeting. 'Welcome to Israel, Mr President . . . and welcome to our old friend, Henry Simpson.' Peritzsky embraced the Secretary of State.

Tim smiled and shook hands politely. 'Thank you, Mr Prime Minister. We're glad to be here in your country.'

'Sit down please, gentlemen,' said Peritzsky, indicating the chairs around a small conference table. Sol Goldblatt joined them, and then, for a few minutes, Peritzsky engaged in light conversation with Tim, congratulating him on his campaign and election. Peritzsky was about sixty-four, and had an animated manner and a mane of long white hair. His face was narrow, his chin sharp, his two front teeth protruding slightly. He had been Prime Minister for seven years, representing a coalition of conservative Orthodox groups.

As the light small talk began to wind down, Tim O'Donnell smiled apologetically. 'I'm sorry this visit came up so abruptly, Mr Prime Minister. I'd have preferred to have more time to travel around Israel.'

Meyer Peritzsky stared back gloomily. 'I am even sorrier. A trip like this could have meant a *lot* of good will – given proper planning. Perhaps, being new to the Presidency, you do not yet appreciate the tremendous publicity value which such a meeting can have. Much could have been done . . .'

The President frowned at Peritzsky's chiding tone. He knew that the Prime Minister's failure to meet them as soon as they alighted probably meant he was pouting.

'Mr Prime Minister,' he said cuttingly, 'this is not intended as any good-will tour . . .'

'But good will has always existed between our countries. Do you not

208

come here in good will, as a friend of Israel?'

The President eyed Peritzsky warily. 'I do not find the reasons for my visit here to be pleasant ones. I would not have made such a trip at short notice unless I felt it a matter of the utmost urgency, Mr Prime Minister.'

Peritzsky shrugged. 'I cannot imagine how anything could be so urgent as to interfere with a properly planned state visit by the newly elected President of the United States.'

'May I come straight to the point of our visit?' asked the President curtly.

Peritzsky waved a hand dismissively. 'Please . . .'

'We have made what we believe to be a major breakthrough in the investigation of the Manhattan murders.'

Peritzsky looked sorrowful. 'A horrible crime, a monstrous atrocity . . . We have wondered why your government had made so little progress, but then you're still working on the Kennedy assassination after how long? Over twenty years?'

The President refused to rise to the bait and damped down his anger. Instead, he handed the blow-ups of the Channel 5 footage over to Peritzsky. 'These are the photos of the killers, taken that day at the school. They wore bandanas over the lower parts of their faces. These are enlargements of just their eyes.'

Peritzsky sorted idly through the photos, handed them on to Goldblatt. 'So, how is this a breakthrough?'

The President remained cool. 'We have also been able to locate the men we believe to be the killers. Here are enlarged photos of the men, shot with a telephoto lens.' He handed over the second set of photos. 'Again, we have enlarged the photos of the eyes. If you'll compare these with the pictures taken in New York, you'll see a most striking resemblance. In fact, it is an exact resemblance. It's a new technique, but one regarded as being almost as infallible as fingerprinting.'

Peritzsky stared at each photo, squinted his eyes, then laid them out in two rows. Sol Goldblatt glanced at them over his shoulder and Peritzsky examined them a second time. 'Certainly they appear to be the same men. A remarkable technique. Do you have names to attach to them? We can get their dossiers sent over by our intelligence people. We hold extensive files on the members of the Palestinian Freedom League.'

The President sat back and put his fingers together. 'These men were not members of the PFL . . .'

'No matter. There are dozens of these fanatical Palestinian splinter-groups. We have them all on file.'

'They are *not* Palestinians, Prime Minister Peritzsky.'

'*Not* Palestinians? Then who are they, if not Palestinians?'

The President took a deep breath. 'We have established beyond doubt that these men are active in a terrorist organization known as Deir Yassin. Is that on your files?'

Peritzsky stared back, for a moment reduced to speechlessness. He seemed to be thinking, trying to recall. Then, 'Deir Yassin?' he repeated softly. Suddenly he jerked his head forward towards the President. 'But Deir Yassin is a group, here in Israel . . .'

'Yes, that is precisely so, and I'm sure your intelligence people must be perfectly familiar with them.'

Peritzsky's mouth dropped open. He ran his fingers backwards through the strands of his long white hair. 'But then you are saying that these killers were *Jews*, from Israel!'

'That's exactly what I regret I have to say, Mr Prime Minister.'

Peritzsky leaped up from his chair and shot out his finger at the President. 'Then it's a lie. A filthy lie. I spit on your doctored-up CIA photos.' He was gasping for breath as, suddenly, he stared at the Secretary of State. 'And you, Henry? Do you believe in this . . . these lies?'

Henry Simpson had bowed his head, overwhelmed by the tension of the encounter and also by his own disgust with it all. He gazed up at Peritzsky. 'Meyer, my old friend, I have to tell you that I believe that what the President is saying is the truth. The evidence is so strong that –'

Peritzsky was appalled. 'So who was your source for this? Who led you to this Deir Yassin?'

'We were approached by a member of the PFL, seeking to clear them of responsibility –'

'The PFL!' Peritzsky screamed. 'Now this I don't believe! You fly 10,000 miles to tell me Jews killed Jews, your proof being the testimony of a Palestinian terrorist and some fuzzy photographs of people's eyes? Do not insult me, Mr President. When you have gained a little more experience in world affairs, perhaps we should have a *serious* meeting. Until then, I'm afraid I must be getting back to work.'

Peritzsky began to walk out of the room as Goldblatt looked on helplessly. But, all at once, Henry Simpson came to his feet, finding any implied insult to the President of the United States intolerable. 'Sit down, Meyer,' he said. 'You haven't listened to it all. There's more to come. If you walk out of that door, you'll regret it for the rest of your life.'

Peritzsky paused, his hand on the door catch, never having heard Simpson so vehement before. He turned and looked round the group at the table, his complexion ashen.

When the President next spoke, he was utterly calm. 'Mr Prime Minister, our identification of the killers as members of Deir Yassin has been confirmed by a fingerprint taken from a lock at the Hillel school. The killers are identified as Amram Yariv, Amos Yaacov and Meir Shemesh. You have seen how the photos match. I can assure you the matches are by no means coincidence.'

Peritzsky, dazed and shaken, returned to the table and sat down as the President continued, 'I know that this must come as a terrible shock to you. I found it hard, so hard to believe myself. But these men are violent, they're professional killers, they're fanatics. The existence of this type of group should be taken as no reflection on Israel. What we require now is your help in bringing these men in. We have them under surveillance in Haifa. We would request the assistance of your security people and everything that you have on file on these three men.'

Peritzsky sat up very straight, stared at the President wrathfully, his head trembling. 'You mean to say you have authorized intelligence operations inside Israel without consulting us? That you have never made any of this known to my government? I must ask you to withdraw all your agents immediately. If there is to be an investigation, any kind of arrest, we will handle it. I am shocked, Mr President. Our security people will, of course, need all your evidence so that we may perform our own valuation. If these men are guilty, *we* will take care of them.' Peritzsky thrust out his chin aggressively.

'Mr Prime Minister,' said the President, 'you put me in a most difficult position. I have no doubt that they are the killers. How can we rely on your intelligence operations when these men have gone undetected in Israel for over a year? This is a matter of grave concern to the American people. Frankly, I do not feel confident in trusting you to bring these men in.'

Peritzsky gasped, stared at the Americans incredulously. 'This is impossible . . . utterly ridiculous.'

The President gave a severe frown. 'Mr Prime Minister, if you will not provide prompt full-scale assistance in the arrest and extradition of these three men, then I am prepared to seek an immediate cut-off of all

American aid to Israel, both military and economic, effective within forty-eight hours. With what I have to tell the American people, there's no question in my mind but that they will give such a move overwhelming support.'

Peritzsky gazed in disbelief, then looked towards the Secretary of State. 'What about you, Henry? Do *you* support such action – as a very loyal friend of Israel?'

The Secretary, deeply anguished, looked at Peritzsky. 'Yes, Meyer, I do. So will the people of America.'

Peritzsky blinked, stood up slowly. 'We are a proud independent nation. I will *not* be dictated to by the American government. You have wilfully sent your agents within our borders. You have violated a trust, a friendship . . . international treaties.'

The President had had enough as he exploded in a rage. 'You *dare* to use those words! And where was trust, friendship and treaty obligations at the time of the uranium hijacking at Beersheba? Why was President Randall never informed of this disastrous blunder on your part? And where did trust stand when you secretly built your own plutonium reprocessing plant, your own bomb? Why did your government hide all this from the American government, which has given you unstinting, overwhelming support during three decades? You've been playing a goddamned nuclear poker game, without the slightest concern for your allies or the rest of the world. I want to see these three men apprehended immediately. The dictation of our policy by Israel has come to an end. I have stood enough!'

Peritzsky had gone as pale as a ghost. He stared down at the photos of the killers. 'We can, perhaps, arrange something regarding the three men. As for the matter of the hijacking that I understand is worrying you,' he picked up the phone and made a brief call in Hebrew, 'your questions will be answered at once.'

It was less than a minute later when Lev Shavinsky came striding briskly into the room.

'This is Dr Lev Shavinsky,' Peritzsky introduced him. 'He served as chief technical director of the power plants. He was chairman of the physics department at Hebrew University, and now serves as my national security adviser.' Peritzsky waved a hand towards the President. 'They wish to know about the hijacking again – all of that. The President seems to doubt our word, thinks we're building a bomb. Can you explain, Doctor?'

Shavinsky flashed his bright white teeth. 'I'm sorry you did not attend Senator Lerner's hearings, Mr President. We went over all of this in great detail at the time. I have very little to add to what I said then. We have never been able to trace the uranium shipment hijacked at Beersheba. We suspect it was flown into Syria, though we have no hard evidence.'

'I think we'd like to have a look at the nuclear power plants, Dr Shavinsky,' said the President sceptically.

'Of course – at any time,' responded Shavinsky obligingly. Then he looked down at his watch. 'Ah, Mr President, it seems I've gone on over-long. You'd requested to see something of the Old City and especially the Western Wall during your visit – or the "Wailing Wall" as it is known to non-Jews. We've arranged for that this afternoon – subject to your approval.'

The President could see that nothing was likely to be settled at today's meeting.

'Thank you, Doctor,' said the President. 'That sounds excellent. I think we'd all like to get out and about, look around. We can resume these discussions tomorrow, Mr Prime Minister – when, hopefully, we'll all be feeling a little more relaxed . . .'

Peritzsky raised himself from his chair, a dark look on his face. 'We, for our part, are willing to talk at any time,' he said.

The President and the Secretary of State stood as well, shook Peritzsky's hand, thanked Dr Shavinsky for coming. O'Donnell looked at his watch. 'Looks like we have time to catch a brief lunch before heading over to the Old City. The Wall is something I've wanted to see for many years.'

As the President passed out of the room, Lev Shavinsky called after him, 'Enjoy your visit, Mr President.'

40

Shavinsky's Porsche went like an arrow through the desert outside Tel Aviv. The wind had been growing stronger by the hour. The desert brush was whipping back and forth, while flurries of sand swept across the two-lane carriageway. Shavinsky could barely see ahead as the swirling sand blurred his view, but he kept a foot firmly on the accelerator. Familiar landmarks were obliterated by the hazy air, and he squinted his eyes, trying to see where he was, as he gripped the wheel.

The car shot through a remote stretch of desert, then screeched to a halt. Beside the road there stood an old wooden tower with a set of windmill sails on top. Shavinsky stared at the water pump with a smile, then swung his car off the metalled surface on to a narrow dirt road whose outline was almost invisible in the haze. Again the car sped ahead, hurtling and jarring over the rust and rocks of the primitive road surface.

Within about ten minutes, the Porsche was racing on to an airfield and heading directly for the main hangar. Shavinsky jumped from the car as a man in beige fatigues ran out. They shouted at one another as the wind buffeted about them, Shavinsky pointing excitedly at the runway before they went together inside the hangar.

It was cool and dark inside, though the blown sand still set up a racket as it scoured the metal exterior of the building. Shavinsky wiped his brow with a handkerchief.

'Where is Amos?' he asked.

'Upstairs,' the man said.

Shavinsky leapt up the stairs, two at a time, and entered a sparsely furnished room where a man lay smoking on a bunk bed.

'Amos! The time's here. We cannot delay a moment longer. Even holding back a few hours could make it too late.'

Amos Yaacov, one of the Manhattan killers, stared at the excited Shavinsky. 'Now? In this wind? There's no visibility. None at all.'

'It has to be now! The timing is exactly right. Just as the plan called for.'

Yaacov lifted a blind slightly and looked out at the storm. 'You want to fly out – in this?'

'There's no alternative,' answered Shavinsky grimly. He picked up an intercom and barked an instruction that the runway lights be turned on and the bomber prepared at once.

'Get ready, Yaacov. We take off in fifteen minutes. Meet me on the field.'

Shavinsky quickly changed into a flight suit and went outside to stand with his hand shading his eyes as he looked out across the airfield. Slowly, a P-38 Wasp came rolling out of the hangar towards the runway, then stopped. A heavy transport vehicle emerged from another hangar and headed towards the plane. Its flatbed was loaded down by a great bulk covered by a tarpaulin. Shavinsky smiled with an inner pride.

He ran into the flying sand, directing the removal of the tarpaulins, which whipped and snapped in the relentless wind. The flatbed, carrying its revealed bomb, was backed towards the plane as the bomb bay flaps slowly opened and an elaborate chromium bomb rack descended from out of the plane's belly. The bomb was jacked up from the bed of the transporter as Shavinsky continued to shout commands against the roaring wind. As soon as the weapon was positioned within the bomb rack, Shavinsky clambered on top of the transporter and carefully began to manipulate various switches. Looking down at the two men, he waved them back with his hand. There was a dull humming as the bomb rose on its rack into the plane. Then the bomb bay doors closed like jaws. The payload was ready for takeoff . . .

Shavinsky jumped down on to the runway and looked back towards the hangar as Yaacov came out, still zipping up his flight jacket. Shavinsky gestured frantically.

'Hurry, Amos!'

Yaacov stared gloomily out at the desert before stepping reluctantly towards the plane as Shavinsky lowered himself into the pilot's seat in the cockpit.

Shavinsky switched on the radio, looked at his watch, checked that the bomb's advanced detonation systems were activated, as Yaacov climbed into the cockpit, brushing sand from his hair, a solemn look on his face. 'What time are we due over Damascus?' he asked.

'At 15.30 hours. The bomb's primed for final activation and ejection,' Shavinsky replied confidently.

'What about Syrian radar?' demanded Yaacov gruffly.

'No worry. Syrian radar will be knocked out in precisely twenty-five minutes. We'll be getting the confirming signal as it happens.'

Yaacov settled into the co-pilot's seat and latched on his seat belt, and as he looked out through the windshield saw that the runway lights were barely visible in the storm. The bomber's fuselage shuddered as the wind surged.

'This is madness, Shavinsky – it's too windy,' he said. 'It's too dangerous for takeoff.'

'Yaacov,' said Shavinsky, 'you are under orders now. Take off we must, and take off we will.'

Yaacov looked at the storm again, listening to the hissing sand. 'It would be difficult enough without the storm – flying at a low altitude with no navigator, no radar back-up at this end and a damned nuclear warhead under our asses. Then this . . .' He waved a hand around the field. 'No, impossible, madness,' Yaacov sighed. He unlatched his seat belt and started to get up.

'What are you doing?' Shavinsky cried out.

'I'm going back in. The flight's cancelled, Shavinsky.' He started to clamber out of the cockpit.

'Get back in your seat, Yaacov. You're going nowhere except Damascus.'

Yaacov, turning about, found that Shavinsky had a .45 automatic aimed at his chest.

'Back in your seat!' Shavinsky waved his gun menacingly, but Yaacov did not move. 'There's no time for talk, Yaacov! Move – or I shoot.'

'You need me, Shavinsky. There's no way for you to get there without me. We have to wait for the storm to clear. When that happens, I'm with you.' Yaacov turned his back and resumed climbing out of the cockpit.

Shavinsky screamed, 'I've warned you the last time,' and pulled the trigger. As the bullet caught Yaacov, he fell sideways out of the cockpit and dropped with a thud to the runway, where he lay twitching, blood seeping through his khaki jacket. Above him, the engines of the sleek jet came alive and began to roar. The plane itself started to move to align itself with the runway, then to gather speed and to plunge towards the clouds of billowing sand. As it rose into the grey-white sky, the sound the engines made was swiftly swallowed within the blast of the desert storm.

41

Peter Watkins arrived in Tel Aviv at a quarter past noon, exhausted, jet-lagged, and riddled with tension. He lost not a minute before making a call to the Secret Service at the President's quarters. The President and his party had just finished lunch, the agent who answered told him, so Peter requested that he speak with the President immediately on a matter of the utmost urgency. When the agent came back on the line he said, 'I'm sorry, Dr Watkins, the President just left.'

'Left? Where's he going? I have to know.'

'He and the Secretary of State are being taken on an afternoon tour by Prime Minister Peritzsky. They'll be visiting the Old City and winding up at the Western Wall of the Temple of Solomon. You only missed them by five minutes . . . Dr Watkins? . . . Dr Watkins?'

Peter had dropped the receiver and sprinted across the airport lobby, breasting the dense crowds of passengers and waving frantically for a taxi. He had to get to Jerusalem.

In Jerusalem itself, the President was feeling slightly happier with the way the day was going. Prime Minister Peritzsky seemed to be unbending a little as he pointed out this and that antique feature or sacred site. As they finally approached the Western Wall, Peritzsky and Sol Goldblatt escorted the President, Secretary Simpson and their party towards where it loomed up awesomely. Many dozens of Jewish men of all ages, dressed in their traditional black clothes, were worshipping, reading the Talmud or kissing the stones. According to tradition, Peritzsky explained, any prayer said before the Wall will pass through the stones and enter the buried Holy of Holies. A prayer in writing, slipped between the stones, will reach God. If the President wished to offer such a prayer as a non-Jew, then he could write it on a slip of paper and he, Peritzsky, would be honoured to slip it between the stones on his behalf. The President turned away from his entourage where they stood by the rails that separated secular from sacred ground, and whispered to himself. Then he took a pen from his coat and wrote on a scrap of paper: 'Peace on Earth', looking more like a self-conscious boy than a man who carried the responsibilities of the world on his shoulders. He folded the slip carefully, but as he turned to pass it to Peritzsky, was startled to see Peter Watkins leaping from a taxi and running through the crowds of tourists and worshippers. He froze with the paper in his hand as Peter cried out loudly to him, 'Mr President! Mr President!' Even as Peter shouted a burst of gunfire from two automatic weapons indiscriminately raked the entourage of the President and his host, Prime Minister Peritzsky, as well as the nearby worshippers. The security police and Secret Service sprang into action to return the fire, but a total panic had broken out in the whole area before the Wall as people ran in every direction, confused and screaming, some of them falling and bleeding.

Peter Watkins was himself on the ground, the shoulder of his jacket discoloured by a spreading stain of blood, his arm feeling as if it had been torn out at the socket. Nevertheless, he managed to regain his feet, and then saw Tim O'Donnell lying only a few feet in front of him.

Tim's face was very pale, his blue eyes quickly clouding over. He smiled weakly and, in a whisper, said, 'Peter . . . Why are you here?' Then he reached up the hand which still held the crumpled slip of paper but, before Peter could take it, his arm fell back, his eyes shut and he died before Peter's helpless gaze.

The rest was a nightmare blur. As the entire area was rapidly cordoned off and people huddled, shocked or lamenting, over the dead and injured, and police scurried about with walkie-talkies, Peter was led gently away by a Secret Service official. A terrible nausea overcame him in the hot car. He tried to grasp an understanding of what had happened, but his mind could not take in even his own stained jacket or his hands wet with fresh blood. He had a brief image of Tim's dying face, but then the pain from his wound reasserted itself excruciatingly. He slumped over and lost consciousness.

42

At the Mount Zion Hospital, the wailing of ambulance sirens filled the air. Peter was vaguely aware of the pandemonium about him as he was wheeled into the emergency room. He opened his eyes briefly to find the Secret Service agent who had helped him to the car standing beside him. Peter asked, in a faltering voice, 'The President . . .?'

The agent frowned, looked down. 'The President is dead, Doctor.

There was no way to help him. Mr Secretary of State Simpson too.'

Peter stared up at the ceiling in a daze. Tim and Henry both dead? He looked at the agent. 'Then Michael Lerner . . . he's President now. Are they swearing him in?'

The agent stared down at Peter, his own face narrow with shock. 'We just got a report from Washington. Michael Lerner was shot outside his home – within the past hour. His condition's not yet clear, and the information conflicts, but the Georgetown Hospital is holding out small hope for his survival.'

Peter sighed, his face empty of emotion.

'High-level conspiracy,' remarked the agent bitterly.

A nurse came up to Peter, needle in hand. 'We're taking you into surgery now, Dr Watkins,' she said.

Peter remained unconscious for thirty-six hours after surgery. He had lost a lot of blood. When he eventually came to, he was immediately aware of a weakness and pain – especially of a pain in his shoulder. He felt he was pinned down to the bed. A door opened and someone came to lean over him. Peter looked up, squinting his eyes, and saw Ronnie Montgomery.

Ronnie spoke almost in a whisper as he said, 'You're awake . . . finally. You know how long it's been?'

Peter stared back at him, barely understanding. He wanted to sit up, to speak.

'Just you lie still, now,' said Ronnie gently. 'Do you remember anything that happened?'

Peter's voice was faint and hoarse inside his own head. 'The President's been killed,' he said slowly. 'I tried to reach him –'

'It's all right, Peter. It's all right.'

He began to remember running towards the Wall, calling out to the President, then the sound of shots, but then he drifted back into a haze of unconsciousness.

When Peter next awoke, it was dark outside but a light was on in his hospital room. He saw that his chest was bandaged, his arm in a sling. An intravenous tube ran into his other arm. When a nurse came into the room, he looked at her, deeply puzzled. 'Where is this?' he asked.

'In hospital, in Tel Aviv.'

Peter stared in bewilderment. 'What's . . . wrong with me?' he asked haltingly.

She took the food tray away and made him wash down four large pills with some water. 'You got yourself shot, when you tried to reach the President, to help him. Don't you remember?'

'Me, shot?' He stared. 'I don't remember. I wanted to help the President. My arm hurt. There was blood . . .'

'You got a bad hit in the shoulder, and another in your right arm. The doctor was amazed you were able to move at all.'

'Move?'

'You went on to the President and held him in your arms.'

'I did?'

She smiled gently. 'Yes.'

Not long afterwards, Ronnie came in with a newspaper, and he held it out. Under a huge headline – PRESIDENT O'DONNELL KILLED IN JERUSALEM – was a news photo of the President cradled in Peter's arms.

'You're a hero, Watkins!' said Ronnie, making the effort to sound jolly.

Peter stared at the picture in blank amazement, and then another headline caught his eye: VICE-PRESIDENT SHOT IN WASHINGTON – RUSHED TO GEORGETOWN HOSPITAL.

'Michael . . . is he?'

Ronnie patted his shoulder gently. 'He's alive – in hospital. We're getting hourly reports. His condition's unstable, but he's holding his own.'

'He must live . . .' But Peter's eyes closed as the sedative hit him again.

On the morning of his third day in hospital, the curtains were wide open. Peter had woken to see the sun rising over the low white city. He felt better, his thoughts seemed clearer. What was more, he was hungry. The nurse entered the room and gave him a shot. Then breakfast was brought in and she helped him to eat. He could still barely sit up. Then Ronnie, smiling brightly, came in at the door.

'What in hell are you doing in this country?' Peter asked.

Ronnie laughed. 'I've been around while you've been sleeping,' he said. 'Never mind if you don't remember. I'm here to keep an eye on an old buddy. You're a lucky man. Either one of those shots –'

'Tim should have lived,' said Peter, suddenly more lucid. 'I really thought I'd got to him in time.'

'You did everything possible, Peter.'

'And then Michael as well –'

'He's OK, Peter. Lerner's OK. His condition's stabilized. Two major wounds, but the operations came off well.'

221

'He'll be a fine President,' Peter smiled.

Ronnie looked nervously out of the window. 'Peter, you should know this – Michael Lerner may not be able to assume office. A lot's been happening –'

Peter stared back incredulously. 'But how . . . what could stop . . .' He trailed off, tired with the effort of conversation.

Ronnie sat down beside the bed. 'In those first few hours after the killings, nothing was clear. There were reports of Michael Lerner being shot, of him being dead. All hell broke loose in the Capitol, and under the Constitution, if the President and Vice-President are dead or incapacitated –'

'Not Lusk!' Peter cried out. It hit him like a bolt of lightning. 'Jesse Lusk . . . as Speaker, next in line for the Presidency.'

Ronnie sighed. 'During this period of uncertainty, someone had to take charge. Jesse Lusk assumed the role of acting President – though he'd never been sworn in. There was a lot of controversy, what with no one knowing how badly Michael Lerner was wounded, whether he'd live. So Lusk took charge, like it or not.'

Ronnie stood up and gazed out at the city, seeming deeply worried as he continued, 'After the shootings, Lusk summoned a joint session of Congress which was televised nationwide. He charged the PFL with being behind the latest killings, just like those in New York, he said. He ranted and raved like any demagogue, claiming that the Syrian and Libyan governments had prior knowledge of the attack and demanding that US forces be put on an immediate war footing . . .'

Peter felt his heart sink, then he managed to sit bolt upright in concern. 'But this is crazy. We know it wasn't the PFL, but Deir Yassin again! We know that, Ronnie.'

'You know it and I know it. But Jesse Lusk is a powerful man – and a powerful speaker.'

'Something has to be done,' said Peter, grabbing at Ronnie's arm.

'I've tried to talk sense to a few key members of Congress, make the facts clear.'

'And?' Peter asked, a desperate look in his eye.

'I thought I was making progress till the furore about a nuclear bomber came up.'

'Tell me,' said Peter, his voice fading.

'That's one of the reasons I'm here. A plane has crashed in the desert, about twenty-five miles south-east of Nazareth, in northern Israel. It was discovered yesterday afternoon.'

222

'A plane?'

'Not merely a plane. It was carrying a small nuclear warhead of the home-made variety. It didn't go off, but it might have. It was primed. Prime Minister Peritzsky, who's still in hospital, claimed it as an unprovoked Arab attack on Israel. The Knesset was called into an emergency war session. Jesse Lusk immediately offered full US support for any Israeli military initiative.'

'Dear God!' said Peter in a whisper.

'As for you, Peter, you have to stay calm. You're still weak. The doctors say –'

'That was Shavinsky, Ronnie. Shavinsky and Deir Yassin were behind the bomb. I know it. Aida called me, just before I left Washington. There was no time to tell you.'

Ronnie stared at him blankly.

'Yes, yes,' said Peter excitedly, moving too quickly and wincing with pain. 'The crew was ready to transport the bomb. That's what Shavinsky told Liza that night in the warehouse.'

'Shavinsky!' exclaimed Ronnie.

'Yes, *he* was the man at the warehouse – he's Liza's brother! Shavinsky was behind it, behind the bomb. We've got to tell them – it was him!'

But Ronnie was gone from the room, running down the echoing corridors of the hospital and out at the entrance, praying that there might still be time.

43

Peter awoke quite early next morning. He was able to sit up in bed stiffly but with less pain. He felt eager to get out of the hospital now, and back to America. He was missing Aida terribly, but that aside, he also knew that Washington must be going through one of the greatest crises of modern times with him stuck here, 10,000 miles away.

Peter buzzed the nurse and asked to have the TV above his bed turned on. He wanted to see what was happening, feeling he'd all but lost touch with the outside world. As the nurse turned on the set, it came up with a special news programme from America, taped late the previous afternoon in Washington. Peter frowned as he saw the round white face of Jesse Lusk, who stood before the members of the US Senate, gesturing emphatically.

'Could you turn up the volume?' Peter asked the nurse softly.

She did so, and he heard Lusk saying, '. . . and just as these Arab terrorists would kill innocent children in a quiet schoolyard, innocent helpless children, so, too, they would strike down the President of the United States with their bloody deeds, a man, a father of young children, and a friend.' He paused. 'Yes, Tim O'Donnell was my friend, someone I admired from the time he arrived in Washington, a man whose dedication and ideals I came to share. And Tim O'Donnell was a friend of Israel, a supporter of that tiny helpless land, the refuge of the Jewish people who wandered homeless for so many centuries. It was for this support, this unswerving devotion to Israel that Tim O'Donnell died in Jerusalem two days ago – cut down by the savage forces of Arab violence.'

As Peter watched the screen grimly, he thought of the bitter irony which lurked behind Lusk's remarks. As he sank ever more deeply into his fit of despondency, there was a sharp rap on the door. Ronnie stood there, a sheaf of papers in his hand and an expression of bright excitement on his face.

'Well, look at you,' he said. 'I can see you're starting to revive.'

'Where did you get to?' asked Peter curiously.

Ronnie drew up a chair. 'Well, as soon as you told me the connection between Shavinsky and the bomb yesterday, I figured I'd better check out this plane crash. The Israeli government's been keeping it very hush-hush. They'd only revealed that the plane was Syrian and had a Syrian pilot. So I drove out to Nazareth myself yesterday.'

'And got to see the wreck?'

'No, it's been sealed off by Israeli military intelligence. I also asked to see the body of the pilot, but they claimed it had been burned in the wreck. That puzzled me. How could they know he was Syrian if the body was burned?'

A flicker of the old excitement was growing steadily stronger in Peter's eyes. 'But, surely, the plane must've been positively identified as Syrian, some kind of Russian jet.'

'No. It was American. One of those P-38 Wasps we gave Israel a while back. We got reconnaissance shots of the wreck as soon as we heard about it. Here are some of the photos and the report.'

He handed several papers over to Peter, who spread them out before him on the bed cover.

'Then it had to be from Israel,' Peter said. 'This was Shavinsky's work. He dispatched the bomber, probably timing it to coincide with the confusion after the assassinations.'

'Not merely his project – he piloted the damned plane! That's probably why it crashed. He wasn't a very good pilot, I'm told.'

Peter raised himself abruptly. 'Shavinsky? In the plane? You mean he's the dead . . . But how can we –'

'It took some doing, but I located the shepherd who first found the wreck. He'd even climbed in and lifted the pilot's body out of the cockpit. There had been no fire, he said. The pilot was a tall blond man

225

in his middle thirties, very pale complexion. I showed him a press photo of Shavinsky. "That's the pilot, right enough," he said.'

Peter whistled. 'It's absolute dynamite.'

'So I went to the Israeli government, demanded to see Dr Shavinsky immediately. They claimed he was out of the country, denied the shepherd's story.'

'There's no point then,' said Peter tiredly. 'It's too late.'

'Don't you underestimate Ronnie Montgomery. I've been very busy since we last met. I got on the phone to Senator DeAntonio in Washington. He's one of the few who see straight through Jesse Lusk, and he's been very sceptical about this supposed nuclear bomber "captured" by the Israelis. His first step was to demand an immediate high-level investigation into the whole incident.'

'But that'll take time. The Israelis will cover up . . .' said Peter anxiously.

'Not after last night. DeAntonio called a press conference and released the CIA report on Deir Yassin . . . everything about the Manhattan killings and the uranium hijacking . . . everything we went over in the Subcommittee hearings.'

'But would anyone believe it?'

'Frank DeAntonio is one of the most trusted men in Washington. When he talks, they all listen. Plenty of people have been wary of Lusk. I'll tell you, there was total chaos after the news conference. DeAntonio pulled out all the stops, implying that Deir Yassin was in all likelihood behind the assassination of President O'Donnell. He charged Lusk with deliberately holding back the CIA reports for three days to try and secure a war declaration.'

'How did the Senate take it?'

'Like the biggest shock since Pearl Harbor. But there was more. The Senate and House held a joint emergency session last night, after DeAntonio's news conference. There was a terrific uproar over Jesse Lusk's tactics, the cover-up and so on. DeAntonio charged Lusk with improperly assuming the office of President, having never been sworn in, and said he had visited Michael Lerner, who was recovering rapidly. The talk about Lerner being severely incapacitated was being put out by Lusk's people all along.'

'Will Michael be able to serve when he does get better?' Peter asked hesitantly.

Ronnie smiled. 'That's what I'm here to tell you. Jesse Lusk was censured by a full vote of the House a few hours ago. He's been removed from his post as Speaker with a full investigation pending. Michael Lerner was sworn in as President at 3.45 a.m. Eastern Standard Time. Senator DeAntonio was, as Senator Pro Tempore, sworn in as Vice-President, and will serve as acting President until Michael Lerner's released from hospital.'

The expression on Peter's face was one of such incredulity that Ronnie laughed as he continued, 'Oh, and before it slips my mind, there's one more little thing to tell you. President Lerner called me a short while back and asked me to put it to you that you might care to serve as his chief foreign-policy adviser. That is, as soon as you're fit to do so, of course.'

Peter lay back on the pillow, suddenly overwhelmed and exasperated with impatience. 'All I ask you is to get me out of here and get me home,' he said.

'Could be you're just about ready for it,' said Ronnie, looking at him appraisingly.

'Ready for it?' said Peter. 'Ready for it? There's the best tonic a man could need or wish for waiting for me back there.'

'And I'm sure she'll be pleased to see you too,' said Ronnie.

'Yes,' said Peter. 'I've got a marriage to be getting on with. Damn it all, I'm still owed a honeymoon.'